WEDDING NIGHT STRANGER

MR. BUCHANNAN
- Small Town Billionaires -

ALICIA NICHOLS

This book is a work of fiction.

All the characters, organizations, and events portrayed in the novel are either products of the author's imagination or are used fictitiously. Sometimes both.

Copyright © 2023 Alicia Nichols

Cover copyright © Alicia Nichols

An Alicia Nichols Production

All Rights Reserved

The distribution of this book without permission is a theft of the author's Intellectual property. If you would like permission to use the material from the book (other than for review purposes), please contact info@alicianicholsauthor.com. Thank you for your support of the author's rights.

First Worldwide Edition: March 2023

Version 1: March 2023

MORE BY ALICIA

Doctor's Heat (Dr. Wright, Book 1)
Get it for FREE Here:
https://getbook.at/doctorsheat

Daddy's Off Limits (Complete Series)
Read It Here:
https://mybook.to/DaddysOffLimits

Darwin Brothers (Complete Series)
Read It Here:
https://mybook.to/DarwinBrothersBoxset

Dr. Park (Complete Series)
Read It Here:
https://getbook.at/DrParkBoxset

Dr. Stone (Complete Series)
Read It Here:
https://getbook.at/DrStoneBoxset

Dr. Wright (Complete Series – Vol. 1)
Read It Here:
https://getbook.at/DrWrightBoxset

Dr. Walker (Complete Series)
Read It Here:
https://getbook.at/DrWalkerBoxset

Dr. MacLean (Complete Series)
Read It Here:
https://mybook.to/DrMacleanBoxset

Dr. Pierce (Complete Series)
Read It Here:
https://mybook.to/DrPierceBoxset

Dr. Blackmore (Complete Series)

Read It Here:
https://mybook.to/DrBlackmoreBoxset

Dr. Grant (Complete Series)
Read It Here:
https://mybook.to/DrGrantBoxset

Dr. Hayes (Complete Series)
Read It Here:
https://mybook.to/DrHayesBoxset

Dr. Campbell (Complete Series)
Read It Here:
https://mybook.to/DrCampbellBoxset

Dr. Hale (Complete Series)
Read It Here:
https://mybook.to/DrHaleBoxset

Dr. Costa (Complete Series)
Read It Here:
https://mybook.to/DrCostaBoxset

Dr. Duncan (Complete Series)
Read It Here:
https://mybook.to/DrDuncanBoxset

CONTENTS

CHAPTER 1 1
CHAPTER 2 15
CHAPTER 3 27
CHAPTER 4 39
CHAPTER 5 51
CHAPTER 6 65
CHAPTER 7 75
CHAPTER 8 87
CHAPTER 9 99
CHAPTER 10 111
CHAPTER 11 125
CHAPTER 12 137
CHAPTER 13 149
CHAPTER 14 161
CHAPTER 15 171
CHAPTER 16 181
CHAPTER 17 193
CHAPTER 18 205
CHAPTER 19 217
CHAPTER 20 229
CHAPTER 21 241
CHAPTER 22 253

CHAPTER 23 267
CHAPTER 24 279
CHAPTER 25 293
WHAT'S NEXT? *305*
    SHIVER OF DESIRE 306
ALICIA'S AUTHOR NOTES *307*
ACKNOWLEDGEMENTS *317*
OTHER BOOKS BY ALICIA *319*
    COVETED 319
    DR. WALKER 320
    DR. PIERCE 321
    DR. CARTER 322
    DR. MACLEAN 323
    DR. BLACKMORE 324
    DR. WRIGHT 325
    DR. PARK 326
    DR. GRANT 327
    DR. HAYES 328
    DR. CAMPBELL 329
    DARWIN BROTHERS 330
    DADDY'S OFF LIMITS 331
CONNECT WITH THE AUTHOR *333*
REVIEW THE BOOK *335*

FREE GIFT

Hi my lovely!

Thank you for reading my book!

Stay up to date with everything going on in my world. Exclusive books, giveaways, tons of new reads, chapter reveals, and so much more.

Plus, I'll send you my exclusive ebook "Coveted (Dr. Stone, Book1)" that is available nowhere else, absolutely FREE, of course!

Just sign up and enjoy the love and steam:

https://dl.bookfunnel.com/46pg16ndzd

Much love 🖤

Alicia Nichols

To love.

CHAPTER 1

- SAVANNAH -

"Are you fucking kidding me, Kayden? You choose the day of our wedding to tell me that you've gotten another woman knocked up?"

Kayden took a step towards me and frowned. "Can you please keep your voice down? People are going to hear."

"I can't believe you." I threw my hands up in the air, my heart pounding wildly against my chest. "Do you think I care that people know? It's only going to be a matter of time anyway."

He bridged the distance between us and reached for my hand. I snatched it away and took a few steps back, pushing my veil away from my face. "Don't touch me. I don't want you anywhere near me right now."

Kayden's frown deepened. "Baby—"

I pointed a finger at him and bristled. "Don't you dare baby me. I forgave you for this before, Kayden, and you told me you were never going to do it again."

"I wasn't planning on it, but I ran into Macy at the bar two months ago, and we got to talking—"

I held a hand up, the fire in my veins turning molten. "Wait a second, Macy? *As in your ex-girlfriend's sister, Macy?*"

Kayden shoved his hands into the pocket of his pants. "Yeah, I had no idea she was back in town."

A low ringing began in the back of my head.

This was not happening.

Not here, not now.

Not me.

It couldn't be.

I was in the middle of some twisted joke, and I had no idea when the punchline was.

Or why I seemed to be it.

"The woman you slept with and got pregnant is your ex-girlfriend's sister?"

"When you put it like that, it sounds bad."

"How else am I supposed to put it?" I balled my hands into fists at my sides. "Why don't you tell me how you want me to phrase it in a way that makes it seem okay?"

It was taking every ounce of self-control I had not to punch Kayden squarely in the face. The only thing keeping me from causing any more of a scene was knowing that deep down, a hundred guests were gathered and milling around the courtyard of the local B and B. Soft strings of music were playing and somewhere in the house, a priest was getting ready to join the two of us in holy matrimony.

Meanwhile, I was trying to keep it all together and emerge with a shred of dignity intact. Over, and over, I kept trying to figure out what was wrong with me, or what I had done to deserve this. The longer I stood there staring at the man I was meant to be spending the rest of my life with, the worst I felt about the entire thing.

I wanted a hole to open up and swallow me whole.

"Jesus, Sav. I don't know. It's not like I planned for this to happen, okay? Macy was supposed to be different, not like the others—"

I held a hand up and sucked in a harsh breath. "Did you just say others? As in you've cheated on me more than once?"

Given that I had known who Kayden was from the start, having forgiven him for cheating before, I shouldn't have been as surprised as I was. Unfortunately, it was one thing to forgive him for a single lapse in judgement years ago.

It was another thing entirely to realize it was ongoing.

And with many different women.

Jesus.

My heart felt like it was breaking into a million pieces, and my head was still spinning.

Why?

Why was this happening?

Kayden reached for my arms and I was too shocked to resist. He pulled me to him. "How can I make this better? Tell me what you want me to do, and I'll do it."

I shook myself back to reality and pried myself away from him. "Why were you planning on marry me if you were just going to sleep around?"

"What are you talking about, Sav? I love you."

"You love me? How is this love? You don't destroy the people you love."

"Sav, I—"

"Get the fuck out of my hotel room."

"Sav, come on. Don't you think you're overacting?"

My hand connected with his cheek before I knew what I was doing. It left an angry red mark on his face. His hand moved to his cheek, and he rubbed it gingerly. "What was that for?"

"It's the least you deserve." I stood up straighter and folded my arms over my chest. *"Get out."*

Kayden spun on his heels and hurried out of the room, the door clicking shut behind him. A heartbeat later, Gemma came into the room, her blonde hair falling out of her elaborate bun, and a confused look on her face. She dragged the train of her pink dress inside before slamming the door shut behind her.

"What the hell is happening? Kayden just got into his car and took off without talking to anyone."

I sank into the nearest chair and stared at her. "He just told me that he got Macy pregnant."

Gemma jerked back, and her eyes widened into saucers. "Macy as in his ex-girlfriend's sister Macy?"

I nodded and ran a hand over my face. "I don't want to deal with the guests downstairs. Can you please get them all to leave? Make something up if you have to."

Gemma cleared her throat. "Your aunt is singing karaoke downstairs. I'm not sure how you want me to deal with that. You know how she gets when she has a mike."

"Great, just what I need."

As if having to deal with the town's gossip and pity about my canceled wedding wasn't going to be bad enough. With a sigh, I stood and hurried past Gemma, my wedding gown trailing behind me. On my way down the stairs, I got a few curious looks from the wait staff who were dressed in a standard black and white uniform. In a daze, I made my way out into the courtyard, where chairs were lined up on either side of the aisle, leading up to an arch that was made up entirely of flowers.

The sight made knots form in the center of my stomach.

Do not cry. There will be time to cry later. One crisis at a time, okay, Savannah?

WEDDING NIGHT STRANGER (MR. BUCHANNAN)

Scanning the people milling out in the courtyard, I spotted my aunt on the makeshift stage in her red sequined dress, arguing with the band. She glistened underneath the late afternoon sun, her makeup running down her cheeks. I gathered up my dress, stepped onto the stage and snatched the mike out of her hands.

I had known my aunt was going to pull a stunt like this, since she always did, but I didn't have the energy or the patience to deal with her.

Not today.

Not like this.

She twisted to face me, a furrow appearing between her brows. "You're not supposed to be up here."

"I know that. Neither are you. I told you no karaoke, remember?"

Alexandra Parrish tossed her hair over her shoulders. "Darling, I know what you said, but you can't deny the people what they want. People love to hear me sing."

"No, they don't, and the wedding is off anyway, so it doesn't matter."

Alexandra huffed and placed both hands on her hips. "What do you mean it's off? What did you do?"

"Thank you for assuming it was something I did rather than asking if I'm okay." I tossed the mike over to the band and pointed in the direction of the exit. "I'll be in touch about the rest of your payment."

Hastily, they began to gather their instruments, their heads bent the entire time. Before they left, my aunt snatched the mike out of their hands and began to sing, loudly and offkey. She was my mom's sister and had raised me after my parents' passing. I wrapped my hands around the mike and tried to wrestle it out of her hands. "Let go."

"No. I have to sing."

"You do not, Ti. Just let the damn mike go."

The two of us struggled until I tripped on the dress and went sailing backwards, and into the wedding cake.

Bits and pieces of it were all over my wedding dress and drooping down the sides of my face when I stood up. It took every ounce of self-control I had to push back the tears. I dug my nails into the inside of my palms, the roaring in my ears growing louder. Of all the times to pull a stint like this, my aunt had to pick today of all days.

It was the icing on an already spoiled cake I didn't want.

Fucking perfect.

My aunt hid the mike behind her back and gave me an apologetic smile. "You still look beautiful, and I'm sorry, dear, but you know how important my music career is to me. I can't let anyone get in the way."

I pulled a chunk of cake out of my hair and threw it onto the floor underneath me. "You know what? Do whatever you want, mom. Just keep me out of it."

With that, I climbed off the stage and onto the grass. As soon as I landed, my heels sunk into the ground, and I heard a cracking sound. The ringing in my ears kept getting louder as I huffed and struggled until I pulled my feet out, sans the shoes and walked over to Gemma. The back of my eyes burned, but I kept counting backwards in my head and comforting myself with thoughts of ice cream.

Large quantities of it while I sobbed into a tub.

Why the hell hadn't I listened to my gut when it came to Kayden?

Gemma stood by the gates of the courtyard, ushering people out. I held my head high and didn't meet her gaze as I walked past.

I didn't realize what I was doing until I got into the car and backed out of the parking lot, nearly knocking a man off his motorcycle. Then the car lurched forward, and I had both hands on the steering wheel, and the music turned up.

WEDDING NIGHT STRANGER (MR. BUCHANNAN)

What the fuck was I going to do now?

I was supposed to be standing across from Kayden underneath an arch made entirely of flowers while everyone looked on and smiled. I wasn't supposed to be gripping the steering wheel of my car in a death grip while my mind spun and raced, trying to make sense of the day.

None of it felt real.

It couldn't be.

Trees and houses whipped past me in either direction, all blending into a flurry of shapes and colors that were indistinguishable from each other. Once I pulled up outside the house, I was breathing heavily as I reached for my purse, my fingers trembling. Bare-foot, and in a dress covered in cake, I walked up the driveway, with as much strength I could muster and pushed the key into the lock.

One more step, and I could break down.

As soon as the door opened, I had a perfect view of our open-concept kitchen. On a table next to the counter were the wedding gifts. I took one look at them piled up on top of each other and burst into laughter. While I was relieved that Kayden hadn't moved in yet, since he had planned to move in after the wedding, the sight of all those gifts had gotten to me.

A glaring reminder of what was snatched out from under me.

I fucking hated Macy.

And I wanted to scream and cry and punch something.

Anything to keep me from dwelling too long on the hollow ache in my chest.

Frantically, I clawed at my hair, pulling out pin after pin until hair tumbled down around my shoulders, little pinpricks of pain shooting up and down my scalp. Once I was done, I fished my phone out of my purse and listened to it ring.

Although the last thing I wanted was to be alone in the house I bought to start a life with Kayden, I had nowhere else to go. Since my aunt lived out of her suitcase in the hotel where she worked, and Gemma's cramped studio apartment barely fit one person, much less two, it was the only option I had.

Briefly, I considered calling my dad, but I hadn't seen him in years.

"I'm still at the B and B. It turns out there's a lot of details to go over if you cancel a wedding out of the blue. Are you---are you laughing?"

"You piled the gifts on top of a table and color coordinated them," I wheezed out, in between giggles. "That's such a you thing to do, Gem."

"Sav, I'm a little worried."

I drifted over to the window and pushed the curtain aside. "Worried? Why would you be worried? It's not like I had to break up with my fiancée on the day of my wedding because he cheated on me. It's not like the worst that could happen has happened or anything."

"I'm trying to finish up here, and I'll be right over."

My laughter trailed off and turned into tears. "Why? So, you can see what a mess I am? I don't want anyone seeing me like this."

Least of all deal with all the pity and confusion.

Gemma was my best friend and had been since high school, but I was suddenly glad she wasn't here to see me fall apart. Having been forced to keep it together for the past hour while I wrestled with my aunt and, I didn't want to bottle everything up.

Not when everything was threatening to spill out of me all at once.

And I wouldn't be able to control it.

I wasn't even sure I wanted to.

WEDDING NIGHT STRANGER (MR. BUCHANNAN)

Calling off the wedding was bad enough. Realizing that I was going to be forced to see Macy parading around town and rubbing it in my face was worse. In a few months, everyone was going to see Macy's bulging stomach and make assumptions about why Kayden and I had ended things on the day of the wedding. I barely listened to Gemma talking as I went through the fridge until I found a bottle of wine. Using my teeth, I forced it open and took a long sip.

It burned before settling in the pit of my stomach.

"...forget about him anyway. He doesn't know what he's missing out on."

I took another swig and drifted back to the font window, overlooking the rows and rows of Victorian style houses. I'd chosen the neighborhood because it looked idyllic and magical, like somewhere Kayden and I could build a life together and start a family. Now, I couldn't stop seeing him with his arm draped over Macy's stomach and a bright smile on his face.

Goddamn bastard.

How could he do this to me?

I stared at the house across the street and continued to sip on my drink. When the blue front door opened, and a tall, dark-haired man stepped out, my mouth fell open. With his broad shoulders, sharp jaw and slicked back dark hair, he was easily the most handsome man I'd ever seen.

In his expensive suit, with a tie hanging askew around his neck, he looked out of place in the neighborhood. He spoke rapidly into his phone, then pulled the phone away from his ear and scowled.

Who was this man?

And why couldn't I stop staring at him?

Considering I'd just had my heart broken, at the altar no less, I knew I shouldn't be ogling my new neighbor. Yet, the longer I stood there, trying to force myself to move away and yank the curtains shut, the less inclined I was to do that. Gemma was still talking about something, but her voice was a dull roar in the background.

Until she repeated my name a few times.

"Huh? What?"

"I asked if you were okay. You went quiet all of a sudden."

I stood up straighter and took another long sip. "Yeah, I got distracted by the new neighbor across the street. He looks like he should be working on Wallstreet or something."

"Why are you checking out your new neighbor?"

"Because he's hot. Why shouldn't I?"

"Okay, yeah. You definitely need a pick me up after the day you had. Is there anything you want me to grab for you on the way over?"

"No, I need you to do me a favor when you get here."

"Anything, what do you need?"

"I want you to knock me over the head, hard. And if I mention anything about getting with a man ever again, I want you to tie me up to a chair until I get some sense knocked back into me."

Gemma chuckled and pressed on her horn. "I can definitely do that."

"I'm being serious. No men, ever."

I studied the handsome stranger as he paced from end of his porch to the next, idly aware that I wasn't *really* breaking my new rule, I was just enjoying the view. He slipped his phone into his pocket, tapped something against his ear then scowled into the distance.

It looked like I wasn't the only one having a shit day.

"Hold on. I'm getting a notification." I pulled the phone away from my ear, stared at the message on my phone and a lump rose in the back of my throat. "It's an email from the hotel that I booked for our honeymoon. They're going all out for the Valentine's theme."

"Fuck. Do you want me to call them?"

I sniffed and pressed the phone back against my ear. "I'll do that later, after a few more bottles of wine."

"Bottles? How many have you had?"

I squinted at the bottle in my hand. "Half a bottle, but it's not doing anything."

With a frown, I set the bottle down on the floor and made a beeline for the kitchen. While I was rummaging through the fridge, the refrigerator light flicked on and the power went out. I was plunged into semi-darkness, with small particles of light pouring in through the open curtain in the living room.

Great. Because I need electricity problems to deal with on top of everything else. Fucking perfect. Can anything else go wrong today?

I swung the refrigerator door shut and used the back of my hand to wipe my mouth. On my way back to the window, eager and desperate for some light, I lost my balance and flew backwards. Flat on my back, staring up at the cream-colored ceiling, I placed my phone in the center of my chest and buried my face in my hands.

"What the hell happened? Are you okay?"

"I slipped and fell on the dress," I told Gemma, in between my hiccoughs. "Gem, I'm beginning to think that I'm cursed or something. And I'm pretty sure something happened to the electricity because the power is out."

"Babe, you're not cursed. You're just having a bad day."

Gingerly, I pushed myself up to my feet and ignored the little pinpricks of pain dancing up and down my arms. When I drifted back to the window, the neighbor was still standing there, facing the house, with his back facing me.

"Tell me more about the new neighbor," Gemma urged, in a low voice. She muttered something into the background, and I heard cars rushing past her. "What does he look like?"

"Tall, broad shoulders, dark hair," I responded, with a tilt of my head. "I'm too far away to tell, but I think he's got blue eyes."

"What makes you think he should be on Wallstreet?"

"He's wearing a suit that looks expensive, more than I could make in a lifetime," I replied, after a brief pause. "And he looks furious. I would hate to be on the receiving end of that conversation."

"Yeah?"

"Oh, yeah. He's definitely telling someone off."

"What about his ass? Does he have a nice ass?"

I studied his back, a smile hovering on the edge of my lips. "Yeah, I think so. Gem, what am I doing? Why am I checking out a complete stranger?"

Considering how many phone calls I had to make in order to pick up the pieces after leaving Kayden, it was better if I got started. The sooner I got through it, the sooner I could put it all behind me and figure out what I wanted to do next. But as I stood there, unable to look away from my attractive new neighbor, I realized I had no idea what that was.

I had no big dreams.

Nothing that drove me forward.

Only a mountain of debt, a house I could no longer afford, and a married life that I was never going to get to live.

The tears came again, and my shoulders shook. Out of the corner of my eye, I saw a flash of movement and realized the neighbor was staring straight ahead and looking directly at me. Panic blossomed within me as I threw myself onto the floor, heart pounding wildly against my chest.

"Shit. I think he saw me looking at him, Gem."

"I doubt he can tell from there."

"I can never leave the house now," I whispered, with a sigh. "Which is probably for the best anyway since I'm sure everyone is already gossiping about the wedding."

"If it makes you feel better, I think they'll let you keep the presents."

ALICIA NICHOLS

CHAPTER 2

- ASHER -

I placed a hand in my pocket and stood up straighter. "That's not the kind of news I want to hear, Will. Do you have any idea what kind of damage this is going to do?"

I'd gone through every inch of the house, rifling through every nook and cranny for any kind of clue as to their whereabouts but none of it made me feel better.

On the contrary, it made me feel worse about being duped.

I had had the wool pulled over my eyes, and I had never even suspected them.

With a frown, I twisted to face the Victorian house I now owned and surveyed it intently. Months ago, I had chosen the property myself, knowing it would be the perfect headquarters for my project. With several bedrooms and bathrooms, a picturesque and idyllic view situated in the middle of the town, it had been exactly what I needed in order to help me get into the right mindset of starting my own server farm, using water to cool the servers.

Or so I thought.

I had half a mind to take a chainsaw to the whole thing and set it on fire.

But collecting the insurance was going to be painful and unnecessary, prolonging my stay here.

I spun back around to face the front, and the rows of manicured lawns and two story houses and paused. In the sun-soaked distance, I saw a flutter of movement in an upstairs window followed by the rustling of a curtain. Then the movement stopped altogether, making my frown deepen.

Was I going to have to deal with nosy neighbors on top of everything else?

Considering the size of the town, and the number of looks I'd already gotten, I shouldn't have been surprised. The neighbors probably already knew what happened.

With a slight shake of my head, I made my way back into the house, the door clicking shut behind me. Once it did, I glanced around and studied the tiny particles of light dancing on the hardwood floors. Such a waste. Already, this was the worst investment I'd ever made, a money pit I wanted to rid myself of.

"Will, I need you to stop right there. I don't care about any of the goddamn bi-laws or whatever fancy terms you're going to use, I want results. It's what I pay you and your team for."

And right now, they were making me wonder why I'd hired them to begin with.

What was the point of a team of highly qualified, overpaid professionals if they weren't going to get me the results I wanted?

"Mr. Buchannan, we have been trying to figure out what went wrong since you called me a few hours ago, but—"

"I don't want buts," I interrupted, pausing to kick off my shoes. "I want to know what the hell happened. How wasn't anything flagged?"

"We ran every background check possible, sir," Will replied, sounding out of breath. "It was a legitimate business proposal."

I paused to kick off my shoes and left them by the door. "So, you're telling me there's nothing I can do?"

For the life of me, I couldn't imagine how they'd done it.

WEDDING NIGHT STRANGER (MR. BUCHANNAN)

Months ago, when Jeffrey my best friend from college and Caroline, my girlfriend, approached me with a business investment, I'd been intrigued. For weeks the two of them took me out to all of my favorite spots in the city, plied me with drinks and showed me one proposal after the next. I'd spent the entire time reviewing the details in my head and running it by my legal team.

It had been an exciting prospect, and a way for me to branch out.

I was always looking for the next challenge, and the next big thing.

Caroline and Jeffrey knew this all too well, and they had known exactly how to get to me. Between the dinners and my personal relationship with both of them, I'd been too blind to see the truth. Two hours ago, I'd driven up to the town of blue breeze, an empty house and no sign of either of them.

And I'd been on the phone with my lawyer ever since.

Every phone call and message to Jeffrey and Caroline went unanswered, leaving a pit in the center of my stomach.

What had they done?

And why hadn't I caught onto it sooner?

That's why you get for trusting your best friend and girlfriend with a large business venture. You should've gone with your gut, Ash, instead of letting them sweet talk you.

Will cleared his throat. "There's more, Mr. Buchannan."

"Of course, there is," I replied, stiffly. "How else did they screw me over?"

"We've checked the account, sir. All the money has been transferred into an offshore account, and we haven't been able to trace it."

I should've known that making Jeffrey a business partner was a mistake.

I had known it in my gut, but I had ignored my instincts.

Goddamn rookie mistake.

I balled my hand into a fist at my side. "I see."

"And they didn't do their do diligence where the wellness center is concerned," Will continued, the words tumbling out of him in a rush. "There's been some dispute over the land where it was built."

I ran a hand over my face. "Tell me something good, Will. You know I like good news."

"You can still open the wellness center as planned, and we are working to find a loophole for the dispute. Most likely, we'll have to settle."

"Consider it done. I want this problem solved. What else?"

"Mr. Buchannan, I got a call from the police today and the FBI."

I switched the phone to my other ear. "Why?"

"You're being investigated for fraud and money laundering charges," Will whispered, his voice rising towards the end. "I've taken the liberty of hiring a private investigator. It turns out that Ms. Caroline and Mr. Jeffrey were involved with some very…powerful people."

Fuck.

As if the two of them stealing money and leaving me in the dust wasn't bad enough. The two of them had been on my side for years and had seen the amount of sacrifices I'd made for the sake of the company. I had worked hard since college, pouring my blood, sweat and tears to built it from the ground up, and I couldn't believe it could all be undone because of a single, deadly blow.

Bastards.

"Tell the investigator to dig deeper," I told him, calmly. "Tell him to find out whatever he can because we're going to use it against them."

"Sir?"

"I know the two of them have secrets," I added, after a brief pause. "There's no way they can pull off something like this and not have skeletons in their closets. Find me something good, Will."

"Yes, sir."

"Have the lead investigator for the FBI call me directly."

"Sir, as your lawyer, I should advise you against it. It's not advisable to communicate with the FBI given the nature of the allegations—"

"I have nothing to hide, and I'd like to be kept in the loop either way. I'll be expecting his call."

"Agent Lawry, sir. She's in the area, and she will probably want to talk to you in person."

"You can stay on the phone if you want," I offered. "Although I don't think it'll be necessary."

I came to a stop in front of the window, with a direct view of the neighbor's house. I saw another flash in the downstairs window, and a glimpse of a white dress before the curtains rustled closed. By tomorrow, I expected the entire town was going to be talking about me, and the real reason I was there.

If they weren't already.

Nothing rocked a small town like a scandal.

And being in the center of one was the price I had to pay in order to see this project through. Since I'd already rented out the house for an entire year and made several other financial commitments to the project including taking over the wellness center as way to integrate myself into the community and make money while doing it, the last thing I wanted was to throw in the towel. In a few days, the news would become public knowledge, hitting my reputation, and the company's.

Being conned out of money was not a good look for an insurance brokerage company.

Nothing I said or did was going to change that.

There's got to be some kind of explanation. They wouldn't just betray you like that.

"I'm staying to see this project through," I said, pausing to stride back into the kitchen. I rummaged through the shelves until I found a bottle of whiskey. After pouring myself a generous amount, I tossed it back, allowing it to burn a path down my throat before it settled in the pit of my stomach.

The longer I stood there, listening to Will discuss contingencies and legal strategies, the worse I felt about the entire thing.

Why hadn't I seen the truth about the two of them sooner?

I prided myself on being able to see right through people, but when it came the two of them, I ignored all of the warning signs. Everything from the quick looks the two of them shared to the whispered conversations when I stumbled upon them.

The realization left me with an ache in the center of my chest. I set the phone down on the counter and took the velvet box out of my other pocket. Once I propped it open, the diamonds glistened and shone underneath the light.

A furrow appeared between my brows as I reached for my other phone and dialed Caroline's number. It rang a few times before it went straight to voicemail. Heart thumping against my chest, I tried Jeffrey again only to be told the number had been disconnected.

Wherever they were, they were somewhere far away, spending my hard-earned cash. While I had spent the past few hours trying to come up with every excuse to justify what they'd done, I couldn't do it anymore. I was going to make sure my investigator found the skeletons they were hiding.

And when I did, I was going to make sure I buried them.

They might have seen me as an easy target, but I was going to prove to everyone they'd just made the biggest mistake of their lives.

WEDDING NIGHT STRANGER (MR. BUCHANNAN)

A short while later, someone knocked on the door. I pushed myself off the counter and in the doorway, there was a short woman in a suit with bright blonde hair and a no nonsense look, her bright eyes wide and assessing. She glanced over my shoulders before taking a step back and holding her hand out.

"Agent Lawry, I presume."

"Mr. Buchannan, thank you for taking the time to meet with me."

"I'm more than happy to help with the investigation, Agent." I gave her hand a firm shake before pushing the door open. "Won't you come in?"

"I'd rather we talked outside."

I nodded. "Of course. Please, have a seat, Agent."

Once she selected a chair on the front porch, I went back inside and snatched the bottle of whiskey off the counter and retrieved two glasses. Agent Lawry sat with her back erect, hands folded across her lap and was studying the terrain intently. As soon as I sat down, she let her hands fall to her sides, and her eyes flicked over the bottle before moving to my face.

"Can I interest you in a drink, Agent?"

She shook her head. "No, thank you."

I shrugged and poured myself a generous amount. "I already told my lawyer that we are going to be cooperating with the FBI, and the local police for whatever you need. I have nothing to hide, Agent. And I'm sure your investigation will support my claim."

"Mr. Buchannan, you were with Ms. Caroline Bennett, weren't you?"

"Yes."

"And you went to university with Mr. Jeffrey Palmer?"

I eyed her over the rim of my glass. "I'm sure you didn't come here to ask me questions you already have the answers to,

Agent. You already know I knew Ms. Bennett and Mr. Palmer well, or at least I thought I did."

Agent Lawry's eyebrows drew together. "And you still maintain that you had no idea they worked for the mob?"

"None whatsoever. Tea?"

"Excuse me?"

"Since you won't have a drink with me, Agent, because you're on the clock, I'm sure a cup of tea won't do any harm."

"Mr. Buchannan, this isn't a social call."

I set my glass down and brought one leg up over the other. "I'm well aware of that, Agent, but I was taught to make my guests comfortable."

Agent Lawry frowned. "Is this a joke to you, Mr. Buchannan? Because these are some very serious accusations."

I placed a cigarette between my lips and watched her through a thin plume of smoke. "I can assure you that I'm taking these accusations very seriously, Agent. I've worked hard to build my company, and I have no intention of allowing my mistake to undo everything I've done."

"Even if it means having to put your girlfriend and friend in jail?"

"Ex-girlfriend and former friend."

"You don't seem upset by what they've done." She sat back against her chair and linked her fingers together. "Is there anything you want to share, Mr. Buchannan?"

"It's Asher."

"I beg your pardon?"

"I don't like being called Mr. Buchannan outside of the office," I replied, pausing to take another long drag and exhale. "Agent, if I had something to hide, would I be sitting here with you, offering my help?"

Making an enemy of the police and the FBI wasn't the smart move.

She and I both knew it.

Good thing for her, I didn't need Agent Lawry to like me to do her job. But I did want her to believe me, otherwise she was going to make things hard for me. With another look in her direction, I stood up and put out my cigarette. Then I made my way inside and rummaged through the fridge. I returned with a pitcher of lemonade and a plate of cookies.

"My housekeeper made these." I set the tray down and made a vague hand gesture. "Please."

Reluctantly, Agent Lawry reached for a glass and took a small sip. "I'll need to interview your housekeeper."

"Of course."

"And any other staff you've hired."

I raised an eyebrow. "Including the staff that's been hired here at the wellness center?"

Agent Lawry set down her drink and cleared her throat. "Were you part of the hiring process?"

"No, I employed an agency. I can provide you with their information."

She reached into her blazer and pulled out a notebook. A furrow appeared between her brows as she patted the rest of her pockets. Wordlessly, I held out a pen to her and waited for her to take it. Her gaze flicked up to mine before she began to jot things down.

"I'll need to see the wellness center you've built," Agent Lawry continued, without looking at me. "And all of the paperwork, including the paperwork for the house you've rented."

"Of course, but I'd like to keep the entire thing discreet. This house was meant as a base for myself, and my business partner to stay in while we were overseeing the project."

Agent Lawry stopped writing and looked up. "Discreet?"

"My lawyers have assured me that I can still run the wellness center as planned. It's my other project that's going to be on hold for a while. I'm sure you can understand why I don't want the negative press surrounding the wellness center, and I'm sure you don't want anything or anyone interfering with the investigation."

Agent Lawry stared at me and didn't say anything.

I leaned back against the chair, a smile hovering on the edge of my lips. "I'm happy to wait while you clear everything with the higher-ups."

She muttered something underneath her breath and took a phone out of her pocket. Slowly, she rose to her feet and climbed down the steps. In the middle of the path, she stopped and glanced at me over her shoulders, the phone pressed to her ear. I studied her and gave nothing away.

Was she inclined to believe me?

Lock me up without a backwards glance?

Were things a lot worse than my lawyer made them out to be?

Not knowing was driving me crazy, but I pushed it all down and sat there, taking long drags of my cigarette and trying to calm myself down.

A flicker of surprise moved across her face before she ended the call.

Agent Lawry climbed back up the stairs. "You've got fans in the bureau, Mr. Buchannan."

"I'm always happy to help." I shrugged and poured myself a drink. "Will there be anything else, Agent? I've got a lot of details that need my attention."

Agent Lawry straightened her blazer. "Of course. I'll be in touch, Mr. Buchannan. Thank you for your time."

I rose to my feet and nodded. "You're welcome, Agent."

With that, she spun on her heels and left.

On her way to her car, she passed an elderly couple, dressed in matching suits, with a small dog in tow. The two of them walked faster, pausing to give her a look over their shoulders.

Once they were gone, I went back into the house, dragging my suitcase behind me.

I ignored the low ringing in the back of my head and pulled out my laptop.

But I couldn't stop thinking about Caroline and Jeffrey.

And what they had done to me.

After leaving Will a message, I spent the rest of the day staring at the screen and wondering how to spin this entire disaster. Returning to the city wasn't an option, not when I had a wellness center to run and an image to maintain. I couldn't run from my problems.

As far as I was concerned, the only way to move forward was to proceed as planned.

As if I hadn't gotten stabbed in the back by the two people closest to me.

You can think about that later. Right now, you need to focus on keeping your head down and figuring out to make this project a success.

I was going to make sure something good came out of this.

It was what I did best, after all.

ALICIA NICHOLS

CHAPTER 3

- SAVANNAH -

"Stop looking at me like that and give me another drink."

With an exhale, Robbie reached behind him and poured me another generous amount of tequila. My hand darted out, and I snatched the bottle out of his hand. He gave a slight shake of his head and walked to the other end of the bar, where a group of women were waving and giggling.

Conversation rose and fell around me while I sat there, drowning my sorrows in one shot of tequila after the next.

While the alcohol did nothing to quell the growing ache in my chest, or the heaviness in the center of my stomach, it was better than sitting all alone in my cold and damp house. Having spent the past few hours pacing and ripping the gifts open while Gemma sat on a chair watching me, I'd had enough.

I'd had enough of her pity, of the voices in the back of my head, and the itching sensation crawling up my spine. Against my best friend's advice, I'd stormed out of the house, and she'd followed close behind. In silence, Gemma had driven me to O'Malley's, the closest bar and ushered me inside. As soon as I set foot in the bar, I'd known it was a mistake.

Several pairs of eyes had turned to me and gawked.

In my wedding dress, with my hair piled on top of my head and no makeup, I was attracting a lot of attention even without the food I'd gotten out. Half of me had been tempted to turn around, gather up my dress and run back outside. The other half of me had lifted my head up and made a beeline for the bar, ignoring the whispers and lingering looks.

Everyone was going to talk anyway.

Why should I care what they said?

Except I did, and I hated every single second of it.

Gemma sat at a booth a few feet away watching me while nursing her own drink. Now and again, she got up to talk to me, but I waved her away and kept my attention focused on my drink. While I appreciated her being there and wanting to keep an eye on me, I didn't feel like talking.

Or explaining why I felt the need to be alone in the middle of a bar.

All I knew was that the more I drank, the less I felt.

Everything was a dull roar in the back of my head, and I liked it better than the silence or the feeling that I wanted to rip off my wedding dress and collapse into a heap on the floor.

Keep it together, Sav. Kayden isn't worth of all the heartache anyway.

But my heart didn't seem to care either way.

I kept replaying our conversation in my head and seeing his face as he told me, apologetic but determined. On my fifth shot, I was beginning to wonder if I had imagined the entire relationship between me and Kayden and allowed myself to build it up into something it wasn't. With a scowl, I looked down into my shot glass and pictured Macy's smug face.

Fucking moron.

I had known she was trouble the minute she breezed back into town.

But I'd told myself it was nothing to worry about.

"You could get another drink, you know."

I glanced up and found myself looking at the neighbor from across the street. Up close, I realized he had an angular face, a square cut jaw and a smooth chin. His blue grey eyes stayed on my face while I studied him as he leaned over the counter, the first few buttons of his shirt undone.

Shit.

He was exactly kind of distraction I was looking for.

And he looked sexy underneath florescent lighting.

I sat up straighter and pushed my hair out of my face. "The tequila isn't bad, but what do I now? I'm a terrible judge of people, so I'm probably not the person you want to go to for drink recommendations either."

He raised an eyebrow. "It's a little late for an existential crisis, isn't it?"

"Or early depending on who you ask." I snatched my glass of the table and tilted it in his direction. "You look like you're having a shit day too."

He shrugged. "I'll turn it around."

"That makes one of us." I tipped back the drink and sighed. "Do you know how much this dress cost?"

A furrow appeared between his brows. "Should I?"

A group of people jostled past us, and he leaned forward, offering a scent of his cologne, musk and sandalwood. The knots in the center of my stomach unfurled, replaced with a swarm of butterflies. He shoved one hand into the pocket of his trousers, the picture of confidence and charm in his pressed suit and dark, unruly hair.

Goddamn it.

"It cost a lot," I told him, after a long pause. "That's why I'm wearing it. Considering how much it cost, I thought why the hell not?"

He signaled the waiter and tilted his drink in my direction. "I'll drink to that."

"You think you know a person, but how well do we really know people, even when you're prepared to spend your life with them? We can never truly see what's on the inside, we can only make guesses."

A short while later, a takeout bag was set down on the counter in front of my neighbor. He finished his drink, took out his wallet and handed the bartender the money. Then he turned back to me and gave me a look that had shivers racing up and down my spine.

"I'm Asher by the way."

I leaned forward and raised my voice over the music. "I'm Savannah." Without warning, I stood up and swayed on my feet. "And I was just going to walk home."

"Me too."

After a quick glance at my shoulders at Gemma, I took out my phone to shoot her a warning about what I was planning. In silence, I wove in and out of the crowd of people, ignoring the smell of fries and hot wings lingering in the air. Outside, the night air was brusque, the smell of flowers lingering in the air. In the distance, a wolf howled, and I shivered.

Asher draped his jacket over my shoulders. "Do you always go to the bar in a wedding dress, or were you really just trying to get your money's worth?"

I shoved both hands into the pockets of his jacket. "Today was supposed to be my wedding day, but I had to call off the wedding because he was a lying piece of shit."

I had no filter with several drinks in me, but I couldn't bring myself to care. It felt good to call Kayden what he was, not gonna lie.

"You're better off."

I tilted my head in Asher's direction and studied him underneath the moonlight. "I hope so."

"You definitely are," Asher assured me, without missing a step. "You dodged a bullet, Savannah. I know it doesn't seem like it now, but it doesn't make it any less true."

I sighed. "Thanks. How about you?"

Asher grunted and didn't say anything.

"You're dressed in a suit and picking up takeout from a bar. Shouldn't you be on Wallstreet somewhere, or in a big corporate office running an empire from behind a fancy desk?"

Asher twisted to face me, surprise lingering in his eyes. "You got all of that from talking to me for a few minutes?"

"I like watching people."

"Sounds like you like stalking people."

"It's not stalking. You're in a public place."

He laughed and shook his head. "I'm here because for business," Asher replied, after a lengthy pause. "But I'm pretty sure my suit didn't make as much of a statement as your dress."

"We're definitely going to be the talk of the town tomorrow."

Asher stopped and looked at me. "In that case, we better give them something good to talk about."

My breath hitched in my throat. "What did you have in mind?"

"Let's go to the pier."

I nodded, slowly. "Sure, why not? It's not like I have anywhere else to be."

"That's the spirit." Asher gave me a quick wink before he made a sweeping hand gesture. "After you."

The streets ahead were empty, with only streetlamps on either side of us. Asher took long, brusque strides while I tried to keep up with him, the butterflies in my stomach beating mercilessly the entire time. A small voice in the back of my head kept telling me to turn around and go home, sleep off the hangover and get to work tomorrow, but I shoved it down.

I deserved to have a nice night out with an attractive stranger.

Especially after the night I had.

Shut up, conscience. So what if I like him because he's hot? I need this.

"You know, people who allow you to take out mortgages on your house should be held liable too," I muttered, mostly to myself. "They should assess what kind of person you are, and the person you're going to live with before agreeing to anything."

"It wouldn't accomplish anything."

"Maybe, but at least I wouldn't be in debt from a house I can't afford, and a wedding that never happened."

In the distance, the water loomed and glistened. At the edge of the sand, I paused and gathered my dress up. Asher waited next to me, his expression thoughtful as he gazed out at the water. Then he took off his shoes and motioned for me to do the same. My toes sank into the warm, squishy sand, and I wriggled my feet.

"Getting screwed over is shit, but I think you can always make the most out of it," Asher offered. "It makes you wiser, and it really shows you what you're made of."

"What are you made of?"

Asher's lips lifted into the ghost of a smile, but he didn't say anything.

In silence, we walked along the edge of the water.

Now and again when the water moved over my bare feet, I shivered. Asher was quiet as he walked alongside me, but I felt his eyes on me. Every inch of him radiating sex appeal, and the butterflies in my stomach returned. Eventually, we circled back to the pier, and Asher helped me brush the sand off my dress, his skin burning through the thin fabric.

In the middle of our street, I stopped and peered up at him. "Are you going to invite me in for a drink?"

Asher's eyes moved over me. "Okay."

My heart was thundering wildly against my chest as I followed him down the driveway and up the front stairs. A part of me couldn't believe I was about to walk into a stranger's house, knowing what I wanted him to do me. The other part of me had been picturing his mouth on mine all night.

And his hands all over me.

The low thrum of anticipation in the center of my stomach grew as reached into his pocket, pulled out a key and unlocked the door. Then he motioned for me to step in front of him, giving me another whiff of his intoxicating cologne. As soon as he stepped in behind me, he flicked on a lamp, casting soft shadows across the wall.

"I'll pour us a drink." Asher brushed past me and into the kitchen.

I cast a quick look around the empty house before I twisted my arm over my head. "Did you just move in?"

"Something like that."

With a huff, I slid the zipper down and over my back. Hastily, I shimmied out of the dress, leaving me in lacey, see-through night gown with black lingerie underneath.

I placed both hands on my hips and cleared my throat. "I have a better idea."

Asher was pouring whiskey into a glass when he looked up at me. His eyes became dark and hooded as his gaze raked over me, and slowly, he set the bottle down. He wandered over to me, the look in his eyes making the desire in my stomach molten. He stopped a few feet away, and his bright eyes moved over me, leaving heat wherever they went.

"Are you going to say anything?"

"Your ex is an idiot," Asher replied. "You look as good in that dress as you do without it."

Color crept up my cheeks. "Thank you."

"I'm not the solution to your problems, Savannah." Asher came closer, so we were inches away, and the hairs on the back of my neck rose. "I'm a distraction, a temporary fix at best. Do you understand that?"

I released a deep, shaky breath. "Yes."

"Good. I wanted to be sure you understood before I did this."

Without warning, he took me into his arms and kissed me so thoroughly my toes curled. I pressed myself against him while the blood in my ears roared, and every inch of me sang. Asher growled into my mouth and hoisted me up, so my legs were wrapped around his waist.

Every last part of me yearned for him.

For his touch, for his mouth on every inch of my skin.

Until I could forget that this day ever happened.

He carried me inside and set me down on a king-sized bed with black sheets. Wordlessly, he stepped away and began to undress, his eyes never leaving my face. I sat up on my legs and reached for him. I pulled his shirt up over his head and had a brief glimpse of smooth, tanned skin before he was on top of me again, claiming me as his. Every sweep of his tongue, every touch, every growl drove away my doubt, my insecurities.

So there was nothing else left except for his strong, muscular body pressed against mine, making me feel things I'd never felt before. Kayden's touch had nothing on Asher, and as Asher's fingers glided over my skin, leaving goosebumps everywhere he touched, it was easier than ever to forget I'd ever been almost married. When he sank his nails into my waist, I lifted my hips up off the mattress and moaned.

"You taste better than I thought you would," Asher said into my skin. He sat up, and I did the same. His eyes didn't leave my face as he pulled my nightgown up over my head and tossed it onto the floor. My bra followed shortly after, allowing my breasts to spill forward.

Raw hunger was carved onto every inch of his face as he pushed me back onto the mattress. "You were right. I definitely like this idea better."

I blew out a breath. "You smell amazing."

Asher pressed hot, open-mouthed kisses down the length of my neck and over the slope of my chest. He stopped at my stomach before peering up at me, sending another thrill racing through me. Then his teeth were grazing my skin. Every inch of me was flushed and humming with energy as he nibbled his way down my body, then used his teeth to pull my panties down over my thighs.

Fuck.

I couldn't get enough of Asher.

I wanted more.

I *needed* more of him.

When he kissed me again, I forgot why I was meant to be miserable, and the fact that I had to go home to an empty house. Once he inserted two fingers in between my wet folds, it didn't seem to matter that I was with a stranger on my wedding night, or the fact that in a few weeks' time I was going to be alone for Valentine's Day.

Instead, all that mattered was his fingers felt inside of me, stoking the fire burning in the center of my stomach. He lowered his head and kissed me, and all I could think about was how good he felt, and how glad I was that I'd invited myself into his house and taken off my dress.

Being with him was much better than the alternative.

And it felt better too.

Asher propped himself up on his other elbow and kissed me. He nipped on my lower lip, and when my lips parted, his tongue darted in, exploring every inch of my mouth. The taste of whiskey and mint washed over me, making wave after wave of desire build within me. I could barely hear past the pounding in my ears.

Suddenly, I was falling, hurtling over the edge as my orgasm ripped through me. Asher's fingers moved faster and with more purpose as his mouth moved from my mouth to my chest. With a growl, he took one nipple between his teeth and tugged. Then he reached for the other one and bit down, hard.

Dual waves of pain and pleasure ricocheted through me.

I linked my arms over his head and whimpered. "*Oh, fuck.*"

"We're just getting started," Asher promised, in a thick voice. Once my nipples were as hard as pebbles, he removed his fingers and positioned himself in front of me. In one quick move, he thrust into me until he reached the hilt. Then he pinned my arms up over my head and growled.

Goosebumps broke out over every inch of my bare skin.

I loved hearing the effect I had on him and knowing I was driving him as crazy as he drove me gave me a strange sense of satisfaction.

He was all that mattered, especially as his heavy breathing reverberated inside of my head. I squirmed against him and bucked, eager to feel more of him. "Asher, please.'

"I love how you sound when you beg." Asher eased out and slammed back into me, his eyes swimming with desire. "You like this, don't you?"

I breathed. "Yes. Yes, I do."

Asher brought his head to a rest against the headboard. "You're so tight, Savannah. And so wet. *Fuck.*"

I lifted my hips off the mattress and whimpered. "Oh, Asher. Oh, yes."

He released my hands, and they came up around his shoulders and squeezed. Together, we moved, the bed dipping and creaking underneath us. Abruptly, he changed his pace and began to move with wild and animal-like abandon. I raked my fingers over his back and struggled to breathe while my lungs burned.

It felt like I was going to explode into a million tiny pieces.

But I didn't care.

Not if it felt this good.

Asher grunted and circled his hips. "Fuck, Savannah. Fuck me."

My name was a chant on his lips as his arms trembled. Another orgasm ripped through me, making my writhe and spasm as I struggled to catch my breath. Beads of sweat glistened on Asher's forehead as he pressed it to mine and jerked against me. His entire body shook as warmth pooled between my legs.

Wordlessly, he climbed on top of me and collapsed onto the bed.

I held my arms out at my side and stared at the ceiling.

Every part of me tingled and thrummed with pleasure.

I had just had the best sex of my life, and I had no idea how I was supposed to feel about that. Asher was meant to be a one-night stand, but a small part of me found myself wishing he wasn't.

And it bothered me to no end.

CHAPTER 4

- ASHER -

I groaned and lifted a hand up to my forehead. Bright spots danced behind my eyelids, and the lawn mower in the distance is like holes are being drilled into the back of my head. With a growl, I swung my legs over the side of the bed and run a hand over my face. Slowly, I forced one eye open and wait for the room to stop spinning.

Then I opened the other eye and glanced around.

My clothes were scattered throughout the room, and a distinct fruity smell lingered in the air. I craned my head over my shoulders and stared at the empty spot next to me, relief flooding my system. Thankfully, I didn't have to deal with any awkward conversations while trying to figure out how to get her out of my house. Gingerly, I rose to my feet and blinked. On my way to the bathroom, I picked my phone up off the dresser and peer at the screen.

Already, I had several emails waiting for me.

While I waited for the water to heat up, I scrolled through the messages and typed up quick replies. Once I was done, I drew back the curtain and stepped in. I scrubbed every inch of my skin, but I could still smell her on me, an intoxicating combination of peaches and honey.

Last night was incredible.

However, I was thankful that she'd had the good sense to sneak out in the morning. Not only did I have no interest in going through a whole spiel about why the two of us weren't in any shape to get involved, but I also had no desire to explain why I wasn't the kind of guy to date.

No matter how great she was in bed.

As soon as I washed the soap out of my eyes, I started replaying our night together, everything from the sight of her in that wedding dress, to being pinned underneath me, her hair fanned out around her. But the more I stood there, thinking about the events of the previous day, the more surreal everything felt. Eventually, I pushed myself off the wall, got out of the shower and reached for the towel.

You got a better distraction than you were looking for, eh?

With a slight shake of my head, I finished up in the shower and then paused to peer at myself in the mirror. There was a small red mark on my neck, and I had scratch marks all over my back. I huffed.

Savannah was a lot wilder than I thought she would be.

Knowing that she was at the bar trying to get over her almost wedding, I hadn't known what to expect. As soon as I saw her standing in the middle of my living room in a nightgown and lingerie that showed off every curve and a generous amount of tanned skin, all I had known was that I wanted her.

Badly.

And in spite of the fact that we'd spent all night in my room, on the bed, in the bathroom, in the shower and against the wall, I still craved her.

Like an itch that wouldn't go away.

She was a lot better than I had given her credit for.

I reached for my toothbrush and squeezed a generous amount of toothpaste. Once I was done, I gurgled some water and spat it back out. When I set foot in the bedroom, the smell of her hit me again, turning the blood in my veins molten. After a quick glance at my watch, I strode to the closet and scanned the clothes there. As soon as I stepped out of the bedroom and into the kitchen, I was ready to face the day and pour all of my focus and energy on the wellness center.

WEDDING NIGHT STRANGER (MR. BUCHANNAN)

It was the only reason I was still here, and the only thing that mattered.

Getting the wellness center up and running was my number one priority while I figured out how to navigate the mess regarding the server farm. I knew that the wellness center was more of a front while I endeared myself to the locals, yet I was grateful to it for providing me with the distraction I needed.

And to keep me from going insane while I stayed in the house that was meant to be a home away from home while the three of stayed here and oversaw the project.

Jeffrey and Caroline had probably never even believed in the server farm.

While I waited for the coffee to brew, I scrolled through my phone and answered the rest of my emails. Over a cup of coffee, with early morning sun pouring in through the open windows and dancing on my hardwood floors, I planned for my day. Everything from a phone call with my lawyer to a virtual meeting with the board of directors was set up before I took my final sip.

I washed my cup, put it away and strode towards the door.

In the doorway I paused, took a look in the mirror above the table and fastened a button on my suit jacket. Then I stepped outside and pulled the door shut behind me with a click. Outside, the morning sun was high in the sky, with a few grey clouds gathering on the horizon. In the distance, I saw a group of women in matching track suits keeping up a steady pace.

All of them waved at me on their way past.

I gave them a blank look before getting into the car.

The world outside whizzed past me in either direction while I fiddled with the knob. I settled on a rock station, leaned back against my leather seat and drummed my fingers against the steering wheel. Little by little, signs of life were unfurling around me, with a school bus trailing behind, a group of people crossing the road, and a man in neon shorts who was tugging along a rabid looking dog behind him.

It really was like something out of a hallmark movie.

I couldn't tell if it was a good thing or a bad thing, but as long as this town and its people didn't get in the way of my plans, I didn't care.

Lockwood Creek wasn't anything at all like I imagined with its idyllic Victorian style houses, miles of green foliage and a view of the sparkling water. While I had been reluctant to invest in a project in a town I had never heard of and which produced little results when I looked it up, Caroline and Jeffrey had insisted it was part of the appeal all along.

It was untouched.

At least they had gotten that part right.

Once the light turned green, I pressed on the gas, and the car lurched forward. I continue to drive past rows of houses which eventually gave way to shops and boutiques, displaying everything from clothes to jewelry to dog food. On the other side of town, I came to a stop in front of a small plot of land, with a two-story stone building in the center of it overlooking the water. For the first time since I arrived in Lockwood Creek a day ago, I was beginning to see the appeal.

The wellness center had the best view and was ideally situated.

I had a chance of turning this around after all and not just save face.

The board was going to be pleased.

When I got out of the car, I spotted a group of people on the other side of the street, with their heads bent together. They kept glancing at me then back at the building, their expression growing more and more animated. I slipped a hand into my pocket, climbed up the stairs and pushed the door open. The smell of incense hit me first, followed by the soft strings of music. All of the curtains in the main room were left open, offering a view of the water and allowing sunlight to pour in and bathing the plush leather chairs and couch in a warm, buttery glow.

Behind the front desk, a woman stood with her back facing me, and a pair of headphones around her ears. She pushed herself up onto the tips of her toes, giving me a generous view of the tattoo on the small of her back. When she spun around, set the box down and glanced up at me, her expression froze.

Hastily, she yanked the headphones off, color staining her cheeks. "What are you doing here?"

"I could ask you the same question."

Savannah fished her phone out of her pocket and jabbed it. "We're still working on a few kinks here. That's why this is a soft opening. You should come back tomorrow."

I raised an eyebrow. "Why would I do that?"

Savannah cleared her throat. "Look, I really don't want to get in trouble with the new boss, okay? I haven't met him yet, but I heard he's a hard ass, and a real stickler for the rules, and I really want to leave a good impression."

"I wouldn't worry about that if I were you."

Savannah tilted her head to the side and stared at me. "Why not?"

"Because you've already left a *really* good impression," I told her, before covering the distance between us. I held a hand out. "We haven't been formally introduced. I'm Asher Buchannan, the hard ass."

In a daze, Savannah slipped her hand into mine. "You're the new boss?"

"In the flesh." I released her hand and glanced at the shelves of products behind her. "I see you've already started setting out our products. That's good."

Savannah stood up straighter and cleared her throat. "Well, this isn't awkward at all."

I glanced back at her and smirked. "It's only awkward if we make it awkward."

Savannah blew out a breath. "Ash—Mr. Buchannan, I wouldn't have slept with you if I knew who you were obviously...I really hope what happened last night doesn't affect our work relationship."

"Not at all."

Savannah blinked. "Really?"

I paused and nodded.

I was not the kind of man who liked to mix business with pleasure, not with the plethora of complications that came with it, but I was smart enough to know that it was too late to take it back.

Or undo what had been done.

The only way to move forward was to pretend like it never happened.

Regardless of how much I enjoyed it.

"You're not going to chew me out or write me up or anything?"

"I've read your CV, and I know you're the most qualified person here to be an office manager. Why would I write you up?"

Color crept up Savannah's neck and stained her cheeks. "I...well, there's no reason, I guess."

"Exactly. There's going to be a staff meeting in fifteen minutes. I expect you to let everyone else know and make sure they're in the conference room next to my office. Thank you."

With that, I spun on my heels and walked away. In my office, I studied the area, taking in the comfortable chair behind a mahogany desk, the empty shelves pressed up against the walls and the small table with a printer and fax machine in the back, set up next to a mini fridge, and a door that led into my own bathroom.

"Ms. Parish, would you come here for a second?"

Savannah materialized next to me, a notebook held against her chest. "Sir?"

"Since you've got a good eye for things, I'd like you to decorate my office. I want it to look less like an advertisement and more like an actual working space."

Savannah jotted something down. "Yes, sir."

I moved, so I was standing behind the desk and looking directly at her. In her knee length skirt with a cream-colored button-down shirt, and the early morning sun slanting in behind her, she was even more beautiful than I remembered.

And more of a problem than I thought.

I was here to work not get distracted by my new office manager.

"Oh and there's no need to call me sir," I added, my eyes moving over her face. "I think we know each other a little too well for that. Mr. Buchannan is fine."

"Will you be needing anything else, Mr. Buchannan?"

"I'll need resumes for an assistant."

"I'll have them ready for you by end of the day tomorrow."

I sat back in my chair and linked my fingers together. "It's good to see you again, Savannah."

Savannah's flush deepened as she hurried out of the office. My eyes fell to her hips, and I watched the sway of them, picturing her as she writhed on top of me. I gave a slight shake of my head and booted up my laptop. While I waited for it start, I drummed my fingers against the desk and kept stealing glances at Savannah. Through my big glass window, I could see the entire workspace, offering me a clear view of what was happening. Having put away the headphones, Savannah was now re-organizing the shelves behind the desk, a look of fierce concentration on her face.

I couldn't stop looking at the single line of sweat forming down the front of her neck and slipping in between her cleavage. With a frown, I sat back in the chair and lick my lips, imagining myself calling her in here and ushering her into the bathroom. When she bent over the front counter, I saw her covered in a thin sheen of sweat and pressed against my bedroom wall while I thrust in and out of her.

Jesus.

Why was I reliving our night together like some lovestruck teenager?

Savannah and I had both fallen into bed together out of desperation and loneliness. While I know she had spent the entire time trying to get her ex and her heartache out of her system, I hadn't minded. I myself wanted to lose myself in her to forget all about the betrayal of the two people closest to me, and the fraud charges hanging over my head.

And it had worked.

For a few blissful hours, I hadn't thought about anything other than how wet and tight she was, and how good she looked bathed underneath the light of the moon. In the early morning sun, she looked even better, especially with her hair piled on top of her head, showing off her long slender neck. When she went back around the desk, I caught a brief glimpse of the bite marks on her neck.

And it filled me with a strange sense of satisfaction.

She hadn't wiped away all remnants of last night either.

Why did that please me more than it should?

I snorted, turned my gaze away from her and focused my attention on the laptop. While I answered the remaining few emails, I kept thinking of her, and our night together. I heard her breathy whispers and moans reverberating in my head, and I frowned. After a small pause, I downed an entire bottle of water and pushed away all thoughts of her to the back of my head, finally getting some work done.

Until she came into my office and knocked on the door.

She set down a stack of papers and straightened her back. "These came in for you earlier, Mr. Buchannan. Someone from the town council dropped them off and said they were for the permits for the ground around the wellness center and the water server farm."

"Thank you, Ms. Parish. That'll be all."

The plan was already being set in motion.

Because of the server heating problem, I have every intention of purchasing the water rights in the whole area to install computer servers under water.

Hence a computer server farm.

But neither Savannah nor anyone else needed to know this.

Yet.

Not when it was only going to raise concern about the impact on the town's reliance on fishing and tourism.

When I came out of my office for the meeting, Savannah stood outside the door to the conference room, one hand on her hip, and the other holding the same notebook against the center of her chest.

Goddamn lucky notebook.

On my way past, I brushed my fingers against hers, and I was reward with a hitch of her breath. She waited until I moved to the front of the room before pulling the door shut behind her. A group of fifteen men and women, all in khakis and button-down shirts stood in front of me, wearing identical expectant expressions.

"I'm glad you're all here," I began, in a loud voice. "As you all have heard by now, I'm your new boss, Asher Buchannan. And I will work you to the bone, but I'm also a fair boss unless you give me a reason not to be."

Nervous laughter rose through the group.

"There's no reason we can't make this place a success and put Lockwood Creek on the map," I continued, my eyes moving around the room and lingering on Savannah. "I've already met some of you. As for the rest, I'll get to know you as we work alongside each other. Be punctual, be consistent and be loyal. Those are my mottos. Breaking those rules will result in immediate termination."

A heavy silence settled across the room.

"We're not off to a good start with the soft opening, but I'm sure we can turn our luck around tomorrow. Let's brainstorm ideas strategies during another meeting later today."

A murmur of agreement rose up.

"Let's give Lockwood Creek something to talk about," I finished, pausing to give everyone around the room my signature determined look. Immediately, most of my employees stiffened. One by one, they filed out the door, with Savannah lingering in the back.

"Ms. Parish." I gestured to her, and she hurried over, a furrow between her brows. "When you're done reviewing the resumes, send the ones you think do well to my office when you're ready. Thank you, Ms. Parish."

WEDDING NIGHT STRANGER (MR. BUCHANNAN)

ALICIA NICHOLS

CHAPTER 5

- SAVANNAH -

"Gem, I really can't talk about this right now." I glanced over my shoulders at the wellness center and frowned. "I don't want anyone to overhear me."

"You shouldn't have sent me that message then."

I blew out a breath and glanced back ahead of me, at the sidewalk where people lingered and enjoyed the warmth of the afternoon sun. "I'm still trying to process it."

"I still can't believe that you went out to get shit faced on your wedding and ended up sleeping with your boss. What are the chances of that happening?"

"Slim," I replied, with a sigh. "It's not like I knew."

"I can't tell if you have the worst luck in the world or…"

"Or what?"

"Yeah, I've got nothing. You definitely have the worst luck in the world."

I ran a hand over my face. "That's not even the worst part. He's got all these plans, Gem for the town, and for his computer servers…this is going to destroy Lockwood Creek as we know it."

Or it was going to run the town into a ground, turning it into little more than a commercial district for the rich and powerful, making my hometown nothing more than a shell of its former self. Considering who Asher was, and what he was here to do, I shouldn't have been surprised I had taken it upon myself to research the permits that were left on his desk the other day. I had known from the minute news began to spread that things were going to change, but I hadn't imagined anything like this.

Asher was going to put his servers underwater.

It was going to destroy marine life.

I had applied for the job because I needed it, but needing the money didn't mean I had to turn my back on my principles.

Not if I could help it.

Asher either didn't know about the severe impact his plans were going to have, or he didn't care. Either way, I had been turning the matter around and around in my head, until I came to the decision that it was up to me to make him see reason. Using my intimate knowledge of the town, I was going to show him around and make him put faces to the names. Since he planned on turning the entire town inside out, the only way I could think of stopping him was to humanize the town to him.

Show him it wasn't his playground to mold or shape as he pleased.

But I had no idea where to start.

"I'm sure it's not that bad," Gemma replied, in a low voice. "The mayor wouldn't have agreed to this if he didn't know what Asher's plan was."

"Maybe he doesn't know the extent of the plan or how bad the damage is going to be," I argued, with a quick look over my shoulders. "I know I'm meant to be working for him and everything, but what if I'm supposed to do this?"

"Huh?"

"What if the reason I got this job is to stop him? It's worth a shot, right?"

"This isn't your fight, Sav."

"If I don't fight for this town, who will? It's our home, Gem. We have to do something."

"I hate when you go into Earth warrior mode," Gemma grumbled, underneath her breath. "I can't promise I can help, but let me know if you need anything anyway."

"Thanks, I've got to go because my lunch break is almost over."

"Try not to get fired on your first day, okay?"

"He's not going to fire for me for fighting for my home."

Or at least I hoped he wouldn't.

Hours later, after dealing with an endless barrage of complaints from the staff regarding space, lack of proper equipment and conflicting schedules, I slumped behind my desk and brought my head to a rest against the counter. With an exhale, I lifted my head up and saw Asher coming out of his office, looking especially good in his suit, with his sleeves rolled up to his elbows.

I couldn't stop staring at his muscular forearms.

Or imagining them pining me to the bed while he had his way with me.

Goddamn it.

Why was I still thinking about our night together?

I needed to get Asher out of my system before he started causing some real problems.

He came to a stop in front of my desk, his eyes never leaving his phone. "I know it's not your job, but I was wondering if you could find someone willing to help."

I stand up straighter. "What do you need, Mr. Buchannan?"

"A tour guide. I need to familiarize myself with the town, and the way it works if I'm going to be spending some time here."

"I'll do it."

Asher glanced from his phone and arched a brow in my direction. "You want to be my tour guide?"

"This is my hometown, and I know it like the back of my hand."

Showing him around gave me the perfect opportunity showcase Lockwood Creek in all of its glory and convince him to make some adjustments to his plan.

Or throw it right out the window and pretend it never existed.

Asher's eyes moved over my face. "Alright. I'm going to go home and change. I'll meet you in an hour."

"Isn't it a little late to be fishing?"

"The sun hasn't set yet, so there's still time to catch something," I replied, with a smile. "Do you see how many fishing boats there are? Lockwood was built as a fishing town, so we rely on the water as a source of income."

Asher nodded. "I don't think I've seen so many seafood restaurants in one place."

I matched my pace to his and made a sweeping hand gesture. "Did you know that coastal waters don't just support many fish species, but they also provide a breed habit for eighty five percent of migratory birds?"

"Uh-huh."

I held up my hand and began to tick things off. "It also helps prevent erosion and filters pollutants—"

"If I wanted to know the importance of coastal towns, I would've stayed home and watched a documentary," Ashery interrupted, pausing to give me a pointed look. "Fascinating as your plethora of information is, can we get back to focusing on the actual town?"

I cleared my throat. "I'm not just giving you information. I'm giving you facts. Humans need water to survive. A lot of the fisherman here have families that rely on and need them, some of them even work at the wellness center like Cameron."

"I did pay attention in science class, Ms. Parish."

"I thought we weren't going to make things awkward."

Asher slowed his pace and twisted to face me, the afternoon beginning its descent behind him and bathing the world in a kaleidoscope of pinks and purples. "We're not."

"Outside of the office, I'm not Ms. Parish."

Asher grunted. "Fair enough."

I ignored the dipping of my stomach and set off at a brusque pace. "You know Lockwood isn't just a good location for your wellness center. We also get a lot of tourists over the summer, people who want to escape the city and relax by the water."

"There's beaches for that."

"A lot of those places are too expensive now," I pointed out, pausing to gesture to a group of kids with their legs dangling over the edge of the pier. "Scientifically, it's been proven that being near a body of water is both relaxing and healing."

"I did build a wellness center here, so I'm well aware of the benefits of water."

I faltered and missed a step.

After passing rows and rows of shops, all of whom called out to me my name, I realized I was stalling. Given that I'd only been given an hour to change and do some quick research before passing by Asher, I hadn't been able to cram enough information into my mind.

Now, I was grasping at straws, and Asher didn't look impressed.

If anything, he looked unimpressed with my efforts at changing his mind.

But he didn't give anything away.

Instead, he let me lead him around to point out information, such as obscure facts about the town's history and the rumors that it was founded because of Spanish treasure stolen by pirates. Asher hadn't shown any kind of interest when I told him the story, leaving me to lapse into silence and glance away.

Shit.

What was I supposed to do now?

I couldn't admit defeat after a single day.

Before the sun dipped below the horizon, we circled back to the pier, and I came to a stop near the edge of the water. A lot of the fishermen were still there, their pants rolled up their knees, and their weathered faces marked by the sun. Asher twisted to watch as they left, his eyebrows furrowed together. When he turned to look at me, a shiver raced up my spine.

"I know what you're trying to do, Savannah."

"I'm showing you around the town."

"You don't like my plans for the water, do you?"

"As a matter of fact, I don't. I don't think you've thought this through."

Asher raised an eyebrow. "Is that so? And what makes you think I haven't?"

"Because you don't care about the devastating impact on the environment, the economy of the town or the people who live here."

A muscle ticked in Asher's jaw. "I never said I don't care. All investments come with a risk."

"So long as the money outweighs the risks it's fine, right?"

"I wasn't aware you were well versed in business," Asher commented, dryly. "Are you telling me how to do my job?"

"I'm not telling you how to do your job. I'm telling you how to be a human being."

"I don't tell how to do your job," Asher replied, without missing a beat. "You may think you have all the facts, but you're only looking at it through one lens."

"Enlighten me then."

Asher tilted his head to the side and studied me. "What do you want to know?"

"Why are these servers so important?"

"Because this is important, especially for a town like Lockwood. Imagine having far less technical problems with our machines and devices. Imagine the developments and advances we could make if we had better coolers for our servers."

"Why does it have to be the water? We're managing fine without it."

"Because we don't have any other options," Asher replied, without missing a beat. "But once this project succeeds, everyone is going to want to implement this."

"Everyone? As in all over the world?"

"Exactly."

"What about marine life? Haven't we already devastated our waters enough?"

"It wouldn't be entire bodies of water, only certain sections of them."

"And what about the fish? How are you going to stop them from chewing on the wires?"

"We're working on a developing a non-hazardous material to make sure they don't choke. As for the water temperature, we're working on this new technology to make sure that the servers don't affect it so much that it becomes unlivable."

I make a low choking sound. "Oh, at least you're taking that into consideration."

"This really bothers you, doesn't it?"

"Of course, it does. How can it not bother you?"

"I've done my research, Savannah. I know the impact this is going to have on the environment, but at the end of the day, I'm a businessman, and I make decisions based on what's most beneficial."

"Beneficial to whom?"

Asher's face gave nothing away. "It is practical and beneficial to anyone who uses computers."

"It doesn't sound like it's worth the risk."

"It is. Your emotions are just clouding your judgement."

"At least I've got them."

Asher bridged the distance between us, only leaving a few inches of space between us. His smell washed over me and butterflies erupted in the center of my stomach. "Don't mistake me being a good businessman for being devoid of feelings, Savannah. The two are not mutually exclusive."

"Sounds like you're deflecting."

"As opposed to being stubborn like you?"

I sucked in a harsh breath. "I'm trying to fight for my hometown. I don't think there's anything wrong with that."

"No, there's nothing wrong with that, and I understand why this is important to you, but it doesn't change anything for me."

"If you give this town a chance—"

"I'll what? Settle down, put roots down and have a family? Realize corporations are the big bad?" Asher is standing directly in front of me, and his eyes are filled with a strange glimmer. "Look, I knew it was going to be difficult for the townspeople to come to terms with this, it usually is, but like I said it doesn't change anything."

I pressed my lips together and didn't say anything.

But I really wanted to wipe that look off his face.

Even more than I wanted to kiss him.

Damn it, Sav. Get a grip. He's your boss, and the person trying to run this town into the ground. You could not have picked a worse person to be attracted to.

"It should."

"A lot of things should happen," Asher agreed, the ghost of a smile hovering on his face. "It doesn't mean they will. I spent months negotiating this deal with the mayor, Savannah, and I've got a lot riding on this."

"So, you're going to prioritize the business over the welfare of a town?"

"This town is going to benefit from the changes, and it could use an update."

I stared at him through hooded eyes and counted backwards from ten.

While I could tell Asher was taking me seriously, it was also becoming clear to me that his back was against the wall. He had his own company, and an entire board to answer to, after all. I, on the other hand, wasn't held back by the same restrictions he was. Regardless of how sympathetic Asher was, I couldn't blame him for choosing to put the interests of his company first.

He wouldn't have gotten to where he was without that nononsense attitude.

No matter how much I hated it.

"I'm not going to give up," I told him, taking a few steps back and folding my arms over my chest. "I think you can understand why."

"It's your choice, Savannah. By all means, if you can find a solution that gets us both what we want, everyone would benefit, don't you agree?"

Silence stretched between us.

But I didn't like it one bit, especially because I still felt the energy between us.

A living breathing thing I couldn't ignore.

"Haven't you ever been in a situation like this?"

"I can't say that I have."

He was even more of a closed off grump than I thought. Although I had gotten glimpses of that the previous night, with him keeping his secrets guarded close to his chest and spending most of the night with a blank look on his face, I hadn't imagined it was this bad.

Still, I wasn't going to be deterred.

I wouldn't let myself be.

"It's still early," Asher pointed out, after a lengthy pause. "Why don't we continue with the tour?"

"Why?"

"Because you are a local," Asher responded. "And I like to see things through a different lens."

"Could've fooled me," I muttered, darkly.

In silence, Asher fell into step beside me, his hand inches away from mine. I resisted the urge to reach between us and see if he still felt the same. The burning fire I'd felt the other night was dying down, little by little, the longer I stayed in his company and turned his words over and over in my head.

Changing his mind was going to be a lot harder than I thought.

At the end of the tour, we walked back to his house, and I lingered at the bottom of the stairs. "My issues with your vision aren't personal."

"I'm not going to fire you if that's what you're worried about," Asher said, without looking at me. He pushed the door open with a creak before twisting around to face me. "There's a reason I never mix business with pleasure, and I'm sure you can understand why."

My throat turned dry. "Of course."

Why was I still attracted to him after spending the past few hours trying to talk him out of destroying the town?

It didn't make sense.

"I'll be asking someone else to show me around from now on," Asher added, with a grunt. "Thank you for the tour."

"You're welcome."

He gave me one final look before pushing the door open. It clicked shut behind him, plunging me into silence. I stared at the door for a while, replaying our night together, before I spun around and hurried across the street. Gemma was waiting for me inside of the house, with Chinese takeout on the counter. She stopped with the chopsticks halfway to her lips and raised an eyebrow.

"Why do you look like you want to kill someone?"

"I might kill my boss." I peeled off my sweater and tossed it on the table. "What are you doing here?"

"Still have that bug infestation in my apartment, remember? And since you have all this free space, I thought it would be okay if I stayed here."

"I am not doing your dishes or your laundry."

Gemma slurped on her noodles and snorted. "You don't even do your own dishes and laundry."

"Still a valid point." I pulled the container towards me and peered into it. "I don't think a tour of the town helped, Gem. I think I might have made things worse. I basically accused him of being an emotionless robot who only cared about money. And I gave him the worst tour of his life. I kept spewing off facts instead of impressing him."

Gemma choked back a laugh. "And you still have a job? You must've left a hell of an impression last night."

I scowled. "I thought we weren't going to talk about that."

Gemma pointed her chopsticks at me and swallowed a mouthful of food. "You said you don't want to. I never agreed. You can't expect me to."

I leaned against the counter and push the food around. "There's nothing to talk about. He and I work together, so we're going to have to pretend it never happened."

Because even with his back against the wall, I could tell Asher wasn't the sort of person who gave up easily.

Gemma reached for a glass of water and eyed me over the rim. "So, you want to tell me that you're going to ignore the best night of sex of your life?"

"I didn't say that."

She reached across the counter and patted my hand. "Honey, you didn't have to. I could hear it in your voice, and I saw it all over your face. You are screwed."

"Fuck you."

"I'll leave that to Asher." Gemma gave me a quick wink before dancing out of reach. "I've got to go take a shower."

As soon as she was gone, I brought my head to a rest against the counter and groaned.

I hated when Gemma was right.

ALICIA NICHOLS

CHAPTER 6

- SAVANNAH -

I cleared my throat and clasped my hands behind my back. "So, what do you think?"

Gemma looked up from her coffee cup and squinted. "I think you dragged me out of bed on a Sunday morning to practice your presentation, and I hate you for it."

"You don't hate me." I pointed the remote at the projector and switched it off. "I got you coffee from your favorite place."

I'd spent hours researching the importance of coastal towns in preparation in order to impress him with my knowledge and show him the error of his ways.

Asher Buchannan wasn't going to know what hit him.

Gemma snorted and took a few sips of her drink. "Coffee and pastries aren't going to make up for anything."

"How about the fact that you love me?"

Gemma shook her head. "No, that's not a good enough reason either. You're actually making me consider moving back into my bug infested apartment."

I set down the remote and pushed the curtains open. Bright sunlight flooded the living room and gave it a warm, ethereal glow. "You're just being dramatic."

Gemma ran a hand over her face and set down her coffee. "Sav, Sav, Sav, my dear friend, in all the years we've known each other, when have you ever known me to be dramatic?"

"Most of the time actually."

Gemma stood up and stretched her arms up over head. "That is not true. That's your tired brain talking. You know what you need? You need to stop thinking about this and actually enjoy your weekend."

"I can't, not when I know what's coming."

Knowing I could be the only one to talk Asher out of his plans was exhausting.

I spent all of last week considering the issue and wondering how to bring it up again. Asher, on the other hand, was the picture of professionalism, charm and poise. Half of the female staff was already in love him, and the male staff eyed his car and his clothes enviously.

I couldn't exactly blame them.

In a town like Lockwood, people who looked like they walked off the cover of a men's magazine didn't just show up, set up shop and stick around to see it come to fruition. Most of them tended to leave a few days after they arrived. While I was relieved to see that Asher had a more serious work ethic than all the other air-headed suits, it didn't give me much comfort when I knew what he was planning.

When he wasn't exuding confidence, poise and sex appeal, Asher retreated into himself and became almost unapproachable. During those moments, he turned into something of a grump who stayed in his office all day and hardly spoke to anyone. I couldn't understand if it was because of his need to maintain boundaries, or if it was because he was avoiding me.

Given how poorly the tour went, I wondered if it was the latter.

Yet, Asher didn't strike me as the kind who hid from his problems. On the contrary, I had seen him tackle several budgeting and resource problems head on, without breaking a sweat, and with the same fierce concentration and dedication.

Asher Buchannan was unstoppable.

I only wished he was using his influence and power for something else.

"...are you even listening to me?"

I blinked and fixed my gaze on Gemma. "I'm sorry, what?"

"I said you really need to get laid, so you can stop obsessing over the server farms."

"No, the last time I got laid I got into this mess."

"You're not in this mess. You're wading right into the middle of it and refusing to get out before you do get sucked in," Gemma pointed out, with a shake of her head. "Seriously, Sav. I don't think you've thought this through at all. And I'm not saying this because I don't care about Lockwood. I'm saying this because I'm your best friend."

"You could help me," I suggested.

Gemma snorted, picked up her coffee and mug and downed it all. "And risk being banned from the wellness center? I don't think so. You know I love my massages and spa time."

"Gem, come on."

"Babe, I love you and in spirit, I support you," Gemma told me, before stepping into the kitchen and running the mug under the water. "Physically, I'm going to be in the sauna enjoying the hot steam."

"Don't be a sellout. Think of what we'd be accomplishing."

Gemma chuckled and spun around to face me. "I don't think I've seen you this worked up since you learned that they wanted to add gaming consoles in the library."

"Because they don't belong in the library. They've got their own space."

After months of campaigning and getting people to sign petitions, we had finally gotten enough attention that the mayor had scraped the idea altogether. While it hadn't been easy, I was proud of the good work we'd accomplished by keeping the library a quiet and safe space for the townspeople.

Even if it did mean the younger population wasn't a fan of me.

Gemma came to a stop in front of me and placed one hand on either side of my shoulders. "Sav, you need to consider what will happen if this goes sideways."

"The impact on the town is going to be devastating and—"

"I mean for you," Gemma interrupted, her expression turning serious. "You need this job, remember? You still have the mortgage to pay and unless you can figure out a way to sell your wedding dress, you're going to have to pay it off too."

I huffed. "I know that, but I don't want to feel like a sellout."

"You can figure out a way to take a stand without endangering your job or pissing off your boss."

"How?"

Gemma removed her hands and shrugged. "Beats me. It's too early in the morning for me to come up with ideas."

"It's eleven in the morning. Some people have been up for hours."

"I am not people," Gemma reminded me, with a shake of her head. "And you're lucky I love you, or I would've kicked your ass for waking me up before noon on a weekend."

"You don't really mean that."

Gemma flipped me off on her way down the hallway to the guest room. "I really do. Don't wake me up unless it's an emergency. Good night."

"You don't really mean that," I called out to her retreating back. A moment later, the door to the guest room slammed shut, and I was plunged into silence. With a sigh, I spun on my heels and tidied up the living room. Once I was finished, I went back upstairs and wandered around my room, turning Gemma's words over and over in my head.

Was she right?

Was I being too sentimental and risking my livelihood over a fight that wasn't mine?

Since the mayor was the one in charge of permits, I was sure he had done his due diligence. While I wasn't a big fan of mayor Perkins nor he of me considering how many projects I'd stalled over the years because of my concern, however I did believe that he and I were on the same page. Deep down, we both wanted what was best for Lockwood even if we went about it differently.

And I did understand why it was important to bring in investors and developers. Money had to come in from somewhere.

A few hours later when Gemma came out of her room, looking well-rested, and with a smile on her face, I pulled her into a hug. She chuckled, patted my back and joined me on the couch. For the rest of the night, we made small talk and watched reality shows on TV.

When I went to sleep, I couldn't stop dreaming of Asher.

Of his hands on my body, and his mouth on every inch of my skin.

In the morning, I woke up drenched in sweat, and my entire body was flushed. In the shower, I kept repeating our night together until a low thrum started in the center of my stomach. With a sigh, I leaned against the shower wall and squeezed my eyes shut. Then I scrubbed every inch of my skin, twice, praying the feeling would pass.

Because in order to save the town and keep my job, I couldn't give into my attraction.

Not if I wanted to convince him to abandon his plans.

And not if I had any chance of keeping my job.

As soon as I stepped out of the shower, I felt much better about the entire thing. I hummed under my breath as I got ready and made my way downstairs. Gemma was already in the kitchen, lingering over a cup of coffee and scrolling through her phone. She gave me a small smile on my way past before returning her attention to her phone. On her way out the door, she blew me a kiss, and the door clicked shut behind her.

It's now or never, Sav.

A short while later, I walked into the center with my head held high. I left my bag behind the desk and spent the next few minutes organizing the shelves behind me. Once I was sure no one was coming in through the front door, I ducked out from behind the desk and into the conference room. Moments later, Asher came in, in his usual pressed suit, with his phone held up to his face.

I dimmed the lights when he sat down and stood at the front of the room. "Thank you for coming, Mr. Buchannan."

Asher glanced up, and a furrow appeared between his brows. "Where are the interested clients?"

"They're running a little late," I lied. "But I thought that you and I could talk while we wait."

Asher sat up straighter and pressed his mouth into a thin, white line. Hastily, I switched on the laptop in front of me, and while I waited for it to start up, I pushed the button to lower the blackout shades. Once the room darkened, lit only by the glow of a single laptop, I powered on the projector and sucked in a deep breath.

Here we go, Sav. Deep breaths. You've got this. Swing big.

In a few quick clicks, I had pulled up my presentation, reflected on the empty screen behind me. Asher glanced between the screen and me, a flicker of surprise etched onto his face before he stamped it out.

"The other day when I took you on a tour of Lockwood, I didn't do a very good job of conveying how important the water is to this town," I began, with a lift of my chin. "I told you about how the fishermen rely on the water for their livelihood and that we got a lot of tourists as well."

Asher sat back in his chair and stared at me.

"In fact, tourists represent like eighty percent of the economy," I continued. "And because of that, we're also able to sell and rent a lot of real estate overlooking the water. It obviously increases the price of any property."

I paused and looked at him expectantly.

His face was smooth and impassive, and it still gave nothing away.

I clasped my hands behind my back. "Tourism generates a lot of revenue, Mr. Buchannan as I'm sure you're already realized by now and building a server farm in the water would affect that."

A single muscle ticked in Asher's jaw.

"However, the server farm would also leave a devastating impact on the ecological footprint of the world, and it would affect the wellness center too. People come to this wellness center, primarily, because of the view."

Asher leaned forward and laced his fingers together.

Why wasn't he saying anything?

Half of me wished he would talk, even if it was just to put me in place for dragging him in here under false pretenses. The other half of me was relieved he was listening and not saying a single word.

At least for now.

Eventually, he was going to have to say something.

I linked my fingers behind my back. "But it's not just tourism or the impact on the environment or the livelihood of fisherman, did you know that the local community college also has a marine biology program?"

Silence stretched between us.

"It's one of the few marine biology programs in the country, and it offers an interactive up close and personal view of the water and aquatic life," I added, with a triumphant smile. "Can you imagine what would happen if the water and the ecological systems there were changed because of the server farm? All those marine biologists wouldn't be able to do their jobs anymore."

I lifted my arm up over my head and switched to another slide. "Then there's also the cruise ships that dock here, bringing boat loads of tourists, especially in the warmer weather. There's an entire community that depends on the water, Mr. Buchannan, but I'm sure you already knew that."

Asher unlinked his fingers and let his hands fall to his sides.

A hard knot settled in the pit of my stomach.

It's not too late to backtrack. Tell him it's an office prank or something. He might be willing to brush it off.

Instead, I stood up straighter and cleared my throat. "I'm sorry that I lured you here under false pretenses, Mr. Buchannan, but I did think it was important for you to hear this. No one else is going to tell you the truth because everyone wants this to work, and maybe it will, but I thought you should have all the facts."

With that, I powered off the projector. Asher's eyes stayed on me the entire time as the blackouts rose back up, flooding the room with bright, early morning light.

A clock ticked in the background.

Still Asher said nothing.

I swallowed past the lump in my throat. "In conclusion, I believe that—"

Asher held a hand up and took his phone out of his pocket. He pressed it to his ear and stood up. "Hello? Yes, I've been expecting your call. No, I'm not doing anything important, let me go somewhere quieter."

Without a backwards glance, he pushed the glass door open and spilled out into the hallway. In the doorway to his office, he stopped and threw me a look over his shoulders, his bright eyes regarding me intently. Then his office door clicked shut behind him

I slumped against the desk in front of me.

Shit.

It could not have gone worse.

I could've handled him yelling at me or even giving me a piece of his mind in that cold, precise way of his. Instead all I got was silence, and it kept ringing in my ears as I picked up the laptop and walked back to the front desk. For the rest of the day, I didn't see Asher in spite of my best attempts to gauge his reaction. A few of the other employees gave me sympathetic glances as news of my presentation spread, but no one approached me directly.

And it wasn't until my lunch break that I was able to breathe again.

A warm breeze whipped past me as I sat down on a bench overlooking the water. Over and over, I repeated the encounter back in my head, looking for clues to what was going through Asher's head during my presentation, only to come up empty handed. When my phone rang, and Gemma's name flashed across the screen, the knots in my stomach tightened further.

"Please tell me your day is going better than mine."

Gemma sighed. "I'm guessing it didn't go well, huh?"

I pressed my back against the bench and stared at the water as is it rippled and glistened, shinning underneath the afternoon sun. "That's an understatement. He didn't even acknowledge me, not once."

"What do you mean he didn't acknowledge you?"

"I mean I might as well have been talking to myself."

Gemma let out a low whistle. "Not even a scathing comment about how it isn't your place to tell him any of this?"

"Not even."

Gemma let out another low whistle. "Damn, you really did mess up. Did he say anything afterwards at least?"

"He got up to take a phone call and didn't come back."

Gemma said something in a muffled voice before she came back on. "Well, you could always come and work with me in the flower shop. I could use an extra pair of hands."

I snorted. "Yeah, I don't think that's a good idea. Do you remember what happened the last time I tried to help you?"

"You mean when you sent a funeral arrangement to an engagement party? Yeah, that's pretty hard to forget."

I ran a hand through my hair. "In my defense, I don't get flowers."

"I could put you behind the register," Gemma offered, after a brief pause. "If you really need it."

I lifted my knees up to my chest and brought my head to rest there. "Do you really think he's going to fire me?"

"I don't know, babe, but I wouldn't start planning for employee of the month if I were you."

Out of the corner of my eye, I saw flash of movement and peered. I recognized Kayden's outline in the distance, in a pair of shorts and a t-shirt with his arm draped over a petite redhead's shoulders. Abruptly, I stood up and walked back in the direction of the wellness center, bile rising in the back of my throat.

"I just saw Kayden with some redhead. I've got to go. Talk to you later?"

"Same old Kayden. It figures he would still be sleeping around even after getting someone else pregnant. Good luck, babe."

CHAPTER 7

- ASHER -

"Sit down, Ms. Parish."

Savannah hovered in the door and tucked her hair behind her ear. Reluctantly, she stepped into the office until she was standing inches away from the chair opposite me. My eyes flicked up to hers, and I gave her an expectant look.

She perched on the edge of the chair, a tablet pressed against her chest. "Mr. Buchannan about yesterday—"

"This is a business, Ms. Parish," I interrupted, with a pointed look. "I'm not sure what you were allowed to get away with in your previous employment, but here at the wellness center, we do not make up fake clients to lure the boss into a meeting."

Savannah winced. "I'm sorry."

"It is a waste of talent and time, Ms. Parish," I continued, as if I hadn't heard her. "Not only am I aware of all of the points you made, but I've also had plenty of time to plan and prepare for the server farm. We have plans in place to minimize the damage that'll be done."

Savannah opened her mouth and slammed it shut again.

"As my office manager, your job is to organize meetings, manage databases, book transportation and accommodations during company events, etc. All of these things were made clear to you when you signed the contract, were they not?"

She cleared her throat. "Yes, they were."

I looked away from her and rummaged through the paperwork stacked on my desk. When I pulled out the file I was looking for, I flipped it open and scanned through it. Then I slid it across the desk from her and waited. She shifted from one side to the other and fixed her gaze on a spot over my shoulders.

I could tell she didn't like being in the hotseat.

But I wasn't in a charitable mood after the stunt she pulled in the office, and I had spent all of yesterday trying to come up with a way to get my point across. Considering how few people were qualified to do her job, and how the wellness center wasn't doing as well as I had hoped, I couldn't afford to let her go.

Yet.

However, Savannah was testing my patience, and I was not the kind of man who liked to be questioned in my company, well intentioned or otherwise.

"Ms. Parish, I need you to read over the terms of your contract," I told her, my eyes never leaving her face. "As you can see, I have highlighted a few of the conditions of your employment here."

Savannah's expression turned weary as she leaned forward and skimmed through the paperwork. While she did, I studied her, everything from the hair piled on top of her head, to the crisp and ironed shirt tucked into the waistband of her skirt. Although Savannah knew how to present herself professionally, and she did a good job in other aspects of her job, it was becoming clear to me that she was not the type to fall in line easily.

Nor was she the type to prioritize logic over emotion.

For the life of me, I couldn't understand why a woman like her was ruled by her emotions. Then again, I was the one who hadn't been able to stop thinking about her since our night together. Outwardly, I did my best to project the kind of calm and control I knew was necessary for a man of my position. However, each time I was around her, it was harder and harder for me to remember why I couldn't have her again.

And why I shouldn't want to.

WEDDING NIGHT STRANGER (MR. BUCHANNAN)

Savannah Parish was like an itch I couldn't shake.

Being around her was a test of my patience and my determination to see this project through, with as little trouble as possible, and I didn't like it. Not only was she splitting my focus and making it difficult for me to do my job, but she was also completely unaware of the effect she had on me.

Goddamn it.

Why was I pining after a woman I couldn't have?

Once she was done reading, she glanced up at me, and her expression turned solemn. Even when she was serious, she was still the most beautiful woman I'd ever seen. "I know what the details of my contract are, Mr. Buchannan."

"Then I'm sure you've read over the clause that allows me to add conditions," I pointed out, pausing to lean over the desk. Her floral smell wafted over to me, making knots form in the center of my stomach. "Effective immediately, you are not to abuse your power as my office manager or there will be severe consequences."

"I did not abuse my power," Savannah protested, color rising up her cheeks. "I tweaked the rules a little, but it was for a good reason."

I pursed my lips. "Good reason or otherwise, you abused your power as my office manager. The facts don't change because we want them to, Ms. Parish."

She slumped against her chair.

"In addition to taking your job seriously and having a more limited role in the office, I also expect you to oversee client relations. Considering the wellness center is still trying to find its feet, I'm counting on you to ensure that, when those clients do come, they have a memorable experience."

Savannah nodded. "Of course, Mr. Buchannan."

"You will report to me directly, and you will not take any big decisions without consulting with me first."

Savannah nodded and didn't respond.

I linked my fingers together over the desk and frowned. "You are good at your job, Ms. Parish, and I have gone over your references. You have glowing reviews from all of your previous employers, but you are not untouchable."

Savannah's eyes flashed as she lurched forward. "I didn't think I was—"

"And no matter how good you are at your job, you are replaceable," I interrupted, with another pointed look. "The wellness center will go on with or without you, Ms. Parish. Do I make myself clear?"

Savannah stood up and clasped her hands behind her back. "Crystal clear, Mr. Buchannan."

"Good. Make sure everyone is on time for the meeting later. You're dismissed."

A heartbeat later, she spun on her heels and hurried out of the office, her head held high. Through the glass, I watched her go over to the main desk and settle behind it. Then I lean back against my chair and turn my attention back to the slew of emails, waiting for my response.

Firing people was the part I hated most, especially when it came to small towns.

Many of them had tragic backstories that tugged on the heartstrings.

But I wasn't here to give hand-outs, and considering the delays with my server farm project, I needed the wellness center to do well. Already, the board of directors was breathing down my neck, and my financial department wasn't happy, and the only way to turn that around was to make sure I ran a tight ship.

And that included keeping Savannah in check.

Now was not the time for Savannah to go rogue and make me look bad in the process. Since the fiasco with Caroline and Jeffrey, I was already under scrutiny and didn't need the board questioning my dedication or leadership skills further. Once the entire thing was put to rest, I knew the board was going to rest easy.

Anything else was only going to antagonize them further.

It was what I hired them for.

The wellness center may have been a temporary placeholder that would eventually give way to the server farm, but it didn't mean it couldn't be successful in the meantime. Granted, Caroline was meant to be the one running the place, but I could do this job as well as she could.

Better even.

A few hours later, when I got up and fastened the buttons of my suit, I saw Savannah through the glass. She stood outside the conference room, her back held erect, and her face a careful mask giving nothing away. I picked up my laptop, tucked it underneath my arm and stepped out into the hallway. As soon as I did, she turned her gaze to me, and our eyes met.

For a brief moment, I forget that she and I weren't on the same team.

While she did work for me, and I had feeling she wouldn't knowingly sabotage the center, it didn't mean she couldn't make things difficult. A part of me did admire the loyalty and protectiveness she felt towards her hometown, but I also knew that, while she was at work, there was no room for it.

All she needed was a little nudge in the right direction.

And nothing incentivized people like money.

Considering I knew Savannah was not in a place where she could afford to lose this job, because of her mortgage loans, and the canceled wedding she had to pay off, I wasn't above using this knowledge to my advantage. A part of me felt bad for using this information against her, when I knew it was said in confidence. However, the other, more pragmatic part of me realized it was necessary.

I was, first and foremost, Savannah's boss.

Allowing my personal feelings for her to get in the way of doing my job wasn't a smart move. Regardless of how attractive I found her or how much I sympathized with her crusade, I wasn't going to let it affect my judgement. Not when I knew the hefty price to be paid if I did.

Someday, she was going to be thankful I pushed her.

You threatened to fire her if she doesn't fall in line. I doubt she's going to be grateful for that, regardless of what your intentions were.

During the meeting, while several key employees discussed products and client management, I kept sneaking glances at Savannah and wondering if I had jumped the gun. As a general rule, I didn't interact with my clients outside of work, preferring to keep the boundaries between us clear and separate. Unfortunately, it was too late when it came to Savannah because I had no idea who she was when I met her.

And a part of me wondered if that would've changed anything.

The energy that pulsed and crackled between us was still there, despite my best attempts to ignore it. Every time she was in the room with me, she sucked up most of the oxygen, and it took everything I had to remember why staying away from her was the best course of action. Until she drew closer, and I found myself questioning my judgment all over again.

I had underestimated her effect on me.

And I had no idea how I was supposed to deal with it.

Not only was Savannah smart, quick on her feet and resourceful, but she was also enthusiastic, passionate and not afraid to go toe to toe with people, including me. It was part of the reason why I found her appealing, and why, the longer I sat in the conference room, enjoying the cool breeze wafting in through the window, the less sure I was about trying to bully Savannah into silence.

It was not the kind of boss I wanted to be.

She's not going to give up if you don't, and you've got a lot riding on this, remember? Besides, Savannah is tough. She'll get over it.

Given that she had her job on the line, she was going to have to find a way to make her peace with it.

But I found myself strangely uncomfortable with the idea of being the one to push her into complacency. As soon as the meeting came to an end, I drew some of the employees aside to give them my notes. Savannah lingered in the doorway, talking to a blonde man with broad shoulders and dark eyes.

He smiled at her, and she smiled back, leaving a knot in the center of my stomach. With a grunt, I pulled my attention back to the present and ignored them. Little by little, everyone filed out, leaving me standing in the middle of the conference room, alone. I cast a quick glance around the room before I hurried out and into my office.

Hours later, when the afternoon sun began to dip below the horizon, plunging the world into darkness, my lawyer arrived. He wore his usual pressed navy suit, his hair slicked back and polished loafers that were soundless against the hardwood floors. Through the glass, I saw him study the place and peek into some of the rooms. I stood, walked over to the door and beckoned him into the office.

Savannah was sitting behind the main desk, her fingers moving steadily. She didn't look away when I gestured to the lawyer, and the door clicked shut behind him. Slowly, Savannah blinked, looked around, and a small furrow hovered between her lips. Then she picked up the office phone and called me. I cradled the phone between my neck and shoulders, giving Will a long look in between.

"There was a visitor here to see you, Mr. Buchannan," Savannah told me, in a brusque voice. "I'm not sure where he went though."

"He's in my office, Ms. Parish. Thank you." I ended the call and placed the phone back where it belonged. Carefully, I spun around to face my lawyer and stood behind my desk. "You're not discreet."

Will raised an eyebrow and set his briefcase down on the carpeted floor. "I haven't drawn any attention to myself."

"You look like a lawyer."

"I am a lawyer," Will replied, with a shake of his head. "I wanted to do this in person to prevent any misunderstandings."

"You think the FBI is listening in on our phone calls."

He snapped the briefcase shut and set the folder down on my desk. "It can't hurt to be careful."

I moved from behind my desk and brought my hips to a rest against the desk. "Wouldn't it have been better to have this meeting in a hotel or somewhere less conspicuous?"

Will flipped the folder open and scanned through it. "It would've drawn too much attention to you, and that's the last thing we want."

I folded my arms over my chest. "I take it the case isn't going well."

"We haven't been able to get the charges against you dropped."

I frowned. "Why not? You have all of the paperwork you need to prove my innocence."

"They are still trying to corroborate the story," Will replied, without looking up at me. "I wouldn't worry, Mr. Buchannan. These things take time. They wouldn't be doing their due diligence if they didn't look into everything."

"There's something you're not telling me."

He glanced up at me, a furrow appearing between his brows. "You asked me not to bother you with the boring details, Mr. Buchannan."

"Mr. Turner, I'm being charged with money laundering and fraud because I put my trust in the wrong people. Now is not the time for technicalities. I want to know everything."

Will set down the file and cleared his throat. "Mr. Buchannan, these charges are serious. If you're convicted, you could face up to twenty years in prison."

I pushed myself off the desk and walked over to my freezer. After pulling out a bottle of whiskey, I poured myself a generous amount and hold out another glass to Will who shook his head. While the last thing I wanted was to be in another meeting with Will, hearing news that I didn't like, it was better than not being in the loop at all. I knew my lawyer was competent as was the rest of my legal team, but I wasn't going to sit on the sidelines and watch the life I'd worked to build be taken away from me. With a shrug, I down all of my drink and his, allowing the liquid to burn a path down my throat before settling in the pit of my stomach.

"Have you had any luck finding Caroline and Jeffrey?"

"The investigator believes they're underground, sir," Will replied, without missing a beat. "It'll take some time to flush them out. In the meantime, we're building a case against them."

I eyed Will and frowned. "Is it a solid case?"

And was it going to be enough to clear my name and that of my company's?

Will had gotten me out of messes before but nothing like this.

Never like this.

"We're putting the pieces together," Will assured me after a brief pause. "We'll need to do a lot more digging because they were careful."

I exhaled. "What happens when you do find them?"

"They're going to be brought in to stand trial and own up to what they did."

I scoffed. "I doubt it's that's simple, Mr. Turner. The evidence will have to incriminate them if there's going to be a case. The FBI will be prepared for that."

"They better be. When you do find them, I want to be the first one to see them,"

Will paused and frowned at me. "Excuse me?"

I finished off my drink and set it down with a thud. "I want to be the one who looks them in the eye and confronts them about what they did."

Considering everything the two of them had put me through, the least they could do was tell me the truth about what happened.

Even if it didn't change anything.

Will nodded and stood up. He set the file back down on my desk and held his suitcase in front of him. "I'm sure we can come to some sort of agreement with the FBI. In any case, this is what we've found so far. I'll keep you posted, Mr. Buchannan."

"Next time, if it doesn't need to be in person, I would prefer to have this meeting over the phone or online. I don't want anyone here getting wind of this."

Will grimaced. "It'll only be a matter of time, sir. With the FBI involved, sooner or later, the press is going to get a hold of this, and in a small town like this…"

"I expect you and my crisis management team to stay ahead of it," I pointed out.

With that, I picked up the folder and lowered myself onto my chair. "Good day, Mr. Turner."

Will lingered for a few moments before he hurried out of the room. I glanced up in time to see Savannah stare after him before looking back at my office. Then I swung my gaze back to the folder in front of me and read through it. Everything from my financial records to their last known whereabouts was in front of me.

Yet, it still didn't connect any of the dots.

And until it did, I was going to keep all of close to this vest.

WEDDING NIGHT STRANGER (MR. BUCHANNAN)

There was no reason for anyone in Lockwood Creek to find out about any of this.

Not if I could help it.

ALICIA NICHOLS

CHAPTER 8

- SAVANNAH -

"What are you doing?"

I looked up from my cup of coffee and blinked. "Having my morning coffee?"

"I mean, why are you up so early?" Gemma swung the refrigerator door open and peered inside. "I thought you would want to sleep in after the day you had."

I lowered my cup and stared at Gemma's back. "What are you talking about?"

She wheeled around to face me and made a vague hand gesture. "You know, losing your job."

"I haven't been fired."

Yet.

And I couldn't decide where I was relieved or suspicious.

On the one hand, I was glad that Asher wasn't the type of boss to jump the gun. On the other hand, not knowing what was going to happen next was killing me. Especially because I saw the well-dressed looking man coming out of his office a few days ago. After a quick internet search and I found that the man was Asher's lawyer, the knots in my stomach had only grown worse.

Over the past few days, when I've seen Asher around the center, I've held my breath, not sure what to expect from him.

Thankfully, he had been in and out of the center, attending multiple meetings with suppliers, the city council, and other important figures. Since clients were slow to trickle through the door, he was doing everything within his power to drive more clients through the door.

I felt bad for him.

And it didn't make sense that he was putting in this much effort with a wellness center which, as far as I could tell, was only going to be around for a year. Then again, I didn't have much of a mind for business, and I was sure Asher knew what he was doing.

In the meantime, I was relieved the center was keeping him busy and distracting him from the server farm. Unfortunately, during the few moments when our paths did cross, which was inevitable considering my position as his office manager, I could feel the disapproval and frustration rolling off of him in waves.

On the outside, he gave nothing away, except for his usual charm, poise and control. Now and again, when he looked at me, I saw a flicker of something different, and it made me wonder.

Was he prolonging the consequences to punish me?

To keep me on the tips of my toes, agonizing over whether I still had a job?

Given that he knew how much I needed it, I wouldn't blame him. He was, after all, a businessman and my boss to boot, I expected nothing else.

If anything, I expected more.

Like being called into a meeting to be publicly chewed out and humiliated. Whatever Asher was planning, he was going to have my ass handed to me. And I had no choice but to sit around and wait for it to happen.

Gemma waved a hand in front of my face and frowned. "You haven't heard a word I've said, had you?"

I blinked. "What did you say?"

"I said how the hell haven't you been fired yet?"

"Thanks for the vote of confidence."

"It's not about confidence. It's about being realistic. If I had an employee who pulled that kind of stunt, I'd fire her so fast, her head would spin."

"It's a good thing I don't work for you."

Gemma's frown deepened. "You should be careful."

"Why?"

"Because he's not keeping you around out of the goodness of his heart. Asher Buchannan isn't that kind of man."

"You're acting like you know him."

"We ran in the same circles at some point, but we haven't spoken in years, and if there's one thing I remember, it's that Asher doesn't like looking like an idiot."

I blew out a breath. "I'm guessing he's not going to take that meeting I pulled him into as me trying to help."

"Yup." Gemma brushed past me and poured herself a cup of coffee. "Unless you can convince him otherwise."

"How do you suggest I do that?"

Gemma shrugged and lifted the cup to her lips. "How the hell should I know? I'm a florist, and I don't do office politics."

"Since you were friends, maybe you can put in a good word for me."

Gemma snorted and took a long sip of her drink. "First of all, I doubt that's going to work. Second, I don't think he remembers me."

"You could try."

Gemma sighed and lowered the cup. "If I can, I will."

I smiled at her. "Thanks."

"Yeah, yeah. You owe me."

"I owe you? You're the one staying in my house."

"And offering sage life advice, people usually pay for that sort of thing."

I choked back a laugh. "Are you calling yourself my therapist?"

"A therapist is paid way better." Gemma shook her head and went through the fridge again. "By the way, we should go grocery shopping. We're running low on supplies."

"Let's go tonight. I've got to go get ready for work."

A short while later, I flew out the door with a brown paper bag in my hand, and a hard knot in the center of my stomach as I turned over the conversation we'd just had. The morning sun was high in the sky, hidden behind a few grey clouds as I walked to work, listening intently to the sound of my shoes crunching against gravel. The wellness center loomed overhead, on the outskirts of the town, glistening underneath the afternoon light. I tucked my bag and travel mug underneath my arm and took my keys out of my pocket.

The door made a low clicking sound before I pushed it open.

While I tidied the desk and got the reception area ready for the day, all of the other employees trickled in, one after the other, looking bright and well-rested in their brown and blue uniforms. Once the last of them came in, I stepped behind the front desk and sat down.

I felt the shift in the air before he came in.

Asher looked directly at me before pointing in the direction of his office. I swallowed past the lump in my throat, stood up on shaky legs and reached for my tablet. Then I trailed after him, turning over one scenario after the next. He pushed the door to his office, left it open and strode towards his desk. Wordlessly, he started his laptop and flung the curtains open, allowing sunlight to pour in.

I moved towards the chair opposite his desk.

"Shut the door," Asher instructed, in a clear voice. "You won't be needing the tablet, Ms. Parish."

The hairs on the back of my neck rose as I pulled the door shut and wandered back to the chair. Once I sat down, I set the tablet down in my lap and crossed one ankle over the other. Asher went over to his mini fridge, took out a bottle of water and set it down on his desk. He unfastened the top button of his jacket and sat down.

As soon as he leaned over, I caught a whiff of his perfume, and my heart gave an odd little dip. I dug my nails into the seat underneath me and stiffened. "How can I help you, Mr. Buchannan?"

"Ms. Parish, I don't think I've been unclear with you," Asher began, his bright eyes studying me intently. "In fact, I've been quite straightforward about what I expect from you and your duties around the center."

"Yes, sir."

Asher linked his fingers together over the desk. "Would you say that it's normal to use company resources for your own personal gain?"

I cleared my throat. "No, sir."

"No matter how well intentioned the cause is?"

"Sir?"

Asher sat up straighter and let his hands fall to his sides. "You do come highly qualified, Ms. Parish, but I've made it clear before that you need to have your priorities in order if you want to keep working here."

"I remember, sir."

As if he would let me forget it.

Had he called me in here to rehash the conversation we had last time?

Because it didn't make any sense.

He'd already warned me that I was being watched, and what the consequences were if I set one toe out of line.

"You cannot use company resources to provide an environmentalist agenda," Asher continued, as if he hadn't heard me. "No matter how well-intentioned you think you are."

I lifted my chin up and held his gaze. "Sir, I think it would be irresponsible of me to turn the other cheek while you weren't made aware of the facts."

Asher raised an eyebrow. "Irresponsible? It's not your responsibility to take care of details like that, Ms. Parish. You're an office manager."

"And I've also lived here most of my life. Just because I work for you, Mr. Buchannan doesn't mean I owe you my silence."

"But you do owe me your loyalty."

"Not at the price of my soul," I responded, through gritted teeth. "I know what's expected of me, sir. The terms of my contract are clear, and when you called me in here a few days ago, you made it clear what would happen if I did not stick to my job description."

"Yet, I've heard rumors that you've been talking to people in town about the server farm."

So that was why he had called me into his office, to make sure I wasn't running my mouth.

My eyebrows knitted together. "What I do in my free time is my own business."

"Not if it reflects negatively on the center and by extension me."

"With all due respect, sir, telling people what the wellness center is covering up doesn't reflect negatively. It's the truth."

Asher's eyes tightened around the edges. "You don't have all of the details, Ms. Parish. It's not your call to make."

"Maybe I don't, but it doesn't mean I won't tell people my opinion. In any case, I'm not the one who leaked the news, Mr. Buchannan."

No matter how much I wish I had.

I didn't owe him or this center my silence, but I did respect the code of conduct. Outside of Gemma, who was very good at keeping secrets, no one else knew about the plans for the server farm, and how the water was going to be used for the cooling process. No one other than the mayor that was, and I couldn't see him being the one to tell the townspeople the news.

Not when they would demand his head on a pike if they didn't like the answer.

Knowing the people of Lockwood Creek, they weren't going to be happy about this.

Asher tilted his head to the side and stared at me. "Ms. Parish, I want to believe you, but I'm sure you can imagine why it's difficult for me."

"I haven't given you a reason to."

"Beyond luring me into a false meeting, using a tour to promote your own agenda down my throat and going out of your way to try and make me feel guilty about my plans for this town, you mean."

I jumped to my feet. "I'm a lot of things, Mr. Buchannan, but I'm not a liar."

"Sit down, Ms. Parish."

"I will not."

Asher rose to his feet and frowned at me. "I am not accusing you of anything."

"You are. If you think that I'm using this company to promote my own agenda, you should go ahead and fire me."

"Is that what you want me to do?"

"No, but you're going to go ahead and do it anyway, so I wish you would just get it over with."

"I am not going to fire you, Ms. Parish."

I threw my hands out on either side of me. "Why the hell not? It's not like you want me here. I just make things difficult for you."

"But you are good at your job," Asher pointed out, his eyes never leaving my face. "And good employees are hard to find."

I made a low noise in the back of my throat. "That's bullshit."

Asher stiffened. "I beg your pardon?"

"I think you're keeping me around because you don't want to feel bad about this or something. I don't know. I haven't figured that part out yet."

Asher's expression tightened. "Ms. Parish, I would tread carefully if I were you."

I pressed my lips together and didn't say anything.

"You are here to manage the office," Asher repeated, in a tighter voice. "Not do other people's jobs and definitely not to tell me how to do mine."

"That's not what I was trying to do."

Asher raised an eyebrow. "Ms. Parish, why did you take this job? Besides the obvious reason."

"I took this job because I thought it would be a good idea to work in a wellness center."

And in a small town like Lockwood, I didn't have a lot of options.

At least none that fit me.

I didn't want a high stress job with rigid hours and a toxic environment. After weeks of searching, the wellness center's opening made sense especially with my HR degree and my experience in a wide plethora of jobs from managing a vet's office, event coordinator at the B and B to being a liaison between the townspeople and the town council.

I had done it all.

But nothing felt right.

At this point in my life, it was less about finding my passion and more about paying the bills, and I had no qualms about admitting that. My only issue was that I had unburdened myself to Asher in confidence, believing him to be a hot one-night stand, and nothing further. Unfortunately, not only was he proving that he had no problems using that information as leverage, but he also knew how to push.

Asher wasn't here to play.

And it was clear I had struck a nerve.

I couldn't tell if I was happy or annoyed by the knowledge.

Asher cleared his throat. "Ms. Parish, this issue needs to be resolved. I cannot come into work and wonder what agenda you have planned for me today. I run a tight ship, and I don't like insurgents."

"I'm not here to cause any problems," I replied, evenly. "I just think that there's more to the story here."

Asher tilted his head to the side and motioned for me to continue.

"Let me show you around the town again," I offered, the words pouring out of me in a rush. "I know that we had to cut it short last time, and you had a very specific idea in mind of what you wanted to see, but this time is going to be different."

It had to be.

Because I had one more shot to make him see reason before it all went down the drain. Given how important time and money was to a man like Asher, I doubted he was going to give me a third chance. For a while, he stared at me, his face giving nothing away.

"Will you stop bringing this up if I agree to go on another tour?"

"I'll try."

Asher snorted. "Something tells me that I'm not going to get another answer out of you."

I gave him a small smile. "Probably not."

"Alright." Asher sat back down and linked his fingers together. "I have a few meetings lined up later tonight, so I won't be able to stay long."

"You won't regret it, I promise."

Asher gave me a strange look and didn't say anything.

Hastily, I made my way out of his office and into the hallway. During the walk back to the main desk, I resisted the urge to glance over my shoulders to see if he was watching me. Having my office behind my desk, while unusual, suited me just fine, especially in the absence of a receptionist.

I liked being situated in a unique vantage point, giving me a view of the sidewalk on one hand, and a view of the water behind me. Being able to see the employees and clients come and go made my job much easier, and it definitely didn't hurt that the desk overlooked Asher's office, and he never lowered his blinds.

Most days, I found it distracting.

Today it was welcome, especially when a steady stream of clients came in, and he didn't look up from his laptop. I kept sneaking glances at him, in between greeting clients, but I couldn't figure out what he was thinking. Asher was as much of a mystery to me now as he was when I first met him, only I couldn't seem to shake him.

No matter how much I wanted to.

WEDDING NIGHT STRANGER (MR. BUCHANNAN)

Underneath the grumpy, no-nonsense exterior was the man I had a great night with, and I knew he was still in there somewhere. While I knew I wasn't in any kind of place to get involved with a man, Asher or otherwise, it didn't mean I couldn't spend time with him in the hopes of helping him see Lockwood the way I did.

Being drawn to him was one thing.

Acting on that impulse was another.

And if there was one thing I prided myself on it was the ability to keep myself in check.

Asher Buchannan was attractive and mysterious, there was no denying that, but there was too much at stake for me to ignore everything else. By the end of the day, I had all but convinced myself that the electricity I felt between us that first night was as a result of the adrenaline of the day and way too many drinks.

As I was tidying up the desk and packing up my things, Asher walked past, and I caught a whiff of his cologne, a heady mixture of old spice and sandalwood. It made the butterflies in my stomach erupt into a frenzy and had me wondering if being alone with him was such a good idea after all.

Show him the town, change his mind, and you'll be home before you know it.

This was going to be a breeze.

CHAPTER 9

- ASHER -

"What makes you think they're going to respond now?"

"Incentive," Will replied, in a muffled voice. Something crashed in the background, and his voice came back on, clearer than before. "We need to draw them out into the open."

"I doubt they're going to fall for it. Caroline and Jeffrey are not going to risk themselves unless they have a good reason to," I responded, with a quick look in the mirror.

I was a little too under-dressed for my liking, but considering I was meant to be going on a tour of the town, for the second time in two weeks, I had no idea what I was meant to be wearing. Given that I was doing this under protest, and with the goal of appeasing Savannah, I had chosen a button-down shirt and dark jeans.

With a frown, I turned away from the mirror and set my phone down on the dresser. "Has the investigator had any luck?"

"No, they've covered their tracks well."

"What about their suspected ties to the mob? You mentioned that the investigator heard rumors."

"Nothing to corroborate their ties either."

"The FBI isn't sharing that information?"

"Not yet."

I still had a hard time wrapping my head around the fact that they had criminal ties. That Caroline and Jeffrey had betrayed me in order to squeeze as much money out of me as possible left a bad taste in the back of my mouth. Coming to terms with the fact that they were part of a much larger and more dangerous organization was concerning, to say the least.

I wanted them brought to justice as much as anyone else. More, considering how dangerous they were.

How had I not seen it?

Because they knew how to play you. They preyed on your weakness, on your desire to be accepted for who you are, and they exploited it. You couldn't have seen the truth even if you wanted to.

And I wasn't sure how much good it would've done without any proof.

I had imagined an entire life for myself, with the two of them by my side.

Now, I was stuck in the town overseeing a wellness center I wanted no part of, all in an effort to save face and prove to the board of directors that I can handle a crisis. Leaving without seeing this through was only going to cause more damage than good, and it was a loss I couldn't afford.

Not if I wanted to come out of this stronger.

And better.

For the life of me, I still couldn't understand why Caroline had pushed for us to set up a wellness center, if they never planned to come to town with me to begin with. Initially, she'd pitched it as a way to make easy money, something to pass the time while we got the server farm up and running.

Now, I was beginning to wonder if the wellness center was meant as a front for something else.

Had the plan been to use the center as a front to launder money?

Fuck.

"Something will turn up sooner or later, Mr. Buchannan," Will replied, after a lengthy pause. "We will have those charges dropped. It's all circumstantial evidence anyway."

I shoved my hand into my pocket. "It doesn't change the optics. Without Caroline and Jeffrey, even with the charges dropped, this still looks bad. If I'm going to clear my company's name and mine, this needs to go away. Now."

"Yes, sir."

"Continue working with the FBI and see what they come up with. Combining resources is the best way to get this resolved quickly."

"Mr. Buchannan, working with the FBI—"

"Is in all of our best interests. Whatever issues you have with them, you need to set them aside for the greater good. I don't want excuses, Mr. Turner. Get it done."

With that, I ended the call and pocketed my phone.

On my way down the stairs, the phone rang again, and I fished it out of my pocket with a frown. "What do you want?"

"Is that any way to greet your baby sister?"

I pulled the phone away from my ear and placed it back. "I thought you were my lawyer."

"If that's how you talk to your lawyer, you don't pay him enough."

"How's mom?"

"On one another of her wellness retreats. She misses you."

"I'll try and visit soon."

"How's your new project going?"

"There are a few unexpected hiccoughs. Nothing I can't handle."

The doorbell rang, filling up the empty house. I wrenched the door open and switched the phone from one ear to the other. "Hold on a second, Liz."

Savannah stood in my doorway, bathed in the soft glow of the setting sun, in a dark short sleeved dress. Her hair fell in loose curls around her face, giving her a vulnerable and more youthful look. When her eyes flicked up to mine, a half-smile on her face, my stomach gave an odd little flip.

I frowned at her. "You're early."

"Better early than late, right?"

I grunted and pushed the door open. "Let me finish this phone call, and we can go."

She stepped in and brushed past me, her floral scent sending another jolt through me. I stared at her back as she wandered into the living room and surveyed the area. "Liz, can I call you back later?"

"Are you with a woman? Who is that?"

"None of your business."

"That doesn't sound like Caroline," Liz continued as if she hadn't heard me. "Did the two of you finally break up?"

"Don't sound so excited about it."

"I'm not. Okay, I kind of am. She was not the right woman for you. I like the new one already."

"You haven't even met her."

"Doesn't matter. Anyone who can make you sound this flustered is a keeper."

"I'm not flustered," I told her, in a low voice. "She's my employee, and a local who is showing me around."

"Uh-huh, sure."

"I'll call you later," I added, before ending the call. "Would you like a drink before we go?"

Savannah stood up straighter and cleared her throat. "No, that's okay. I thought we could start at the water. It's beautiful when the sun is setting."

I snatched my keys and wallet off the table and gestured to the door. "I don't understand why another tour matters."

Savannah gave me a warm smile. "You'll see."

She stepped back onto the porch, and I followed her. Once the door clicked shut, I fell into step beside her, a warm breeze that smelled like wildflowers and honeysuckle rustled past us. I shoved both hands into my pockets and matched my pace to hers. Savannah didn't say anything as she led me out of the residential suburban area and into the main part of town.

In the center of town, with shops on either side of us, she came to a stop and gestured to a large tower. "This was one of the first buildings constructed in Lockwood Creek. The clock still works, and so does the bell. It was initially intended to warn the townspeople when danger was coming."

"Danger?"

"A lot of pirates used to stop here to try and steal crops and kidnap people," Savannah explained, her expression growing animated. "Legend has it that the sound of the bell used to scare some of them because they were superstitious."

"Superstitious pirates?"

Savannah nodded, eagerly. "Yeah, it's weird, right? But pirates had all kinds of superstitions, and the founder of the town, Tyler Lockwood, figured that out pretty early. He was the one who discovered that they believed the sound of the bell was used to summon the spirits of the dead."

I made a low grunting noise and said nothing.

Savannah let her hands fall to her sides and led me away from the tower and towards a gothic style building a few streets away, with hundreds of steps leading up to large French doors and two marble pillars.

"This is the town council. It is said to have been built by a Spanish prince who wanted to impress a local woman and win her hand in marriage."

I raised an eyebrow. "Him being a prince wasn't enough?"

"He was in exile," Savannah explained, with a sweeping hand gesture. Underneath the pale light of the moon, I studied the building and tried but failed to picture why anyone would go through all of that trouble for one woman.

Especially when that women clearly didn't reciprocate feelings.

I didn't need to hear the rest of the story to know the truth.

"Sounds like he wasted his time and his money," I replied, with a shake of my head. "He would've been better off without her."

Savannah frowned. "I think it's romantic."

"It's costly." I glanced around at the shops on either side of the street. "What about this street? Does it have any kind of history?"

Savannah came to stand next to me and sighed. "No, but I do have more stories about the pirates."

I cast a quick glance in her direction. "You really like those stories, don't you?"

"What's not to like? Those stories have adventure, danger, romance and the triumph of good over evil."

I scoffed and didn't say anything.

Given that Savannah had been screwed over, and on the day of her wedding no less, I had expected her to be more cynical. Instead with every word, and every story, I began to realize just how much of a dreamer she really was.

She had her head in the clouds, and she didn't seem to mind one bit.

To my surprise, I didn't mind it either.

I liked listening to her tell stories, and I liked watching her face light up, and the rise and fall of her voice as she wove everything together. She spoke at length about the history of pirates, and the role the water played in shaping the town's history until we were on the shoreline again, glancing at the water bathed in the glow of the moon. Savannah paused to look out at the tide, a thoughtful expression on her face.

I had never seen anything like that.

In spite of my better judgement, I kept sneaking glances at her instead of the water. "Let me guess. You're about to tell me that the water is important because of the history."

Savannah rolled her eyes at me. "It is, but I wanted to tell that you there about a local legend around here. People believe that there's Spanish treasure buried in these waters. Washed up and buried with time."

"Because of the pirates?"

"You can tease me all you want, but a lot of legends and myths are based in truth," Savannah said, twisting to face me. "Or some version of it."

"Exactly."

As charming and enchanting as Lockwood was, with its centuries' old history, and its strong ties to the community, it didn't change the fact that it was a means to an end for me. I came to this town because I had been lured here under false pretenses and promised a groundbreaking business venture. The only reason I hadn't packed up and left was because the wellness center gave me the excuse I needed to stay behind and see the server farm project come to fruition.

Once it was done, I had every intention of hightailing it out of there and back to the city. Having made a bad investment, the last thing I wanted was to continue to be reminded of it and find myself sinking further and further into the quicksand. I had nothing against Lockwood Creek, nor its residents, but another tour of the town wasn't going to change my mind.

I still needed to turn this around for myself and my company.

And in time, I hoped that Savannah was going to understand that.

Savannah looked back at the water and inched away from me. "Did you know that this town has a long history with Valentine's day? Legend has it that Saint Valentine himself paid a visit to this town, before he was imprisoned, and he said that he could feel the spirit of love here."

"I feel like you're making all of this up."

Savannah choked back a laugh. "I had a feeling you were going to say that, but I'm really not. This town has a lot of myths and legends."

"I can see that."

I turned when I felt Savannah's gaze on mine, and the rest of my sentence faded away. My entire mind went blank when she looked at me, and I found myself grasping at straws, trying to remember why I was there in the first place.

Why did she have such a strong effect on me?

I was here to expand my business not start another relationship.

And after Caroline, I wasn't sure I wanted to get involved with anyone.

Ever.

The longer I stood there, looking back at Savannah, the more conflicted I felt, like I was on the outside looking in on a stranger. Eventually, she exhaled and glanced back out at the water, her expression turning sad.

"I was supposed to have my honeymoon during Valentine's," Savannah revealed, her voice growing quieter towards the end. "I know it's a cliché, and you probably think it's stupid, but I thought it would be romantic, you know. I wanted it to set the tone for the rest of our marriage to be full of love and romance."

"I don't think it's stupid."

Savannah snorted. "That doesn't sound convincing."

I turned my head to face her and studied her profile, soft and ethereal in the glow of the moon. "I think it was...not well thought out but not stupid."

Savannah's head whipped in my direction, and she raised an eyebrow. "Did you just call me naïve?"

"I did not say that." I shook my head and blew out a breath. "I just mean that you should've thought it through. That's a lot of pressure to put on a marriage right off the bat."

Savannah tilted her head to the side, and her eyebrows drew together. "I never thought of it like that."

"Just a thought."

"Would you still go on that vacation?"

I blinked. "Huh?"

"It's paid for," Savannah explained, color rising up her neck and staining her cheeks. "And non-refundable. I've been wondering what to do for the last few days, and my friend is telling me that I should go. She thinks I shouldn't waste an opportunity like this."

"Where were you going to go?"

"Charleston, South Carolina."

"A little small town southern charm?"

Savannah's lips lifted into a half smile. "That was the idea. Horse drawn carriages, a sunset cruise near Charleston harbor. That whole thing."

"You really do have a thing for small towns and their charm, huh?"

Savannah nodded and glanced away. "I do. I like the sense of community and feeling like I'm amongst family. Doesn't everyone?"

I shrugged. "Not everyone."

I felt Savannah's eyes on my face, studying me. "She really did a number on you, huh?"

"Who did?"

"Whoever broke you heart."

I looked back at her and frowned. "She didn't break my heart."

At least I didn't think she had.

Caroline had hurt me, but I wasn't as devastated as I thought I would be. On the contrary, focusing on making the business a success and recuperating the money she and Jeffrey stole gave me a sense of purpose, and it made me feel better.

And I had no idea what that said about me.

Was I as soulless and indifferent as people thought?

Or had I grown immune to human emotion over time?

"She did hurt you though," Savannah realized, in a hushed voice. "I'm sorry. For what it's worth, I think you're better off without her."

I glanced out at the water and straightened my back. "I am."

My phone rang, slicing through the warm night air. I fished it out of my pocket and squinted in the darkness. When the phone fell out of my hand onto the sand, Will's voice rose through the air, sounding harried and concerned.

"Mr. Buchannan, I'm sorry to bother you, but the FBI wants to schedule another meeting—"

I scooped the phone up into my hand and took Will off of speaker, pausing to shoot Savannah an apologetic look. "I've got to take this."

Once I was far enough away, I ran a hand through my hair. "You cannot start a phone call with that kind of information, Will. I don't want people in this town knowing anything. You know how quickly gossip spreads."

Will exhaled. "I'm sorry, sir, but they're insisting on setting up another meeting as soon as possible."

"When?"

"Tomorrow."

"I'll set up the location. Having the agent over at my house is too risky."

And too exposed.

Considering Savannah had already heard a snippet of the conversation, I didn't want her assuming the worst. I resisted the urge to glance over my shoulders to see what she was thinking.

Was she already turning the matter over in her head?

Did she think I was another white-collar criminal?

A grade A conman?

During my entire conversation with Will, I couldn't stop thinking about it. Once the call came to an end, I walked back to Savannah who was sitting on the sand, her dress fanned out underneath her, and her face gave nothing away. As soon as I came to a stop in front of her, she rose to her feet and brushed off the sand.

"I need to head back. Business never sleeps."

Savannah nodded and adjusted the strap of her bag. "Sure, I think I've shown you all of the good stuff anyway."

"No well where kids discovered the magic of unicorns?"

"That would be the town next to us," Savannah responded, with a distracted smile in my direction. "They've also got a tour of the original influence for the wicked witch of the west."

"Fascinating."

"It can be."

In silence, we walked back to my house, our fingers inches away from each other. Savannah stood at the top step; her arms folded over her chest. "I hope I've given you something to think about."

I pushed the door open and glanced over my shoulders. "You have. Good night…Savannah."

She blinked up at me, a furrow appearing between her brows. "Good night…Asher."

With that, she spun around and hurried across the moonlit street, skidding to a halt outside her own door. Florescent streetlamp cast long shadows across the wall as she pushed the key into the lock and shoved the door open. Savannah went in without a single backwards glance.

I couldn't tell if I was relieved or worried.

CHAPTER 10

- SAVANNAH -

"You can't possibly be this calm about it."

I glanced around and back at her. "Why not?"

Gemma snorted and pushed the salad around her container. "Because I know you. You're a naturally anxious person. You worry even when there isn't anything to worry about."

"Yeah, so?"

Gemma glanced up from her container and set it down on the bench next to her. "So, there's no way you're not freaking out about this."

I looked back at Gemma and raised an eyebrow. "Since when you are so desperate for gossip?"

Gemma shoved my arm. "Since you started holding out on me. What's going on?"

"Nothing."

"Liar."

I sighed and inched closer to her. "I don't think I should be talking about this in public."

"Because of…oh." Comprehension dawned on Gemma's face. She shifted closer to me and lowered her head. "What did your mom's friend say?"

I studied the group of teenagers across the street before I looked back at my friend. "If the FBI already knows about him then I'm sure the Sheriff does too."

Gemma snorted. "You're giving him too much credit."

"I contacted an old friend of my mom's. Retired CIA."

She let out a low whistle. "This is some real spy novel shit. Why the hell have you been holding out on me?"

"Because he said there was nothing to tell."

"And you believed him?"

"Howard has never lied to me before."

Given how close he and my mom were, I had known that I wanted to contact him the minute I overhead Asher's private conversation. Not only was Asher living in town and trying to invest in it, but I was also working closely with him which put me directly at risk if anything went sideways.

And I didn't like being kept in the dark.

I had spent half the night, after leaving Asher at his house, debating whether or not a phone call to Howard was worth it. Since the FBI were already involved, I doubted there was anything I could do to help, not as far as I could tell at least. An hour ago, after a quick chat with Howard, during which I hid in the storage room on the far side of the building, I still had very little to go on.

As far as Howard's contact was concerned, everything about Asher was above board, up until an investment in Lockwood Creek that was under investigation.

Unfortunately, Howard's contact hadn't been able to provide any more information, and he himself was reluctant to pursue it further in order to protect his source and make sure I wasn't endangering myself. A part of me had been tempted to push, to see how far Howard was willing to go, and how much I could uncover, but the other part of me was afraid of what I would find. Besides, it was enough for me to learn that Asher was a legitimate businessman who had never been under scrutiny before.

Considering what little I knew about his personal life, it was something of a relief.

And it explained why he was closed off and reluctant to share things about himself. I imagined being under investigation by the FBI was hard enough without unwelcome attention, and I doubted that Asher wanted me poking my nose where it didn't belong.

Again.

Given that I liked working at the wellness center, and the paycheck kept me from drowning in debt, I couldn't afford to play with fire.

Why did I always have a habit of sticking my nose where it didn't belong?

As far as I was concerned, everyone was entitled to their secrets and just because we had one amazing night together, it didn't mean I was entitled to rifle through and find all of the skeletons in his closet.

He's your boss, remember? As long as neither you nor anyone in town is in danger, that's all that matters. Everything else is just noise you need to tune out.

"For someone who claims that you don't only think of him as a boss, you sure do spend an awful lot of time talking about him."

"I do not."

"Don't get caught up in this shit," Gemma warned, with a frown. "You have no idea what you could be walking into."

"I haven't done anything."

"Uh-huh, sure. Just make sure your hormones don't land you in trouble, okay?"

"If you mention that time in eleventh grade with Chad Cooper again, I am ending this friendship."

Gemma snorted and shoved her container into her bag. "No, you won't. We've been over this already. I know too much."

I threw my head back and laughed. "So, what does that say about me?"

"You also know too much. Face it, babe. You're stuck with me for good now."

Gemma blew me a kiss before she walked way.

I stood up and walked back into the center, with the warmth of the afternoon sun on the back of my neck. I went behind the main desk and put away my lunch bag. Asher came out of his office a few moments later, a furrow between his brows, and a muscle ticking in his jaw. He held his phone to his ear and was muttering something underneath his breath.

He sounded more upset than I'd ever heard him.

It softened some of the resolve I had. He came to a stop a few feet away from my desk and undid the top button on his jacket.

The afternoon was slanting behind him, giving him a warm, ethereal glow. Asher tilted his head to the side and shoved his hands into his pockets. When he ended the call, he looked directly at me, and I couldn't look away.

I wanted to get lost staring into his blue-gray eyes.

Damn it, Sav. Get a grip.

I cleared my throat. "Rough day?"

Asher frowned. "I've been having a lot of those since I came here."

"I'm sorry."

"Not your fault."

"You know what makes me feel better when I'm down? Mickey's."

"The who now?"

My lips twitched in amusement. "It's not a who. It's what. It's the best pizzeria in town. It's owned by this guy who lived all over the world. You're going to love his pizza."

Asher raised an eyebrow. "You want me to go to a pizza place owned by a guy named Mickey?"

I nodded and offered him a bright smile. "Don't be a snob. You'll love it, and it'll get your mind off of whatever is bothering you."

He stared at me for a while longer before he nodded. "Alright, I can pick you up at seven."

A shiver of impatience raced up my spine. "Or we can just meet there."

"I'll probably get lost. It's better if we go together."

"Okay, fair enough."

Hours later, Gemma stood in the doorway with a bowl of cereal pointing at me and laughing. She gave me a slow, devious smirk when the doorbell rang and disappeared.

I raced down the stairs, taking them two a time. When I reached the door, I paused, tossed my hair over my shoulders and did a double take. Asher was dressed in dark jeans, sneakers, a button-down shirt that accentuated his blue eyes, and he was wearing an expensive looking blazer on top.

My heart felt like it was going to jump out of my ribcage and into his arms.

How did he look that good all the time?

"Ready to go?"

I snapped my mouth shut and grabbed my purse off the table. "Yeah, sure."

In silence, the two of us walked to the restaurant, leaving a wide berth of space between us. While there was no denying the pulsing energy between us, I wanted to believe that the two of us could out to dinner and be civil to one another. For the sake of the wellness center, and my own peace of mind, I had to try. Once we arrived at the restaurant, Asher asked for a table in the back, next to the window overlooking the town's clock tower. He took a seat opposite me, picked up the menu and was studying it intently while I tried not to gawk at him.

"So, have you always wanted to be a businessman?"

"Yes," Asher answered, without looking up. "I like watching a business grow from the ground up, and I like being a part of that process"

"I never thought of it that way. How did you make the leap from insurance brokerage to server farms?"

Asher took a sip of water and his expression turned thoughtful. "I want to expand. I don't want to do one thing for the rest of my life."

"I get that."

"Have you always wanted to be an office manager?"

"Nobody grows up wanting to be an office manager, but I like the job."

Asher lowered the menu and signaled to the waiter. "Why is that?"

"I like organizing things and doing things for people. I like making life easier."

Asher motioned to me when the waiter came to a stop in front of our table. After we placed our order, Asher leaned back against his chair and fixed his gaze on me.

It was personal and intimate.

Like we were back in his bedroom, exploring each other's bodies.

I couldn't tell if I wanted to hide or lose myself in his gaze.

But I did know that I liked it, much more than I wanted to admit.

"You don't strike me as a people pleaser."

"You say that like it's a bad thing." I reached for my glass of water and took a few sips. "It's not, by the way. As long as it's something you want."

Asher shrugged. "It doesn't seem like something you want."

"Maybe you don't know me all that well. And you're not as mysterious and grumpy as you think you are, by the way."

Asher waited until the waiter was done pouring the wine before he took a sip. "I wasn't aware that's how people saw me."

I snorted. "You've clearly never dealt with someone who is like you."

Asher snorted back at me. "So, is that why you invited me to dinner? To make a point?"

"I invited you to dinner because you're good company."

"Not bad for a grump, you mean."

I tilted my glass in his direction and grinned. "Exactly."

Asher's lips twitched. "I see."

"There's hope for you yet, don't worry."

"Good because it was going to keep me up at night," Asher commented, dryly. "They should have more of a variety for dessert."

I glanced back down at the menu. "I think it's pretty good."

"You've obviously never tried chocolate covered dates." Asher pushed his menu and glanced up at me, sending a shiver racing up my spine. "It's the best thing you'll ever taste."

"I'm pretty sure I can think of better deserts."

"Such as?"

"Cheesecake."

"Cheesecake? Come on, that's really unoriginal."

I folded my arms over my chest, and my lips twitched. "I wasn't aware we were being graded on originality."

The two of us settled into conversation, making small talk over a large pepperoni pizza and a bottle of wine. When the waiter returned to clear up our plates, Asher signaled for the check and waved my protest away.

As soon as we stepped outside, goosebumps broke out across my flesh, and I rubbed my hands up and down my arms.

Asher draped his blazer over my shoulders. "So, what's next? You are the Lockwood creek expert."

"I should probably get going..." My phone buzzed, and I fished it out of my pocket. With a frown, I scanned the text and exhaled. "Or not. My friend is staying at my house, and she asked me to come back a bit later."

Asher twisted his head to face me. "You're welcome to wait at my house until you can go home."

"Thanks. I'd appreciate that."

A voice inside my head was screaming that it was a bad idea. Somehow, all the wine in my system was telling me otherwise.

WEDDING NIGHT STRANGER (MR. BUCHANNAN)

I knew how great Asher was in bed, and part of me wanted to know if it was a fluke, or the energy between us.

Either way, I knew I wanted him.

So, I led him back to the residential area and onto our street. Asher walked ahead of me, took his keys out of his pocket and pushed the door open. He waited for me to go inside before he stepped in after me. Once he did, his hand darted out and reached for the light switch.

And nothing happened.

"I think the electricity is out. Let me see if I can find some candles."

He returned with a candle, his hand brushing against mine. My breath hitched in my throat when his finger brushed against mine before he drew away.

His face was lit up in orange and red flames as he handed me a glass of water.

I clutched the blazer tighter around me and inhaled the scent of him. "Thank you."

Asher nodded and set the candle down on a table behind him.

He was beautiful, even in candlelight, and the soft glow made everything feel like a dream.

Like if I reached out and touched him, he was going to disappear.

What was happening to me?

Why couldn't I see him as my boss and nothing else?

I knew I should know better, but I couldn't seem to care.

The two of us continued to stare at each other, the thread between us crackling and pulsing. His eyes drifted down to my lips, and the swarm of butterflies in my stomach erupted. He took a step towards me, and my breath hitched in my throat.

Then he covered the distance between us and kissed me, and my head exploded. He made a low noise in the back of his throat before taking the glass out of my hand. Without breaking our kiss, he set the glass of water down behind him, and then his hands moved to my waist.

His touch burned through the fabric of my dress.

I could feel every muscle and every breath, but it wasn't enough.

I whimpered when he drew his mouth away and pressed hot, open-mouthed kisses down the side of my neck. His hands moved from my waist to my butt, and he squeezed, hard. I hoisted myself up, and he caught me, securing my legs around his hips.

My heart was thundering in my chest, and my head was spinning.

Was I really doing this again?

Asher drew back to look at me, his eyes dark with desire. "Are you sure about this?"

I nodded and linked my fingers over his head. "Yes."

"Good." He growled and kissed me again, claiming my mouth his. Then he shifted, footsteps creaking as he hurried into the bedroom. When he set me down on his bed, I sat up and twisted my arms over my head. Asher pulled me to my feet and spun me around, so I was pressed against his front.

Slowly, he unzipped the dress, and it fell to the floor with a flutter.

His hands moved to my waist, leaving a trail of heat in his wake. "You're even more beautiful than I remember, Savannah."

"Asher, I—*mm.*" I squeezed my eyes shut when he undid the clasp of my bra and pulled down my panties, leaving me bare and exposed. I heard a rustle of clothing, and his naked body was pressed against mine.

Flushed and filled with anticipation.

WEDDING NIGHT STRANGER (MR. BUCHANNAN)

He spun me around and cupped my face in his hands. When he kissed me, his mouth moved slowly, gently, like he was learning every last curve and crevice. Each stroke, each touch, each breath drove away any last doubt I had about us.

Or what we were doing.

All I knew was that when I was around him, it felt like my entire body was on fire.

And only he knew how to quench the thirst.

It didn't matter that he was my boss or that he had plans for the town.

We were all that mattered.

His hand dipped below us, and he stroked my center. Little pinpricks of desire danced up and down my skin, making my lungs burst. I clung to him as he slid one finger in then another and stroked me.

Holy shit.

Asher Buchannan knew exactly how to touch a woman.

How to make her pant and writhe for more.

A part of me was embarrassed at the sounds I was making, and how transparent I was being, but the other part of me bucked and writhed against him, needing more friction.

More of *him*.

He pressed his lips to mine, and I moaned into his mouth. His free hand stroked the entire length of my back before moving to my nipples. He flicked one then the other until they were both as hard as pebbles. I raked my fingers over his back and was rewarded with a low hissing sound.

It was like music to my ears, and I wanted to hear more of it.

Of him.

"You have no idea how hard it's been for me to keep my distance."

"I have a pretty good idea actually."

I was putty in his hands, and I didn't even care.

Asher smiled into the kiss as we fell backwards onto the mattress. "You're even sexier than I remember." He climbed on top of me, pinned my arms on top of my head and rubbed himself against me. I moaned and lifted my hips up off the mattress.

"Oh, Asher. Oh, that feels good."

Then I was falling, hurtling towards the edge as the force of my orgasm ripped through me. I called out his name, like a chant, the entire time.

"That's it, baby. That's it. Fuck, you're so wet."

When my vision cleared, Asher lowered his head and kissed me.

Before I could deepen the kiss, he flipped me onto my back. Another holt of electricity and impatience raced through me, and my heart was hammering unsteadily against my chest.

This was the most erotic thing I'd ever experienced.

And I didn't want it to stop. He pressed hot, wet kisses down the length of my back. Wave after wave of desire rose through me as I propped myself up on my elbows and glanced back at him.

Raw hunger was etched onto his face.

I nearly came undone then and there.

My heart was pounding in my ears, and I couldn't look away as Asher positioned himself behind me and gripped my waist. In one quick move, he was inside of me, filling every last inch of me.

"You feel fucking amazing."

Far better than I remembered.

I wanted to bottle his scent up and smell it forever.

"So do you. Fuck, Savannah. You drive me crazy."

Once he began to move inside of me, my head fell forward, and I moaned. I squeezed my eyes shut and ground back against him, relishing every moan and every stroke. His touch burned wherever he touched, and it was all I could think about.

In this room, he wasn't my boss, or the man I couldn't understand.

Instead, he was a man who knew how to take and give, with equal amounts of pleasure and frustration. He eased in and out of me with practiced ease, his grunts making the low thrum of desire in my stomach turn molten. I twisted my arm over my head and over his neck. Then I grabbed a handful of his hair and tugged. He made a noise and nipped on the inside of my wrist.

Holy shit.

Why did it feel so good between us?

Like I was going to explode into a million pieces and not give a damn?

"Fuck, Savannah. You're so sweet." Asher grabbed my wrist and pinned my arm to my back. "I could stay like this forever."

My blood was pounding in my ears. "Maybe you should."

He brought his head to a rest against my flushed, sweaty skin. "I should."

Asher made another guttural sound, and the force of my orgasm washed over me, leaving me panting and breathless. I writhed and spasmed against him while riding out my high. My entire body was trembling when Asher's own release came, and he jerked against me as he called out my name.

By the time I could breathe again, Asher shifted and threw himself onto the mattress next to me. My arms gave out, and I fell face first onto a pillow that smelled exactly like him. When the spots in my vision cleared, I glanced over at him, and his eyes were closed.

His chest rose and fell evenly.

With bated breath, I reached between us and brushed his hair out of his eyes. His expression grew troubled before it became relaxed again. I shifted closer to him and sighed.

What the hell was I doing?

CHAPTER 11

- ASHER -

"What do you mean the investigator lost him?"

"He traced one of Jeffrey's cards, but by the time he got there, they were gone."

I scowled and tugged on my tie. "Of course they were gone. He should've been more careful. Did they leave behind any clues regarding where they were going next?"

"The investigator is interviewing the locals at the motel they were staying at, but no luck so far."

I sat up straighter and ran a hand over my face. "These are not the results I want, Will."

"Yes, sir, Mr. Buchannan."

Through the glass doors, I caught glimpses of Savannah as she sat at the desk, a furrow between her brows. She tilted her head to the side, giving me a generous view of her slender neck, and my frown deepened.

Having an unobstructed view of her desk was proving to be a problem. Ever since we ended up in bed together again, I hadn't been able to stop staring at her.

How had I allowed it to happen a second time?

For the life of me, I couldn't understand.

Granted, Savannah was a smart, funny and beautiful woman, and I admired her passion and loyalty to her town, but she and I had nothing in common. I had only ever lived in the big city, and I thrived on the cutthroat world of business and knew to handle my own in a concrete jungle. Savannah, on the other hand, had only ever known the small-town life.

As far as I could tell, she had barely been outside Lockwood Creek nor did she have a reason to. Considering everything she had ever known was here, and she had even been willing to settle down and start a life with her ex-fiancé here, it didn't make sense for her to move anywhere else.

Even though I could picture her holding her own in the city. A little too clearly if I were being honest with myself.

Not that it mattered, one way or another.

Savannah belonged here, and I belonged in the city.

So, why couldn't I stop thinking about her, and the way she felt when she was pressed against me? Why couldn't I stop thinking about the way she sounded when she pressed her lips to my ear and moaned, and it was the single most intimate thing I had ever heard?

Why had I sat across from her, talking for hours and enjoyed every single minute of it?

Goddamn it.

Savannah was a distraction I couldn't afford; in a package I couldn't resist.

What the hell was the matter with me?

I had bigger fish to fry, including ensuring that my investigator was able to find Caroline and Jeffrey, otherwise, circumstantial or not, these allegations were going to hang over my head and be a blight on the company name. Given the nature of the crime, and the amount of money that had been embezzled, the FBI needed a perpetrator and someone to pin the crime on.

Someone who wasn't me.

It was bad enough that they believed the wellness center and the server farm were a front for illegal businesses. Now, the

FBI were circling and questioning why the initial amount for the projects had doubled in such a short amount of time, and I had no answers for them.

None that made sense.

All I knew was that I had been duped so well and so thoroughly that I had never suspected it until it was too late.

For all I knew, Caroline and Jeffrey could've kept the con going on for a while longer, and I would've been none the wiser. The longer I sat there, listening to Will detail the entire investigation, the worse I felt about the entire thing.

When I looked up, Savannah was staring directly at me.

Our eyes met, and everything else stopping existing.

Will's voice was a dull roar in the back of my head.

Savannah's mouth lifted into a half smile, and a shiver of desire raced up my spine.

What was it about this woman that had me so tied up in knots?

Why couldn't I think clearly and do what needed to be done?

"...I'm sorry, Mr. Buchannan. I know this isn't what you hoped for."

I wrenched my gaze away from Savannah's and cleared my throat. "Has the FBI given you any more information?"

"They're giving us very little," Will replied, after a brief pause. "But I'm sure that we can convince them to give us more. We've been cooperative and helpful, so that's a point in our favor."

"Time is something we don't have a lot of," I pointed out, pausing to rake a hand through my hair. "Comb through the transcripts, my phone, whatever you need. Make this go away, Will. Before things get ugly."

Will mumbled something else before the call ended.

I tossed my phone onto the desk, shoved both hands into the pockets of my trousers and turned to face the window. It overlooked a view of the water, glistening underneath the light of the sun. A flock of birds came out of nowhere, flew up into the sky and called out to each other. I watched as they flapped their wings and flew further and further away, until they became specks on the horizon.

Lucky bastards.

I had spent my whole life working hard to build the company from the ground up and poured my blood, sweat and tears into it. I had even sacrificed a functional relationship with my family to get to where I was, one of the youngest millionaires in the country, and the thought of having it all ripped away by the callous and selfish actions of Jeffrey and Caroline didn't sit well with me.

It made my blood boil.

And thinking of what they'd done made me want to put my fist through a wall.

Repeatedly.

Instead, I pushed down the laptop screen. After patting my pockets to check for my keys and wallet, I stepped out into the hallway. The smell of incense and flowers filled the air, and on my way out, I came across a few clients dressed in long, plush robes with serene smiles on their faces. With a polite smile, I greeted all of them until I made my way to the front desk.

"Any more good resumes?"

Savannah glanced up and stood up straighter. "No, Mr. Buchannan."

"I'll call the employment agency and ask them to send over a few more. Maybe someone from a few towns over." I shoved my hands into my pockets and cleared my throat. "I'm going out for lunch. Can you take my messages while I'm out?"

Savannah nodded, and her eyes lingered on my mouth before moving up to my face. "Of course, Mr. Buchannan. Whatever you need."

WEDDING NIGHT STRANGER (MR. BUCHANNAN)

My stomach gave an odd little dip at the look on her face.

What I need is you sprawled on a bed underneath me, Savannah, with your hands all over my back, and a wicked smirk on your lips, but I know that isn't possible because I was here to get a job done, not get entangled in an office romance.

Getting HR involved in order to make sure our office romance didn't carry as many ethical issues was an option, but it wasn't one I was willing to consider given that Savannah and I hadn't even decided we should be dating.

It was a fling, and that was all there was to it.

With a little more force than necessary, I shoved the thought away and nodded. "Excellent. Thank you."

As soon as I set foot outside, I noticed two things.

One, there were grey clouds gathering on the horizon.

Two, there was a group of people holding up signs and chanting on the other side of the street, and a line of uniformed police officers stood in front of them, looking harried and completely out of their element. I took my earphones out and took step in the opposite direction and paused when I heard my name being called out. With a tilt of my head, I looked over at them and squinted into the distance.

Immediately, I recognized Gemma Hart, holding up a sign with my name on it. After doing a double take, my curiosity getting the better of me, I changed course and walked straight towards them. Once I was a few feet away, a chorus of jeers rose up through the crowd, and they began to stir in anger and frustration.

"Mr. Buchannan, I don't think you should be here for this." One of the uniformed officers, a tall blonde-haired woman with a no-nonsense expression held an arm out and shook her head. "You're not exactly their favorite person right now."

I blinked at her and turned my attention back to the protestors.

Many of them carried signs in bold cursive I couldn't make out. Others held up signs with pictures of the Earth and marine life. Gemma, on the other hand, was looking directly at me, a strange glimmer in her eyes. If it hadn't been for her signature red hair, I wouldn't have recognized her at all.

It had been years since the two of us crossed paths.

And even longer since we were on opposite sides of a cause.

"I didn't expect to see you here."

Gemma's lips lifted into a half smile. "I was about to say the same thing to you. You shouldn't be here, Asher."

"I have a business in Lockwood Creek."

Gemma stepped away from the protestors and made a beeline for me. One of the uniformed officers held a hand out and placed it on her arm. "Where are you going?"

"It's okay, officer. I know her."

He released her, and she covered the distance between us in two quick strides. "Do you even care about the impact your business is going to have on the environment?"

I raised an eyebrow. "Hello to you too, Gemma. It's been a minute. How are you?"

Gemma waved my comment away. "I'm not here for small talk. I'm here because this is an important cause."

"I see you're the one who is leading the protest. Still mad about me sweeping that deal out from under you?"

Gemma scowled in my direction. "I'm not. I'm not in the insurance business anymore. I'm a florist now."

"How do you go from being an insurance broker to a florist?"

"Because I realized what's important," Gemma replied, with a shake of her head. She made a sweeping hand gesture, her eyes never leaving my face. "This is what's important, Asher. The community and being able to fend for itself."

"I just built a wellness center."

"We know about the server farm. One of our friends works for the town council, and they overheard them discussing your plans," Gemma told me, her eyes tightening around the edges. "Do you have any idea what this is going to do, or do you just not care?"

"Look, I've already heard this whole song and dance, and I'm not looking to do it again. I had a team research and look into the risks, and we're going to do our best to minimize the damage to marine life."

"How?"

"I'm not going to discuss the details of my business with you."

"Then you're going to have to deal with protests like this all over town. Today, you're the most infamous man in town."

I shook my head. "You really have no idea what you're getting yourself into."

Gemma pointed at me and frowned. "You're the one who has no idea who you're messing with. The people here stick together. We're not just going to roll over and let you take away our livelihood."

"I'm not taking away anything," I replied, calmly. "There will still be job opportunities, not like the ones you have now, but they will exist. Change has to happen, Gemma. Things can't stay the way they are forever."

"What about tourism? Have you thought about that?"

"Tourists will still be able to come, and the properties overlooking the water won't be affected. They'll just have to move further down if they want to go for a swim. More importantly, this is going to give the technological infrastructure of the town a much-needed boost."

Gemma rolled her eyes. "You always did act like you knew better."

I took a step back. "It was good to see you again, Gemma."

With one last look at me, she moved back behind the barrier and raised her voice, joined by a few others. I walked away from them and resisted the urge to glance over my shoulders. Once I reached the café around the corner, I was given a few withering looks. Whispers started when I walked in and went straight to the register. I ignored everything and everyone as I took my sandwich and sat down.

While I didn't care what people thought of me, I wasn't immune to the heat I was getting. Given the circumstances surrounding the wellness center and myself, the last thing we needed was any more negative publicity. I needed to find a way to put an end to the story or risk more scrutiny from the FBI and another tense meeting with my board of directors. Halfway through my meal, I stood up and walked back outside. I was too worried to eat any more, so I would have to finish at my desk later. On my way back to the wellness center, I saw that the group of protestors had grown in size.

And Savannah was standing next to the officers, making conversation with Gemma. As soon as she saw me, she hurried over. I held the door open, and she ducked past, refusing to meet my gaze.

"What was that? As an employee of the center, you can't be seen with the protestors. It reflects badly on us."

Savannah shrugged. "I wasn't with the protestors. I was talking to Gemma."

"You know Gemma?"

"She's my friend and roommate," Savannah replied, without looking at me. "You know, you could sit down and hear them out. I'm sure it'll make them feel better."

"I'm here to run a business not coddle people and hold hands around the fire."

With a scowl, I strode into my office, and the door clicked shut behind me. Over the next few hours, I made a phone few calls, trying to find someone who could put an end to the protest but to no avail. By the time the sun set below the horizon, they trickled away, little by little until only Gemma remained.

The next day, the crowd was bigger in size, and a lot rowdier.

In the middle of the day, when I stepped outside for some fresh air and saw the news van, and a well-dressed woman holding a mike up to Gemma's face, irritation continued to bubble within me. A few clients, who had crossed the street and were on their way to the wellness center, deviated and went to join the protestors. Throughout the day, more and more clients didn't make it past the front door.

I alternated between watching Gemma's interview on TV and making phone calls to every single person I could think of. Every phone call I made amounted to the same thing. Since Lockwood Creek was a small town, and they were within their rights to protest, provided it didn't get violent, no one was going to be able to stop them.

By the end of the third day, I realized I was going to have to be the one to broker a truce.

Or at least try.

Once I was sure all of the protestors were gone, I walked up to Gemma and waited for her to finish her conversation. She twisted to face me, a flicker of surprise moving across her face. Then she waved at the woman who walked away, her kids in tow, and bridged the distance between us.

"Here for round two?"

"You've been on your feet all day. I'm sure you could use a drink or two."

"Using the Buchannan charm won't work on me," Gemma warned, with a roll of her eyes. "But I won't say no to a drink if you're buying."

I gestured to my car. "After you."

In silence, we walked to the car together, and I held the door open for Gemma. I got into the driver's side, and once the engine revved to life, I eased out of the parking spot and onto the main road.

In the distance, the town loomed, glistening underneath the moonlight. I pulled up to a spot outside the local bar, situated between a restaurant on one side and a laundromat on the other. I parked the car in an empty spot and got out. Gemma followed close behind, her face giving nothing away. As soon as we stepped into the bar, the loud music hit me first, followed by the smell of alcohol and sweat.

Then the two of us were weaving our way through the crowd and pushing past the tightly packed bodies. Once we reached the bar, Gemma pulled out a stool and sat down. I took a seat opposite her and signaled to the bartender, who was standing in front of a group of giggling, red-faced women.

Conversation rose and fell around me, punctuated by the sound of music playing through the overhead speakers.

I called the bartender over and gestured to Gemma. "What are you having?"

"A beer," Gemma replied. "And a burger with fries."

"I'll have the same." I sat back against the stool and glanced around, at the groups of people gathered around the bar, all of them laughing and smiling as they leaned towards each other. Then I swung my gaze back to Gemma and reached for my drink. After a few sips, I sat up straighter and looked directly at her.

"What's it going to take to make this go away?"

Gemma took a long sip of her drink. "Got your attention, huh?"

"You know you did." I took another sip of my drink and made a vague hand gesture. "So, what do you want?"

Our plates were set down in front of us, steam wafting up from the plate of fries.

"You and I both know you're going not going to stop construction on the server farm."

"That's something we agree on."

Gemma sat up straighter and looked directly at me. "Before we talk shop, I just want to let you know that if you hurt Savannah, I will hurt you myself."

"Why am I not surprised that you know Savannah? Everyone in this town really does know each other."

"She's my roommate."

I tilted my head to the side and frowned. "Hmm, I see."

"Yeah, so she's not just someone I know casually. She's also my best friend. Do you see where I'm going with this?"

"I do. I'll keep that in mind."

Gemma cleared her throat. "Now that that's out of the way, let's talk business."

CHAPTER 12

- SAVANNAH -

"So, you just talked shop?"

Gemma nodded and peeled off her sweater. "We tried to reach a truce."

"And?"

"It didn't go well as well as I'd hoped," Gemma replied, with a shrug. "But we agreed to move the protests somewhere else."

I raised an eyebrow. "How did he manage to convince you of that?"

"We're still going to be visible, but we won't be directly across the street from the wellness center. Asher pointed out that any kind of fallout that resulted in the wellness center closing was going to negatively impact the employees too, and we didn't want that. Like he rightfully said, the wellness center is a benefit to the town, and that's not the business we have an issue with. It's only the server farm we want to stop."

I blinked. "Thank you. I know that can't have been easy for you."

Gemma shrugged. "Asher knows what he's doing. Mostly at least."

Ever since their friend L leaked the news about the permits for the server farm, the entire town has been in an uproar, to the point that Gemma had offered to spearhead the protests herself. For the past few days, the server farm was all the town could talk about, and it was causing quite a stir.

I had never seen Lockwood Creek react like this to anything.

Not even the news that a local country music star was passing through for a visit.

Everyone wanted to take up arms against Asher, and his corporation. A part of me felt bad for him because I didn't think it was fair for him to be targeted by everyone in town. However, I also knew if he didn't start trying to compromise and bridge the gap between him and the protestors, it was going to snowball into a much bigger problem.

It was the last thing anyone wanted.

"We sat down and talked about everything," Gemma added, before stepping into the kitchen. She filled a kettle up with water and set it down on the stove. "I also told him that if he hurts you, he'll have to answer to me."

"You didn't have to give that speech, you know."

Gemma shrugged "I know, but I wanted to. He didn't even bat an eye, don't worry."

"Why would I be worried?"

Asher and I weren't together.

While I did enjoy spending time with him, and I loved how he made me feel, I wasn't delusional enough to think it meant anything. On the contrary, he and I had both gone into this with our eyes wide open, and we knew what it meant. A part of me was relieved that there weren't any secrets between us or any mind games that left room for doubt.

When it came to Asher, I knew exactly where I stood.

And I didn't mind.

Or at least I tried to tell myself that I didn't.

Because what was the alternative?

Jumping headfirst into a relationship with my boss?

A man I was just getting to know and who offered very little about himself?

Sleeping with Asher once was justifiable.

And falling into bed with him again was understandable given the heat between us.

Pursing something more with him, on the other hand, didn't make any kind of sense. Not when it was only going to cause problems for the both of us and force me to quit a job I needed.

It just wasn't worth it.

Gemma held a water bottle up to her lips. "Don't you have a job to get to?"

I glanced over at the clock and cursed. "Shit, you're right. I've got to go, or I'm going to be late. Will you tell me the rest of the details later?"

"There are no details. There is nothing juicy to tell," Gemma called out, to my retreating back. "Try not to drool all over him today, okay?"

I flipped Gemma off before slamming the door shut behind me.

A short while later, I arrived at the wellness center, panting and out of breath. Once I pushed the door open, I hurried into the employee bathroom and splashed cold water on my face. Then I tucked my shirt into my skirt and surveyed the outfit. Satisfied, I gave myself a firm nod before hurrying back behind the desk in time to greet the clients who were stepping through the door.

"Mrs. Villeneuve, it's so good to see you again."

"I see the protestors have moved further down." Mrs. Villeneuve set her purse down on the counter and peered at me. "Good for you. Your boss must be pleased."

I gave her a smile as my fingers moved over the keyboard. "He is. Thank you, Mrs. Villeneuve."

Mrs. Villeneuve glanced around before leaning forward. "Is it true that the wellness center is going to be torn down once the server farms are built?"

I cleared my throat. "I'm afraid I can't discuss something like that, Mrs. Villeneuve."

She frowned. "But you love this town. Don't you care what happens to it?"

"Of course I do." I paused and glanced up at Mrs. Villeneuve, her skin weathered with age and the streaks of silver in her hair glistening underneath the late morning sun. "I'm sure it's nothing to worry about, Mrs. Villeneuve. Mr. Buchannan has a plan in place."

Except it was looking more and more like the wellness center was a placeholder.

A distraction while he figured out the water server farm permits.

It had taken me a few weeks to figure it out, but I was beginning to put the pieces together, little by little. And the more I did, the less everything made sense to me. Asher was the kind of businessman who liked to swing for the fences, but he also owned an insurance brokerage company.

None of it made sense.

Nor did the fact that he was staying in a large house all by himself.

"We would feel so much better if someone told us what was happening," Mr. Montgomery added, his head peeking out from behind Mrs. Villeneuve. "You're the only one who talks to us like we aren't idiots, Savannah. What's going on?"

WEDDING NIGHT STRANGER (MR. BUCHANNAN)

Shit.

I should've known that chatting with the clients wasn't a good idea. Especially considering this particular group, who in spite of being charming and friendly, didn't let go of things easily. Since they had little else to do with their time, it made sense that they would latch onto the latest piece of gossip and squeeze till they had every last piece of information they could get.

And I was their means to an end.

Thinking about it made my head hurt, but in spite of my best attempts to steer clear and mind my own business, it was all I could think about. When I wasn't in the center, organizing schedules and putting out fires, it lingered in the back of my head along with my thoughts of Asher, and the spark between us.

I had no idea what the hell I was doing, but I knew it couldn't end well.

Not unless I stopped myself from going further down the rabbit hole.

It's not like Asher owes you any answers anyway, right? Sleeping together twice doesn't mean anything. You need to focus on your job, Sav. That's it.

With a slight shake of my head, I looked up from the screen and let my eyes sweep over the five of them, gathered in a semi-circle in the middle of reception. "I know you're all worried, but there's really nothing to worry about. Mr. Buchannan is a good businessman, and I'm sure he knows what he's doing."

Or at least I hoped to God he did.

Because I couldn't stand the thought that this was all about money for him.

In spite of all evidence pointing to the contrary.

Their voices rose in protest as they all gathered around the desk and frowned at me. I gave them all a bright smile and gestured to the wellness employees, who stepped forward and coaxed them away, one by one until I was the only one left in the lobby. As soon as they were gone, I sunk onto my desk and buried my head in my hands. I hated having to keep things from them, when they had every right to be concerned, but I also didn't want to get in trouble with Asher.

Again.

Considering how many things he let slide, I didn't want him to think I was developing a pattern.

I glanced up, pulled my chair closer to the desk and stared at my computer screen. After a quick look around, I pulled up a tab and drew my bottom lip between my teeth.

"Has the agency sent any more resumes?"

I gave a start and glanced up at Asher's expectant face. "They haven't sent them over yet, Mr. Buchannan."

Asher frowned and looked up from his phone. "Do you know where the agency is?"

"I think it's an online based business, sir."

Asher muttered something incomprehensible underneath his breath. He lowered his phone, tucked it into his pocket and twisted, so he was facing me directly. "I want you to get in touch with them, on every platform necessary, and broaden the search. There's got to be someone who is qualified."

"Maybe if you changed some of the requirements," I suggested.

Asher shook his head. "People need to rise to the occasion. Lowering my standards isn't going to accomplish anything except ensure that the person I hire isn't qualified."

I rose to my feet and cleared my throat. "With all due respect, sir, that isn't necessarily true. I'm sure you can find someone who is qualified, but doesn't have the exact requirements you're asking for."

Asher didn't say anything as he stared at me.

I clasped my hands behind my back, staying firm in my opinion. The butterflies in my stomach beat mercilessly.

When his phone rang, he took it out of his pocket and drifted into his office. I waited until he shut the door behind him before I sat back down. Why was it when he didn't agree with what I said, he always drifted off and pretended like I said nothing at all?

For the rest of the day, I tried to avoid my computer and Asher. Instead, I spent the day roaming around the wellness center and making small talk with our clients. Many of them were old and retired, looking for an escape from the real world and happy to have some company. Others, the more affluential clientele, were more interested in being left to their own devices. I did my best to steer clear of them, save for a few well-placed compliments here and there. By lunch time, I made my way back to the front desk and sat down behind it.

After a quick glance at the door, I ducked underneath my desk and pulled out my lunch bag. The fork was halfway to my mouth when Asher came out of his office and made a beeline for me. Knots formed in the center of my stomach as he came to a stop and gave me a pointed look. Slowly, I set my fork down and stood up.

"Ms. Parish, I'm not sure why I keep finding myself at your desk."

I gave him a confused look.

"A few of the clients asked to meet with me directly," Asher continued, his expression growing more and more irritated. "For some reason, they seem to believe that the wellness center isn't going to be around for long."

"News travels fast, Mr. Buchannan."

"You mean gossip travels fast," Asher replied, pausing to fold his arms over his chest. "Many of them told me that they talked to you first. Do I need to remind you of our agreement, Ms. Parish?"

I frowned. "I only told them that you're a good businessman and that they should trust that you'll do the right thing."

Asher let his hands fall to his sides. "You don't speak for the company, Ms. Parish or me."

"I know."

"Do you? Because I'd rather not pull you into another meeting regarding employee behavior and what's expected of you."

I stiffened. "I'm sure that wouldn't be necessary, sir."

"I think being upfront and honest with the guests is a good idea."

"I'm sure if you…wait, what?"

"I'm sure you did your best in attempting to ensure them that there was nothing to worry about." Asher gave me a pointed look. "I have no intention of tearing the wellness center down."

"Really?"

"Yes, but in the future please remember that I'm running a business, Ms. Parish, not a daycare center."

"Part of running a business is knowing how to deal with clients, isn't it? These are your clients, Mr. Buchannan, and they have the right to express their concern."

Asher took a step and glanced around. "I'd like to see you in my office, Ms. Parish. Now."

Without a backwards glance, he walked away. I waited for a few moments before I hurried after him, pulling the door shut behind me. "I know we don't see eye to eye here, Mr. Buchannan, but we don't have to be on opposite sides of this."

Asher stepped behind his desk. "Not seeing eye to eye is an understatement, Ms. Parish, and it is the least of our problems. I cannot run a business if you keep trying to undermine me at every turn."

"I am not trying to undermine you, Mr. Buchannan. I'm just trying to—"

"Open up my eyes and help me see the truth?" Asher sat down behind his desk. "I didn't hire you to absolve my sins, Ms. Parish. We've already been over the terms of your contract, and you're well aware of what your duties entail as office manager."

I stood up straighter. "Sir, the people of this town deserve to know the truth."

"And what truth is that? That I'm the villain who promised them a wellness center, but is really trying to destroy their economy and take over the water?"

"I'm sure it's not that simple—"

Asher was on his feet in an instant, his careful mask one of cold fury. "You're damn right it's not that simple, Ms. Parish. You have no idea what's happening here, and you are trying to sabotage something that—"

"I'm not trying to sabotage. If you would just listen—"

"—is meant to provide more job opportunities for the residents, and improve the economy but instead you're being narrowed minded—"

"—and sit down with the clients and protestors, I'm sure you could find some common ground—"

"—and you're being presumptuous. What gives you the right to question me?"

I threw my hands up on either side of me and blew out a breath. "Mr. Buchannan, I'm not doing trying to question you or undermine your authority, but I stand by what I said. This is not being handled the way it should be."

Asher's expression hardened. "Ms. Parish, other than your duties as office manager, as I said, if anyone brings up future plans for the wellness center, you should assure them that there is nothing to worry about. No more trying to go over my head or getting our guests worked up."

"Mr. Buchannan—"

He held a hand up and gave me a pointed look. "I will not keep calling you into this office to discuss the same thing over and over, Ms. Parish. You might be qualified and good at your job, but I am not a saint. Consider this a formal warning."

I snapped my mouth shut and stared at him.

In trying to help him, I had struck another nerve.

Trying to navigate things wish Asher was like trying to pick my way through a landmine. Considering how little I knew about him, there was no way of knowing what was going to set him off. Asher sat back down behind his desk and dismissed me with a wave of his hand. I waited for a few moments before I spun on my heels and hurried outside, a low thrum of anger coursing through my veins.

Why was he so dismissive and cold?

Why couldn't he just meet people halfway?

I had dealt with a lot of people over the years but never anyone as stubborn, closed off or as single-minded as Asher. On the one hand, I admired his dedication and his refusal to waver from his beliefs and his vision for the company. On the other hand, I couldn't imagine any of it ending well for any of the parties involved.

For the rest of the day, I sat behind my desk exchanging emails with several local business in an attempt to plan an office outing.

But I couldn't stop thinking about what Asher's words.

When I went back to his office a few hours later to apologize, his door was propped open, and his voice spilled out. "There has to be someone else who can do her job."

Through the slit in the door, I saw his back turned to me, and he ran a hand through his hair. "The wellness center was supposed to the easy part, but I've spent all day fielding clients who are demanding to know the truth."

Asher paused. "There's nothing to tell anyway. Everything I'm doing here is above board, and the mayor knows it. Everyone needs to make their peace with what's happening, and the sooner that happens, the better."

Asher spun around, and I flattened myself against the wall, heart hammering against my chest. "Dealing with them is becoming a headache, and Savannah is only making things worse. She's supposed to make the transition smoother not rile the clients up."

He fell silent, and I heard the rustle of papers.

I swallowed, took a step forward and paused when I heard my name again. Against my better judgement, I pressed myself against the wall and waited.

"Right now, Savannah is more of a problem than an asset. I'll need to review my options before I can make a decision about her future here."

CHAPTER 13

- ASHER -

I stood up and unfastened the button on my jacket. "You told me that this was a done deal, Will. Why haven't they dropped the case yet?"

Will exhaled and sat up straighter. "It's a little more complicated than we thought, Mr. Buchannan. The FBI is having a hard time believing that you didn't know about what they were doing. It seems Caroline and Jeffrey planted some evidence that suggested otherwise."

"All lies, and I'm sure the real evidence can back me up."

"A lot of the evidence is circumstantial, Mr. Buchannan. If it goes to trial, it'll be about what they can make the jury believe."

I folded my hands over my chest. "How do we make the jury believe I'm innocent?"

"Building a good case," Will replied, after a brief pause. "If it comes to that. Given the nature of the case, it's still not clear if the FBI will want to take this to trial."

I stepped out from behind the desk and walked over to the bar. After unfolding my arms, I poured a generous amount of whiskey into two glasses. Then I set one down in front of Will and lifted the other to my lips. The amber liquid burned a path down my throat before settling in the pit of my stomach. With a frown, I patted my pockets for a cigarette. Wordlessly, Will tossed me a lighter, and I caught it mid-air.

I didn't want to go to jail and lose everything I'd worked hard to build.

And all because I'd placed my trust in the wrong people.

In silence, I studied my lawyer through a thin plume of smoke.

Over the years, he had proven himself to a competent lawyer, capable of handling several tough cases thrown his way, including a former disgruntled ex who tried to sue for wrongful termination. Given his discretion, and his cutthroat skills, I believed that Will was the best lawyer for the job. However, over the past few weeks, he had been dropping the ball more often than I liked, and it wasn't sitting well with me. As my lawyer, he should've noticed that something was off about the paperwork that he approved regarding the business venture.

But he hadn't.

Caroline and Jeffrey should've been in my rearview mirror by now.

Instead, they were the gift that kept on giving, and it was getting on my last nerve.

Between the irate clients at the center, the persistent protests being covered by the local news, and Savannah tiptoeing around the office and avoiding me, I wasn't sure what I was supposed to do anymore. Running a business was hard enough without having to face obstacles around every turn, and each time I thought I had a handle on things, another problem materialized.

Fate had a twisted sense of humor making me the punchline.

"There's something you're not telling me." I blew out another ring of smoke in Will's direction. "What happens if we go to trial?"

Will folded his arms in his lap. "Mr. Buchannan, it's better if we don't go to trial. In the court of public opinion, people are not likely to vote in your favor."

I leaned forward. "Because of the seriousness of the case?"

"Because once the prosecutor paints a picture using the circumstantial evidence, it'll be too easy for him to cast reasonable doubt about your role in all of this, and getting them to see past that is going to be difficult."

I pulled the ash tray closer to me. "It's your job to make sure they see me as more than that."

Will stood up and fastened a button on his jacket. "It won't happen, sir."

I flicked away a few ashes and studied his face. "Has the FBI offered a plea deal yet?"

Will pressed his lips together and said nothing.

"They want me to do time and pay a fine, I suppose." I stood up and peered at him. "How long?"

"Ten years and ten million in damages," Will replied, after a lengthy pause.

Before I could respond, the door to my office flew open, and Caroline and Jeffrey walked in. Caroline stepped forward, in her designer top and jeans with her hair piled on top of her head. Savannah was hot on their heels, her cheeks flushed with anger. "I'm sorry, Mr. Buchannan, but they wouldn't wait."

I had no idea what they were doing here, but I was far from happy to see them.

I was tempted to put Jeffrey's face through a wall.

Repeatedly.

"It's fine, Savannah," I replied, without looking at her. "Please hold all my calls and shut the door on the way out."

Savannah glanced between the four of us, a furrow between her brows. Then she took a few steps back and pulled the door shut behind her. As soon as she did, Jeffrey sat down on the couch and crossed one leg over the other. He patted his pocket, took out a cigarette and lit it up, his face giving nothing away.

"We've missed you, Ash," Caroline began, pausing to give me a smile. "So we thought we would come and visit. The wellness center turned out better than we thought."

Will stepped in between us. "I should call the FBI and have you arrested."

Jeffrey blew out a ring of smoke. "But you won't because you don't have anything on us. It's all circumstantial evidence, isn't it, Willy?"

"You want to find out? There's an FBI agent in town right now. Why don't I give her a call? You can't be held on formal charges, but you can be arrested and interrogated."

Caroline looked over at Jeffrey before glancing back at me. "Then you'll never have the evidence you need to clear Asher's name, and his company's, of course. We have information the FBI will find very interesting."

I put out my cigarette and stepped out from behind the desk. "What the hell do you want, Caroline? More money?"

Caroline pouted. "Is that any way to talk to us? We're here to help."

"I don't believe you. You've already screwed me over once."

And they were here to finish the job.

I wasn't going to fall for the same act twice.

Jeffrey stood up and bridged the distance between us. "We didn't have to come, you know. If we wanted to screw you over, we could've stayed away and let the evidence do the job for us. Without enough to pin the job on us, we know you're stuck and will take the blame."

Will and I exchanged a quick look. He came to stand next to me and glanced between the two of them. "What do you want?"

"You can talk to the FBI, tell them we're willing to name names and convince them to drop the charges against us."

Will stood up straighter. "I'm not buying it."

"We'll help you clear Asher's name and that of his company."

"You're screwed, aren't you? Your bosses found out what you did, and they are not happy. A high-profile case like this brings a lot of unwanted attention."

Caroline huffed and crossed her arms over her chest. "Ash, why don't you tell your pitbull to stand down? We're here to help."

Jeffrey draped an arm over Caroline's shoulders and grinned. "Yeah, Ash. Call off your dog unless you're too afraid to play with the big boys."

"I'm not the one who ran away."

Jeffrey's smile turned lethal as he blew a ring of smoke in my face. "No hard feelings, Buchannan. A man's gotta do what a man's gotta do."

"Give me one good reason why I shouldn't call the FBI myself. That will clear my name faster than either of you can."

Caroline and Jeffrey exchanged a quick look before he removed his arm from around her shoulders. She leaned over the desk, giving me a generous view of her cleavage. Her blood red lips lifted into a half smile as she looked directly at me.

I had planned on proposing to her on Valentine's Day.

At the time, I had been able to envision a future for the two of us, starting with the success of the wellness center and the server farm. Unfortunately, the longer the four of us stood there, in complete silence, the more I began to realize how stupid I was. All along, Caroline had been stringing me, and I, her willing puppet, had turned a blind eye to a lot of things.

Up close and personal, Caroline was not as perfect as I thought she was.

Instead of gold, I was realizing she was gold plated and hollow on the inside.

Why had I been so blinded by her before?

"Why don't the two of us talk, alone?" Caroline stood up straighter and gave me another one of her winning smiles, showing off a row of pearly white teeth. "You want a good reason? I'll give you a few."

I stared at her and said nothing.

Reluctantly, Will strode to the door and held it open. Jeffrey scowled before letting his cigarette fall onto the carpet. Using the heel of his shoe, he stubbed it out and gave me a withering look on his way past. Before the door clicked shut, Will tilted his head in Caroline's direction and gave me a meaningful look. Then the two of us were alone together, for the first time in weeks, and I couldn't think of a single reason not to turn them in.

Caroline and Jeffrey deserved to answer for what they did.

And I had a feeling they weren't the least bit apologetic about what they did to me. They were only here because they were desperate or needed something else from me.

Caroline wandered over to my couch, sat down and patted the spot next to me. "Why don't you come and sit down next to me?"

I stepped out from behind the desk. "I know what you're trying to do, Caroline, and it's not going to work."

She took a cigarette out of her pocket and pressed it in between her lips. She leaned forward, and I held a lighter up to her face. Once it lit up, I sat down across from her, pushed a window open and pocketed the lighter. Caroline was a beautiful and generous woman up until people crossed her. Underneath her picture-perfect façade was a woman as cunning as she was dangerous, and a part of me had always suspected it.

After years of watching her rip her competition to shreds, I never thought I'd be on the receiving end of it. Hell, I had even justified her keen and sharp skills as a way to survive in the cutthroat, male dominated industry of architecture. Caroline had gone above and beyond to make sure that I only saw one side of the story, and it had taken her betraying me for to stop turning the other cheek.

Thankfully, I'd spent the past few weeks doing my homework and pushing my investigator to dig up every last piece of dirt he could on her and my former best friend. Yet, in all of the scenarios I imagined, having Caroline and Jeffrey walk into my office at the wellness center waving a white flag was not one of them.

"I just thought we should catch up."

I leaned back against the couch and twisted to face her. "Sure, do you want to talk about the fact that you were screwing Jeffrey the entire time we were together? Or how about the fact that you lied, stole my money and set me up to take the fall?"

Caroline blew out a puff of smoke. "Since when are you so sensitive about these things? You're the one who always said business isn't personal, Ash."

"There's a difference between keeping things professional and stabbing people in the back." I stood up and spun around to face her. "But I wouldn't expect a criminal to understand that."

She stood up, the cigarette held between her fingers. "I'm not a criminal, Ash. I'm just a woman who is trying to get ahead in the world."

"I don't care what you tell yourself to sleep at night, Caroline. It doesn't change the facts."

Caroline studied me, her blue eyes giving nothing away. "You're going to survive this, Asher. Hell, it's even going to give you and your company some exposure. You should be thanking us for what we did."

"You've got a lot of fucking nerve, Caroline. I'm not going to thank you."

Caroline bridged the distance between us and tilted her head back. "Because of your pride? You and I both know that you needed the exposure and even infamy can be spun. When this is over, you're going to be able to expand your company further just like you've always wanted."

"I always knew you were ruthless, Caroline, but this is low even for you."

"You can't tell me you wouldn't have done the same given the opportunity."

"I can, and I will. I've never sold someone else out or thrown them under the bus to make a quick buck."

Caroline snorted. "It's not like you care about the money. You'll more than make up for it, and the board is going to get over it eventually."

"Let's not pretend you give a shit about the money I'll get back or my reputation. We both know that's not really why you're here."

Will was right.

Caroline and Jeffrey hadn't risked federal prison to help me.

Not when they were the ones to put me here to begin.

After weeks of silence, they couldn't be having a crisis of conscience.

Caroline brushed herself against me as she leaned forward and put her cigarette out. Once she was done, she leaned back and stood up straighter. "Is that really how you want to handle this? I thought we could be civil."

"You want to negotiate an immunity deal with the FBI," I told her, with a pointed look. "And you're trying to use me to get them to listen."

"You'd be using me to clear your name," Caroline pointed out. "How is that any different?"

"I didn't throw you under the bus, Caroline. I didn't spend the past two years using you."

Caroline's brows knitted together, and she shook her head. "I didn't spend the past two years using you."

"Bullshit. At least own up to it, Caroline. You me that much."

"It wasn't all a lie," Caroline maintained. "I did care about you, Asher."

"You just cared about the money more."

And I was too blinded to see it.

I was much as to blame for Caroline's deception as she was. From the very beginning, something hadn't felt right, but I had squashed and pushed it away at every turn, doing my best to convince myself it was just nerves. Given that Caroline had been the first woman I'd been serious about in years, I hadn't wanted to believe the obvious. Now that she was back and looking me in the eyes, I couldn't escape it anymore.

Caroline was not the woman I thought she was.

And I wasn't the man she wanted me to be.

I pushed Caroline's hand away and pulled the door open. "We need to finish talking about this."

Will and Jeffrey stood in the blue colored hallway, on opposite sides of the wall, glaring at each other. As soon as they saw me, they straightened their backs and made a beeline for the door. Will stepped in first, and Jeffrey followed in his wake, his face twisted into a scowl. I caught a brief glimpse of Savannah's concerned face before the door clicked shut.

Silence stretched out over the room.

I went to my desk and lowered myself onto the chair. "If you want us to get the FBI to come to the table, you're going to have to prove this isn't some kind of set up. Why not go to the FBI directly?" Jeffrey folded his arms over his chest. "We don't have a direct line of communication. You do."

"You need my help, Jeffrey," I pointed out, pausing to give him a cold look. "The tables have turned, haven't they? The only way I'm going to help is if you convince me that you're worth it."

Jeffrey's scowl deepened. "We don't need to prove anything to you, asshole."

I linked my fingers together and leaned back against the chair. "Then you can go and take your chances on your own. See if I give a shit."

"Jeffrey," Caroline hissed, with a quick look in his direction. "We do need his help."

"I'd listen to her, Jeffrey," I added, my lips lifting into a half smile. "She always was smarter than you."

"He's enjoying this way too much," Jeffrey muttered, pausing to run a hand over his face. Caroline came to stand next to him and squeezed his hand. "Fine, what do you want?"

"Bring us proof that you're serious and proof of Asher's innocence," Will said, his gaze swinging between the two of them. "Then we'll talk to the FBI."

Jeffrey muttered something else, but I couldn't hear him.

Will led him outside, and the two of them stood in the hallway, exchanging angry looks. I stood up, stepped out from behind the desk and looked over at Caroline. When Savannah stepped into the office, a wrapped box in her hand, she saw Caroline's hand brush against mine and frowned.

"I'm sorry, Mr. Buchannan. I had no idea you were still in a meeting."

I twisted to face Savannah and saw the wounded look on her face moments before she stamped it out. "They were just leaving."

"We'll be back." Caroline pressed a kiss to my cheek and smiled. "It's good to see you again, Ash."

On her way out, she stopped to give Savannah, who stood stiffly, a onceover. Then she tugged on Jeffrey's arm and led him away. Will looked over at us, and I gave him a slight shake of my head. As soon as he was gone, Savannah held the box out and wouldn't meet my gaze.

"I saw this the other day and thought of you. When we were at dinner, you mentioned that you loved chocolate covered dates."

I blinked. "You didn't have to go through all of that trouble."

Savannah withdrew her hands and clasped them behind her back. "I wanted to."

I set the box down on the desk behind me and wheeled around to face her. "Caroline and I used to date."

Savannah nodded.

"She's one of the reasons why I came here."

"You did look like you knew each other pretty well."

"I thought we did."

Savannah lifted her gaze up and cleared her throat. "You don't owe me any explanations. You and I aren't together, remember?"

"Right."

Savannah took a step back. "Anyway, I saw the chocolates and with Valentine's coming up, I was afraid that they'd get snapped up."

"I appreciate it, but now is not a really good time to talk."

Savannah nodded and exited the office, walking quickly, and with her head held high. Once she settled behind her desk, I picked up the box and frowned. Savannah and I hadn't met under the best of circumstances and things hadn't exactly gotten better since then. At every turn, she and I butted heads.

She was a thorn on my side.

Yet, I found myself oddly thankful, and I couldn't ignore the swarm of butterflies when I saw her handwritten note and caught a whiff of her perfume.

Savannah had gotten under my skin, and I had no idea how to get her out.

CHAPTER 14

- SAVANNAH -

I tossed a quick glance in Gemma's direction before pushing my way to the bar. There, I pushed my hair out of my eyes and leaned over the counter. Once the bartender, a bright-eyed blond looked over at me, I gestured to the rows and rows of drinks stacked up on the shelves.

The bartender nodded and swung his gaze back to the group of women on the other side of the bar, giggling and bending their heads together. I sighed, spun around and scanned the area around me, taking in everything from the people seated at the booths, overlooking the moonlight streets of the town, to the group of people dancing in the corner, Gemma included among them.

I didn't even know what I was doing here.

But after seeing that blonde draped all over Asher, I needed to forget.

I needed to forget the way she looked standing next to him, and the onceover she'd given me on her way out, sending a shiver of unease racing up and my spine. Not only had I seen right through her, but I'd also received her message loud and clear. While Caroline and Asher might've broken up, for reasons I couldn't determine, it was pretty clear that she wanted Asher back.

And she wasn't going to let anything or anyone get in the way of that.

Including me.

Especially me.

I had no interest in competing with Caroline with her designer clothes, and her petite frame. Unfortunately, the longer I stood there while I waited for another round of drinks, the worse I felt about the entire thing. A part of me knew I didn't have the right to be jealous, but the other part of me couldn't seem to help myself.

Seeing Asher with another woman was disconcerting.

I'd spent the entire day in the office with a strange feeling in the center of my stomach, and a hollow ache in my chest. For the life of me, I couldn't understand it. Although Asher and I had never talked about anything serious developing between us, it didn't change the way I felt when I was around him.

Like I couldn't breathe when he looked at me.

And I could only exhale when he smiled.

I hated it.

Because I knew how stupid it was to get involved with a man like Asher, who was not only my boss, but the reason the town was going to change. Having meet Asher under difficult circumstances, the last thing I wanted was to throw myself headfirst into a new relationship, especially when it was clear he didn't feel the same. As far as I was concerned, Asher and perfect blonde Caroline deserved each other, and he and I were better off staying far, far away from each other.

With a slight shake of my head, I spun back around and gestured to the bartender again. He set the drinks down in front of me with a quick smile. I picked them up and held them close to my chest as I pushed my way back through the crowd. Once I reached Gemma, she plucked the shot out of my hand and downed it back. Then she went back to dancing, her hair whipping back and forth.

I tossed back my own shot and drew myself up to my full height when I saw him.

Asher sat at a table by the window, a beer bottle in front of him and an intense look in his eyes. He was looking directly at

WEDDING NIGHT STRANGER (MR. BUCHANNAN)

me and didn't break my gaze as he lifted the bottle up to his lips and took a long sip. Slowly, he lowered the bottle, and his tongue darted out to lick his mouth, sending shivers racing up and down my spine. My mouth turned dry when his mouth lifted into a half smile, and the rest of the world ceased to exist.

Goddamn it.

What was about this man that made me go weak in the knees?

Why was I so willing to risk my career and my sanity for him?

It didn't make sense.

And there was no denying how much easier it would be not to like him.

With a frown, I swung my gaze back to Gemma and joined the others who were dancing. I lifted my arms up over my head and spun in a circle, aware of Asher's eyes on me the entire time. When I lowered my hands, running them down the sides of my body, I could almost feel myself pressed against him, his hot breath dancing on the back of my neck. Gemma stepped in front of my field of vision, blocking my view of Asher altogether.

"Do you want to leave?"

I shook my head. "He's not going to drive me away. I was here first."

Gemma raised an eyebrow, swaying steadily to the music. "Are you sure you don't want to talk about what you saw? I know it couldn't have been easy for you to see him with her."

I shrugged and looked over her, the swarm of butterflies in my stomach erupting when mine and Asher's eyes met across the room. "It doesn't matter, Gem. We're not together, remember?"

Gemma frowned. "It doesn't mean you can't be upset. You're allowed to have feelings for him."

I shook my head. "Well, I don't, so you don't have to worry about me."

Except we both knew I was lying.

Gemma knew me better than anyone on Earth, and I knew she could see right through me. Fortunately, I also knew that Gemma wasn't the type to pry, not right away at least. She was going to give me a few days to process my feelings then she was going to start badgering me until I spilled my heart out. With a sigh, Gemma stepped away from me and began to dance with a man with shaggy blond hair and jeans that hung low on his hips.

I closed my eyes and moved to the music, but I couldn't stop seeing Asher's face.

Or imagining him with his arms all over me.

Once I opened my eyes, a tall and broad-shouldered man with unkempt brown hair and wearing ripped jeans and a black leather jacket stood in front of me. He gave me a once-over, and when his eyes moved back up to my face, I took his hand and pulled him closer. His smirk grew as I spun around and lifted my hands up over my head. Slowly, I pulled them back down, imagining Asher instead.

As soon as he placed his hands on my waist and ground against me, I knew it was a mistake. Abruptly, I shoved his hands away and frowned. "What are you doing?"

"Come on, baby. I thought we were having a good time."

"I'm not your baby," I snapped, pushing my hair out of my face. "And I didn't tell you that you can touch me like that."

He took a step towards me and huffed. "You don't have to play hard to get."

I snorted and folded my arms over my chest. "Don't flatter yourself."

"Baby—"

"You heard her. She's not interested." Asher materialized beside us, his expression one of cold and calculating fury. He

WEDDING NIGHT STRANGER (MR. BUCHANNAN)

placed a hand on the man's shoulders, and a quick look passed between them. "Why don't you leave her alone now?"

The brown haired man held both of his hands up and stepped back. "Sorry, man. I didn't know she was with you."

"I'm not with him."

His eyebrows furrowed as he glanced between the two of us. Then he shook his head and pushed his way through the crowd, back to a group of guys standing in a circle near the bar. Once they saw him, they hooted and laughed and handed him a beer. I swung my gaze over to Asher who had one hand shoved into the pocket of his jeans, and the other held the beer up to his lips.

He looked effortless, every ounce of him oozing with control and confidence.

I couldn't decide if I wanted to kiss him or push him away.

"I don't need you to save me." I placed both hands on my hips and glared at him. "I had it under control."

Asher lowered his beer and raised an eyebrow. "Having me here didn't hurt."

"Yes, it did. I don't want you doing things like that because it just confuses me."

"Why?"

I let my hands fall to my sides and took a step back. "You know why."

Asher covered the distance between us and studied my face, his gaze leaving pinpricks of desire racing up and down my spine. "I don't."

I swallowed and pointed a finger at him. "Because we both know what this is, Asher, and we can't keep dancing around it."

Asher took another swig of his beer and said nothing.

The energy between us burned and crackled.

But it did nothing to quell the annoyance bubbling up within me.

Why wasn't he saying anything?

Why step in and defend me at all?

Wordlessly, I snatched my sweater off a nearby table and stormed off, without a backwards glance. Outside, I shoved both hands into the pockets of my jeans and made a beeline for the beach, cursing Asher the entire time. Once I got there, I took off my shoes, walked to the edge of the water and inhaled.

"You're a little too close."

My head whipped around, and I saw Asher's vague silhouette, outlined by the silver glow of the moon. My heart gave an odd little dip when he closed the distance between us and came to a stop next to me. He looked out at the water, and his expression turned thoughtful and unguarded.

"Are you following me?"

Asher shook his head. "I love coming to the water. Sometimes, I feel like it's the only place I can think."

"Why do you want to destroy it then?"

"I don't want to destroy it," Asher replied, in a strange voice. "I want to make it more valuable."

"It's already valuable."

Asher titled his head in my direction, and I felt him studying my profile. "You're right."

I twisted to face him, and my breath hitched in my throat. "Thank you."

"I'm not saying it to be nice. I mean it, and the dates mean a lot to me, Savannah. No one has ever given me a gift like that before."

WEDDING NIGHT STRANGER (MR. BUCHANNAN)

"Not even Caroline?"

Asher shook his head. "Especially not Caroline. She's not the woman I thought she was."

"What kind of woman did you think she was?"

"Kind, smart, funny, loyal," Asher replied, his expression growing serious. "Like you. You're all of those things and more Savannah, and it drives me crazy."

My blood was pounding against my ears. "It does?"

"Because I know I can't have you," Asher whispered, lifting his hand up and stroking my jaw. "But every time I'm around you....fuck. It's like nothing else matters, and I don't give a shit about any of the rules or any of the reasons why."

I licked my lips. "You're just saying that because you're drunk."

"It doesn't make it any less true." Asher lowered his head and brushed his mouth against mine. "You taste like strawberry flavored gum. It's my new favorite taste."

I shuddered, bridged the distance between us and grabbed a handful of his shirt. Then my hands moved to the back of his neck and wound themselves through his hair. He made a low noise in the back of his throat that had my pulse racing, and warmth pooling in the center of my stomach.

Suddenly, I couldn't get close enough.

There was too much space between us, too many layers.

I wanted to peel them all away, so there was nothing between us except for this swell of emotion, rising in my chest and threatening to overpower me. With a sigh, my hands moved from his hair, down the length of his back and cupped his behind. He growled into my mouth and the butterflies in my stomach erupted into a frenzy.

Asher hoisted me up, so I wrapped my legs around his waist and lowered me onto the warm, wet sand. When he pressed himself against me, every thought, every doubt flew out of my head. I ran my hands up and down the length of his back until I stopped at his shoulders. With my heart pounding in my ears, I pushed Asher back and stood up. I tilted my head in the direction of the wellness center and licked my lips. He laced his fingers through mine, and we took off at a sprint, breathless and impatient.

It felt right between us, even though it shouldn't.

And I wanted to hold onto that for as long as possible.

His hands were sure and steady as he placed the key in the lock, and it clicked open. As soon as he pulled me in after him, I kicked the door shut with the back of my leg and threw myself at him. He caught me mid-air, and I wrapped my legs around his waist, the pounding in my ears drowning out everything else. Then Asher was everywhere, his hands moving up and down my bare arms as he rubbed himself against my center.

My breath hitched in my throat as he rubbed me over the fabric of my jeans, his touch hot and searing.

I wanted more.

I needed more.

With a growl, I untucked his shirt, and he drew back to let me pull it over his head. It fell to the floor with a flutter, joined by own shirt, leaving me naked from the waist up. Bathed in moonlight, Asher leaned back to study me, and his eyes stayed on my nipples which had turned as hard as pebbles.

I had never more exposed nor more desired in my entire life.

It was a heady and intoxicating combination only Asher could pull off.

He lowered his mouth, took one nipple between his teeth and tugged. My entire body was humming and crackling with electricity as he moved onto the other nipple, and I ground against him.

"I love that you aren't wearing a bra," Asher murmured into my skin. "This is a good look for you."

I threw my head back and gasped when he sunk his teeth into my neck. "It would be even better if I didn't have any clothes on."

Asher dragged his mouth up from my neck and cupped my face in his hands. "Absolutely."

He claimed his mouth with mine while his hands fumbled with the zipper of my jeans. Once he pushed it down to my thighs, he set me down on the floor and took a step back. My eyes didn't leave his face as we both stepped out of our jeans and left them in a heap on the floor. I followed Asher's fingers as they moved to the waistband of his boxers and pulled them down, allowing his erection to spring free.

Holy shit.

I was going to come undone right then and there, and I didn't care.

When he kissed me again, I tasted the hunger and yearning on his lips. One hand moved to my hips, and I jumped up, locking my legs around his waist. The other hand moved between us, pushing one finger in between my wet folds. With a growl, he pushed another finger in and began to move. I clung to him like my life depended on it and threw my head back. The cold glass of the windows dug into my back, but it didn't matter.

In this room, with Asher's smell all over me, nothing else mattered.

Especially not when he knew exactly how to drive me crazy.

With each sweep, each stroke, each touch, I flew closer and closer to the edge. Wave after wave of desire washed over me until it felt like my lungs were going to burst. Then the force of my orgasm ripped through me, and I cried out his name as I rocked against him. The wave of emotion within me only grew stronger. In one quick move, Asher removed his fingers and thrust into me. He eased and slammed back in, so he filled me to the hilt.

I moaned, loudly. "Fuck, Asher. You feel so good."

"I've been thinking about this all night," Asher said, into my skin. He pressed his mouth into my neck and kissed a path up my jaw. "I know you've been thinking about it too. You wanted me to be the one on the dance floor with my hands all over you."

I dug my nails into his back. "I did."

Asher placed his hands on either side of the glass and grunted. "You drive me crazy, Savannah. And you feel so damn good."

My nails move to his waist, and I squeezed, hard. "You feel amazing, Asher."

And I didn't want it to end.

The two of us continued to rock back and forth against each other until I could only hear the pounding in my chest, and the sound of his heavy breathing reverberating inside of my head. He kept one hand on the door behind me, and the other pushed my breasts together and flicked my nipples.

I let my head fall forward and licked a path up his neck and stopped at his ear. Then I took one lobe between my teeth and tugged. Asher made a low, unintelligible sound in the back of his throat and circled his hips. Then I was writhing and spasming as I rode out my second orgasm. Asher's body was slick with sweat as his pace changed, so he was moving with wild and animal like abandon.

It wasn't long before he shuddered and emptied himself into me.

Slowly, he leaned back and looked directly at me.

I held his gaze as I waited for my breathing to even out and wondered what I was supposed to do next.

All I knew was that we couldn't stay away from each other, and at this point, I wasn't sure I wanted to.

CHAPTER 15

- ASHER -

"What do you mean they don't have anything to offer?"

Will exhaled and pushed the file over the table. Then he stood up and leaned forward to flip it open. He took a few of the papers and spread them out, the frown never leaving his face. "These are a few of the statements they've made."

I pursed my lips together, picked up a paper and scanned it. "They're not telling us anything we don't already know."

Will nodded and sat back down across from me. "Exactly. I've asked the private investigator to look into their claims, but they haven't given me anything to work with."

I set the paper down and linked my fingers together. "They're intentionally holding back. Are they stalling for time?"

Will shrugged and leaned back against his chair. "To what end?"

I unfastened a button my jacket and stood up. "I don't know, but they're up to something."

Knowing the lengths Caroline and Jeffrey went to in order to pull off this con, it was clear they weren't done with me yet. Not only were they trying to play the long game, but they were also placing contingency plans in place for themselves. While a part of me understood why they wanted to take their precautions, considering the risk they were taking, the other part of me was tired of doing this song and dance with them.

It was high time the game came to an end.

One way or another.

The only problem was that the FBI was back to keeping information from me. Going straight to them had been right the call, but now that the FBI was icing me out, I had no way of knowing what was happening.

Only that the FBI was likely keeping tabs on Caroline and Jeffrey.

And keeping me out of the loop for reasons I couldn't understand.

Did they still think I was involved?

That I was part of some elaborate set up?

All of my attempts to find some answers had gone in vain.

Since our meeting in my office, the two of them had disappeared, leaving no indication as to their whereabouts. Although I knew they had to still be in town, given that they risked being arrested if they left, it was hard to determine where they were. In a town like Lockwood Creek, secrets didn't stay buried for long with the gossip mill always churning and spitting information out.

Sooner or later, they were going to be found out.

And when they were, they were either going to give us more, or I was going to make the phone call myself. While the FBI wasn't thrilled to let them roam free, they had agreed, with great reluctance, to act as if we had not brought them into the fold. So long as Caroline and Jeffrey were left to believe that they had the upper hand, the FBI had time to investigate their claims and see if what they brought to the table was of any use. Will and I, on the other hand, had spent hours debating the matter of length, and we knew exactly why it was important to keep Caroline and Jeffrey happy.

They were far more valuable to us and the FBI if we cooperated.

I'd been reluctant to trust them, I still was, but I wasn't going to go to jail because of this.

Because, this time, I was making sure I had my own contingency plans in place.

As far as I was concerned, Caroline and Jeffrey were going to get what was coming to them. Regardless of whether or not they provided us with any useful intel, it was only a matter of time before they slipped up and gave themselves away. In the meantime, the FBI and my own personal team of lawyers were combing through the evidence and using every last breadcrumb to build my case.

Unfortunately, it was taking a lot longer than I wanted it to.

Damn it.

I shouldn't have let Caroline and Jeffrey walk out of my office to begin with.

Had I been played again?

So eager to clear my name, save my company and move forward that I'd missed the signs?

"I've tried reaching out using the number they left," Will told me, with a shake of his head. "But either they haven't been checking their messages, or they don't want to meet."

I walked over to the window on the other side of my living room, looking out at my backyard, glistening underneath the light of the late afternoon sun. Then I shoved both hands into my pockets and frowned.

"They're toying with us. This is all a game to them."

Will slammed the folder shut. "I don't like playing games. I've told them what's at stake if this deal doesn't go through, but they don't seem to be taking it seriously."

I spun around to face Will and raised an eyebrow. "They came back into town in spite of the fact that they know the FBI is on their tails. They're risking their own freedom for this chance. They do know what the risks are, but they just don't seem to care."

"Better to betray us than the mob," Will muttered, darkly. He stood up and began collecting the papers on the table and stacking them together. "I'll have one of my associates go through the paperwork again. Maybe they're talking in code, and we missed something."

"What about the evidence the FBI has been combing through? Anything new there?"

Will glanced up, a furrow appearing between his brows. "The results are still inconclusive."

I left one hand in my pocket, and the other curled into a fist at my side. "What does that mean?"

"It means that, for now, the FBI can't do anything. They're probably going to try and compile more evidence."

"Probably?"

Will straightened his back. "They're not really sharing their next move."

"They're closing ranks," I realized, with a frown. "What about a smoking gun?"

Will shook his head. "Nothing so far. Our best strategy right now is to keep trying Caroline and Jeffrey. They won't be able to stay hidden for long and once they come up for air, we need to corner them."

"We need to convince them that coming to us was the right decision," I added. "The immunity deal with the FBI is still on the table, right?"

Will nodded and crossed his arms over his chest. "Only if they confess their guilt of embezzlement, show the FBI exactly how they did it, and provide useful intel about the mob. So far they've met none of those requirements."

"I'll try and get in touch with them. I have to go down to the wellness center. You can see yourself out, right?"

WEDDING NIGHT STRANGER (MR. BUCHANNAN)

Will gave me another nod and didn't say anything.

On my way out the door, I felt his eyes on the back of my head following me until I got into my car, parked at the end of the driveway. When I started the engine, I gripped the steering wheel with both hands and turned his words over and over in my head. Although I didn't like that the case wasn't done yet, I also knew it was in my best interest to have things done right.

Caroline and Jeffrey were going to get caught, and my name was going to be cleared, but it was going to take some time. I settled back against my seat, houses and trees whipping past me in either direction. A block away from the wellness center, as I was driving past, I saw Gemma, and the other protestors, gathered in the middle of a side street with their brightly colored signs, and their loud voices.

Once I drove past them, I saw Savannah standing with them, holding a cup of coffee in her hand, and another hand shoved into the pocket of her skirt, I did a double take. The car slowed to a crawl as I pulled up next to the curb and let the engine idle. Then I switched it off, pushed the door open and walked up to the path leading directly to the wellness center.

I resisted the urge to march back to where Savannah stood, fraternizing with the protestors, to give her a piece of my mind again. Instead, I pushed the door to wellness center and was met with the smell of incense and oil. A few of the employees paused to greet me as I made a beeline for my office. There, I peeled off my jacket, draped it over the back of my chair and rolled up the sleeves of my shirt. After sending Savannah an email, I sat down behind my desk and glared at my screen.

Why was everything so hard?

By now, everything should've fallen into place, allowing me to focus on the server farm alone. Unfortunately, since my arrival in Lockwood, I had been forced to deal with one problem after the next, and each time I put out a fire, another larger one approached, leaving me in a worse mood than before. Having Savannah, as qualified as she was, was not making things easier, especially given her clear conflict of interest.

You could pull a few strings and get her a job somewhere else.

Giving her the opportunity to pay off her debts, and not having to butt heads would be the better alternative. Yet, the thought of not coming in to work every day and seeing her smiling face didn't sit well with me. Over the past few weeks, she was one of the few highlights of my day, and even when I was mad at her, I still liked having her around and knowing she was a few feet away from my own office.

You've got it bad, Buchannan. Jesus, you're like a lovesick puppy or something.

A short while later, I saw Savannah come into the office and toss her coffee cup away. She set her bag down behind the desk, reached for a notebook and straightened her back. I studied her as she stepped into the hallway, headed straight for me. When she stopped outside my door and knocked, my stomach gave an odd little dip. I pushed back my chair, folded my hands in my lap and called out to her.

She poked her head in, her eyes wide and weary. "You wanted to see me, Mr. Buchannan?"

"Come in and shut the door."

Savannah stepped in and let the door click shut behind her. She stood up straighter, her hands on either side of her and fixed her gaze on a spot over the wall. When she swung her gaze to mine, I gestured to the chairs in front of my desk. After a brief pause, she bridged the distance between us and perched on the edge of her seat, her entire body tense and coiled.

It made me feel worse.

Because I kept seeing her half naked, with her face glistening with sweat. I kept replaying how it felt to have her pressed against me while I held her up against the glass door and eased in and out of her. Once she tilted her head to the side and studied me, I remembered how it felt to have her lips on my skin, and a familiar stirring started within me.

Rein it in, Buchannan. This is not the time or the place.

"The agency is going to send over a few new candidates for the assistant position."

Savannah nodded. "Would you like me to sort through the resumes?"

"I'd also like you to sit in on the meetings."

Savannah glanced up at me, a strange glimmer in her eyes. "I don't understand."

"You've got good instincts, Ms. Parish, and I value your...opinion."

Savannah blew out a breath. "Mr. Buchannan, if this because of last night..."

"It's not."

Savannah cleared her throat. "Is this because of your ex and the man who was with her? They're stirring up trouble, aren't they?"

I raised an eyebrow. "Are you spying on me?"

"I haven't been spying on you. I checked up on you because I wanted to be sure that everything was above board."

"It's nothing you need to worry about, Ms. Parish. Everything is under control."

Except it wasn't, and it was unnerving to realize that I wasn't as careful around her as I thought.

"It doesn't seem like it is."

"What, exactly, are you hoping to find out?"

More importantly, how much did she know?

I'd been careful, and we had all agreed to keep the situation under wraps.

Either Savannah had overheard something she shouldn't have, or she had connections of her own.

Savannah held her hands up on either side of her. "I'm not trying to run you out of town, or anything. I just wanted to be sure everything was okay."

I frowned. "Ms. Parish, there are things you need to leave well enough alone."

"It's better than sitting around and doing nothing."

I dug my nails into the inside of my palms. "You don't know a goddamn thing, Savannah. You need to stop acting like you know better."

"You need to do the same," Savannah snapped, her eyes blazing with emotion. "I know a lot more than you think. I know you want me to keep my head down and just do my job, but it's not who I am. I am not the kind of person who won't fight for what's right."

Jesus Christ.

She had the uncanny ability to wander right where she wasn't supposed to and make things worse. I couldn't decide if it made me more attracted to her, of if it made me want to place her in a bubble for her own protection.

Either way, it wasn't good.

"For fuck's sake, you're just creating problems for yourself."

"I could say the same thing about you. I know that the man and woman who were in here the other day are trouble, and I'm sure your lawyer isn't happy about them showing up."

I moved from around the desk and came to a stop in front of her. "How do you know that?"

Savannah tilted her head back to look up at me. "I've got eyes, and I'm a lot more perceptive than you give me credit for."

I couldn't decide if I wanted to kiss her or shake some sense into her.

Goddamn it.

Why couldn't she just have been a mild-mannered office manager who minded her own business?

Why did she know how to get a rise out of me and keep sticking her nose where it didn't belong?

"You have no idea what you're messing with, Savannah," I told her, with a lift of my chin. "You think you're clever for figuring it out? You think it's going to help your town? Well, you're wrong. All you're doing is putting yourself in the crosshairs."

"I am not the one who brought trouble into town."

I stiffened. "I didn't even want to be in this goddamn town to begin with, but I was told of an investment opportunity, and I took it. It's what businessmen do."

"It sounds like you don't want to take responsibility."

"It's still not your goddamn business," I growled, my entire body shaking as red hot rage coursed through me. "I have done my best to be patient, to overlook your indiscretions, but you just do not know how to leave it alone."

"If you were just honest—"

"Honest? Why would I be honest with you? I don't owe you anything—"

"—I could've helped you, we could've figured out a way to navigate this—"

"—and we weren't even supposed to be in each other's lives after that night—"

"—we can still try and figure out how to make things better…"

I held a hand up and glared at her. "Let's get one thing straight. We are not doing anything. You've already done enough. I don't want or need your help."

Savannah took a step towards me and frowned. "Why won't you let me help you?"

"Because you're just going to make things worse. It's what people do."

Savannah shook her head. "Not everyone is like that. Look, I don't know what happened to get you into this mess—"

"We are not going to discuss it," I interrupted her, pausing to take a few more steps back. Once I was safely behind my desk, I sat down, relieved for the space between us, so she wouldn't see how rattled I was. While I wasn't sure what I was expecting out of our conversation together, the last thing I expected was for Savannah to put me on the spot.

It left me feeling unnerved.

Realizing that she had wandered into a landmine, in an effort to save the town she loved, didn't sit well with me. It made me want to rush out of the office, find Caroline and Jeffrey and make them co-operate. Meanwhile, the other half of me considered firing her just to make sure she stayed out of harm's way. Unfortunately, given what I did know of Savannah, I knew it wasn't going to be that simple.

On the contrary, firing her was only going to give her more incentive.

"Are you going to fire me?"

I stared at her. "Not yet, but I would suggest you keep what you know to yourself. Otherwise, you're going to be putting a lot of people in danger."

Savannah swallowed and didn't say anything else.

CHAPTER 16

- SAVANNAH -

"So, what are you going to do?"

I glanced up from my plate of salad and blinked. "About what?"

Gemma snorted, the fork halfway to her mouth. "You know what I'm talking about, Sav."

"I really don't."

Gemma set down her fork and took a sip of her iced tea. "You really are in denial, aren't you?"

"I'm not in denial."

"So, why aren't you bringing up what happened with Asher?"

I shrugged. Halfway through cutting up my chicken, I glanced up at Gemma again, and she was watching me carefully. "There's nothing to tell. I already told you what happened."

Gemma raised an eyebrow. "And yet you still believe this is normal."

I tilted my head to the side and stared at her. "What do you mean?"

"Babe, the two of you have the hots for each other, and you can't stay away from each other. I think it's time to stop denying how you feel."

I reached for my own drink and frowned. "There are no feelings involved."

Gemma's eyebrow rose higher. "Come on, Sav. You and I both know that's not true anymore."

"I have no idea what you're talking about."

Except I did, and I'm a total liar.

The only reason Gemma wasn't pushing me harder was because she knew it wasn't going to get her anywhere. Since we'd spent the past two days dancing around the issue, it was only a matter of time before Gemma brought the topic back. Hell, I'd even suspected that it was the reason why she dragged me out for a girl's night in the middle of the week. Considering how our last girls night went, days before my actual wedding, I knew why she was reluctant.

There were a lot of memories attached to girls' night now.

But it didn't bother me as much as I thought it would.

Being in the same restaurant and sitting in the same booth where Gemma and I had sat across from each other, giggling and making plans for the future, felt surreal, like I was remembering someone else's memories. Although it had only happened a few weeks ago, it felt so far removed from my current life it might as well have been someone else's.

Sometimes, it felt like I was.

I wasn't the same person who once sat across from Gemma, dreaming about Kayden and wondering what our children were going to look like. And I definitely wasn't the person who had debated scaling back my work to allow me more time to spend at home, renovating and decorating until it looked a lot more like a home the two of us could live in. While Kayden hadn't been thrilled about the idea of me being home most of the time, he had tried to support me.

Or at least it's what I thought at the time.

I had no idea he'd had his own plans for the future, plans that didn't involve me or children. In hindsight, maybe the signs had been there all along. With a slight shake of my head, I took a bite of my chicken and began to chew thoughtfully, as if I had all the time in the world. In silence, Gemma sat across from me, shooting me meaningful looks the entire time. Finally, she picked up her own fork and sighed.

"Gem, seriously, stop looking at me like I've grown another head."

"I will when you tell me what's really going on," Gemma said, in between bites of food. "Because I know that something is happening."

I reached for my drink and took a few sips. "Why does something always have to be happening?"

Gemma's eyebrows drew together. "Okay, so if it's not about Asher, what is it?"

I set down my drink and returned to my food.

She glanced around the restaurant and back at me. "Is it being back here? Shit. I pushed you too hard to come, didn't I? And you weren't ready."

I blinked. "No, it has nothing to do with that."

"I know you and Kayden used to come here often," Gemma added, with a frown. "But I thought it would be therapeutic to be back here without him."

"It is."

Her expression softened. "You know it wasn't your fault, right? Kayden was an asshole, and you couldn't have known."

I sighed. "I think I always knew, but I tried to convince myself he could change."

Gemma reached across the table and squeezed my hand. "We all make that mistake, babe. It's not wrong to hope he'll change. Hell, it's not even wrong to try. You saw something in him, and you shouldn't feel bad about that."

Most of the time, I didn't.

At least not since my focus had switched to Asher and the town.

In a weird and unexpected way, Asher was exactly what I needed him to be at this point. Spending time with him, and at the center, even in the midst of our arguing, was providing me with what I needed to switch my focus elsewhere. It was working so well that I'd barely thought of Kayden and our almost wedding at all in the past few weeks. And I couldn't tell if I was relieved or worried.

I didn't want to replace one man for another.

Or use Asher as a placeholder, a temporary reprieve while I picked up the pieces and allowed my heart to heal. While I still had no idea where the two of us stood, even when it was clear we weren't going to be able to ignore the attraction between us, it didn't mean I wanted to hurt Asher or use him like that.

He deserved better.

Especially after what his ex-did to him.

Although he hadn't yet shared the complete story with me, it was becoming increasingly clear to me that she had lured him to Lockwood under false pretenses. Instead of making all his dreams true, Caroline had turned into everything she said she wasn't and had broken his heart in the process.

Knowing what she did to him made me understand him a little better.

And it broke my heart to think of how it must've felt for him.

It was no wonder he was closed off and private.

I had considered acting the same way after the fiasco with Kayden, and if it hadn't been for Gemma and hours of crying into a tub of ice cream, I wasn't sure what would've happened. A part of me still nursed the wounds he inflicted on me, but another, larger, part of me no longer believed it was something I was going to carry around for the rest of my days, and I had no idea what that said about me.

Why was it easy for me to let go of Kayden?

Had I really been clinging to the fantasy of him like Gemma said?

Gemma waved a hand in front of my face. "Hello? Are you even listening to me?"

I blinked and gave her a sheepish smile. "Sorry, I got distracted."

"We can go home if you want," Gemma offered, pausing to give me a smile. "It's the middle of the week anyway, and we both have work in the morning."

"Gem?"

"Hm?"

"How come you didn't tell me that you knew Asher?"

"Honestly? I didn't think it was worth mentioning. He and I did run in the same social circles, but we were never close."

I cocked my head to the side and studied her. "Has he always been closed off, and you know, broody?"

Gemma paused. "For as long as I've known him, yes. I think it has something to do with his dad leaving them when he was younger."

I blew out a breath. "Shit. I didn't know that."

"You and Asher don't spend a lot of time talking. How would you?"

I blew out another breath and sunk lower into my seat. "Fair enough. That's actually true, but it's not on purpose. It's just because—"

"Nothing is going on between the two of you?" Gemma gave me a pointed look. "I don't think you even believe that anymore, babe. And the longer you go without talking about it, the harder it'll be doing something about it."

"Like what?"

Gemma shrugged. "I don't know, you could go on a date or something. See where everything leads you."

I lifted up my drink and eyed her over the rim. "He's my boss."

"That hasn't stopped you from doing other stuff."

I choked on my drink and thumped my chest. Once my vision cleared, I gave Gemma a dirty look. "Sometimes, I wonder if you and I share too much."

"There's no such thing," Gemma teased.

"There definitely is."

When I took a few more sips of my drink, I saw a flash of movement and suddenly Kayden was standing in front of us, in dark jeans, a tight-fitting shirt, and a pair of sunglasses perched on his head. He glanced between the two of us, pausing to give Gemma a bright smile. She scowled at him and looked back at me.

"Looks like someone forgot to take the trash out."

"It's good to see you too, Gemma."

Gemma swung her gaze to him and gave him a look that should've turned him into stone. "Why are you talking to me? Why don't you crawl back to whatever or whomever you were doing and fuck off?"

"I want to talk to Savannah."

"Who said I want to talk to you?" I bite out.

He folded his arms over his chest and cleared his throat. "I got an email from the hotel about our reservation. I know you haven't cancelled it yet."

I lifted my chin up and held his gaze. "Yeah, because I was thinking of going. No point in wasting the reservation."

Kayden studied me, a frown hovering on the edge of his lips. "You don't think we should talk about that?"

I shrugged. "What's there to talk about?"

"How about I buy you a round of drinks from the bar on me?"

Gemma stood up and rolled her eyes. "Make that two rounds. I'm going to get my drink before you change your mind again. Try anything stupid, Kayden, and you'll answer to me."

With that, she sauntered off, tossing him withering looks the entire time. Kayden waited until she sat on a stool at the bar before he slid into the booth across from me. Then he linked his fingers together over the table and leaned back, and I noticed the dark circles under his eyes, and the tight lines around his face.

I squared my shoulders and braced myself.

But it wasn't as hard as I expected it to be.

Being around Kayden wasn't devastating and painful.

On the contrary, it was like looking at someone I didn't recognize anymore, and I couldn't tell if I was relieved or disappointed with myself for not having a bigger reaction. Considering the two of us had been about to exchange vows and spend the rest of our life together, it didn't make sense. However, it wasn't the part that worried me the most. What was worse was that as I sat across from him, I couldn't help but compare him to Asher, and the way he made me feel.

By now, Asher would've already made a comment that would've had me smiling.

"I know I messed up, Sav."

"That's an understatement."

Kayden unlinked his fingers and looked directly at me. "I'm trying to apologize. Doesn't that count for something?"

"It depends."

"On?"

I placed my hands on the table. "Why you really want to apologize. What happened? Did Macy get sick of you?"

Kayden tilted his head to the side, and his expression turned confused. "Macy and I aren't together."

"So, you get her pregnant, and you won't even stick around to help her? I don't even know what you expect me to say to that."

Kayden scowled but didn't respond.

It was a low blow even for Kayden, but it wasn't my business.

And a part of me always suspected he wasn't going to stick around for her anyway. Kayden wasn't the kind of person who liked to take responsibility and did everything he could to avoid it. Before, I had thought of it as a challenge, an obstacle to overcome. Now, it just made me feel sorry for him, and for the first time since I left him, the kernel of relief blossoming in my chest grew.

I had dodged a bullet with him.

But I had also wasted so much time on him.

"I can't be with Macy because I can't stop thinking about you," Kayden told me, his eyes softening around the edges. "And with Valentine's Day around the corner, I've been thinking about you even more."

"What are you talking about?"

Kayden exhaled. "I'm talking about the fact that I screwed up. I never should've messed things up with you the way I did."

"No shit. I'm a catch and you let me go."

Kayden reached for a glass of water and took a few sips. "Okay, I deserve that, but I'm trying here, Sav. I really am."

"Do you want credit for trying or something?"

Kayden's lips lifted into a half smile. "No, but you can at least acknowledge it."

I crossed my arms over my chest and stared at him. "I don't owe you anything and you're have a lot of work to do if you want to convince me otherwise."

"When I saw the email, I realized it was a sign. I knew there was a reason why I hadn't been able to get over you," Kayden continued, the words pouring out of him in a rush. "It's because I'm not meant to."

"What the hell are you talking about?"

"I'm talking about you and I giving it another shot," Kayden revealed, with a smile. "Since you don't want to cancel the trip, I thought we could go on it together."

"Is this your idea of a joke?"

"Why would I be joking about this?"

I made a low noise in the back of my throat, and my arms fell to my sides. "I don't know, Kayden. You have a twisted sense of humor, and I don't know you as well as I thought I did."

Kayden reached across the table and tried to take my hand in his, but I swatted him away. "And I want to fix that. I want us to reconnect, Sav, and find our way back to what we were, and I think the best way to do that is to take that trip together."

I pried my hand out of his. "Let me get this straight. You want us to go on our honeymoon trip but not as a married couple?"

"Well, we have to work our way back to that, but why not? It's a great chance for us to get away and re-connect."

"Why?"

What was in it for him?

Having spent the past few weeks acting like the two of us had never happened, I couldn't understand why Kayden was choosing now, of all times, to try and get me back. He'd gone radio silent after the wedding, I figured he was glad to be rid of me to go bang whoever he wanted without having to lie about it. The last thing I expected was him to approach me and try to win me back. Granted, a couple times I had thought about what it would be like if he did, and how I would feel, but the other part of me had known there was no point.

Kayden wasn't the man I thought he was, and I hadn't stopped thinking about Asher since he sat down. Instead of Kayden, I kept imagining Asher across from me, in his usual dark jeans and flannel, the same serious expression on his face. I saw Asher reward me with one of his rare smiles, and it made the butterflies in my stomach flutter.

Gemma was right.

I did have it bad but knowing it and acting on it were two different things.

And neither of us were in a position to do anything about it.

"What do you mean why? I thought the reason was obvious."

"I guess you're going to have to spell it out for me."

Kayden exhaled and sat back against the booth. "I understand why you're trying to bust my balls, but are you really going make me say it?"

I gave him a blank look.

Kayden sat up straighter and squared his shoulders. "Okay, fine. I did mess up, and I want a second chance. I want to prove to you that I can be the man you want me to be, and I want to earn your trust back."

Out of all the scenarios I imagined, Kayden sitting across from me and begging for a second chance while I sat quietly wasn't one of them. Rather than feeling smug and wanting to rub it in his face, I couldn't muster up enough interest to give him a response. Nor did I know what I was meant to say to him.

Because I didn't want Kayden to be the one sitting across from me.

I wanted it to be Asher asking for a chance to connect.

I wanted Asher to be the who yearned for me.

Who was I kidding?

I wasn't even sure if Asher was ever going to be able to give me what I wanted.

Between the two of us, we carried around a lot of baggage and until we both figured out a way to make our peace with it, it was better if we continued to ignore what was brewing.

"Think about it," Kayden finished, after a lengthy silence. "You don't have to give me an answer right now."

Gemma materialized and placed a hand on my shoulders. "Ready to go?"

Kayden stood up and glanced between the two of us. "I'll see you both around. It was good to see you, Sav."

As soon as he was gone, Gemma sunk back into her seat and rolled her eyes. "You're not really considering taking him back, are you?"

"I see your lip-reading skills have come in handy."

Gemma shrugged and took a sip of her drink. "I told you they would."

"Let's go home." I stood up and reached for my sweater. "I'm getting a headache."

CHAPTER 17

- ASHER -

"Hell no."

Jeffrey pushed himself off the outside wall of the wellness center and straightened his back. "I haven't even said anything yet."

"What are you doing here, Jeffrey? Preparing to disappear again?"

"You know why we're laying low. The FBI probably already knows we're back in town, but they haven't done anything."

"Because you said you'd give up valuable information."

"And we will," Jeffrey maintained, his face giving nothing away. "We're just gathering evidence."

"Bullshit."

His eyes flashed. "I don't need you to believe me. I just need you to make sure the deal stays on the table."

I slammed the door to my car with a little more force than necessary. "And I need you to get the fuck out of my face, but it looks like we're both going to be disappointed."

Jeffrey frowned. "Jesus, man. You don't need to be such a prick about it."

I raised an eyebrow. "How would you like me to react?"

He ran a hand over his face, and his mask fell. "Look, I know everything is fucked up—"

I held a hand up. "You do not get to show up here, trying to use me again and act like you made a small mistake that I 'just need to get over' or get upset when I don't care what you have to say. Be a man and own up to what you did, Jeffrey."

"I didn't do anything."

"Oh yeah? So you didn't embezzle from my company and try to pin the blame on me, then? That's all in my imagination—the FBI is making up stories?"

He frowned, but didn't say anything.

"Why are you at the wellness center if not to cause a scene? Because if you think I'm going to let you take this away from me then you're dead wrong. If you screw me over again, there won't be a single place on this Earth where you can hide."

Because I was going to make it my personal mission to hunt him down if he did.

Having known me since college, Jeffrey knew me well enough to know I wasn't bluffing. If anything, allowing him to stand across from me, knowing what he did, was about as generous and forgiving as I was going to get.

Especially when I'd thought about putting his head through a wall.

But it wasn't going to make me feel better, and it wasn't going to change what he did.

"I'm trying to make things right."

I stiffened. "You're trying to make things right because you and Caroline realize you have no life left after this because I won't sit down and just take the blame for what you did. You want to come out of hiding, that's all. What's the matter, Jeff? Is she bored of you already?"

A muscle worked in Jeffrey's jaw. "It has nothing to do with that."

"Like I give a fuck either way. I've got a business to run, so if you're done wasting my time."

His hand darted out to stop me, and I gave him a cold look. Hastily, Jeffrey withdrew his hand and curled it into a fist at his side. "Look, regardless of why we're doing this, the important thing is we are. It should count for something, shouldn't it?"

"You want props for this? Are you fucking kidding?"

Jeffrey folded his arms over his chest and stared at me. "No."

A group of women in matching track suits walked past us, exchanging quick looks as they did. Once they were gone, I fixed my gaze on the wellness center, where Savannah was propping the front door open, allowing the warm, ocean breeze to waft in. She glanced up, and I held her gaze for a few seconds before looking away.

As much as I hated to admit it, having her nearby helped.

Even if the thought left me feeling more confused than relieved.

"Aren't you going to say anything?"

I snorted. "Believe me, you don't want to hear what I have to say."

Jeffrey took a step towards me, and his expression tightened. "Why don't you just go ahead and say it? We both know you want to."

"You are a backstabbing piece of shit, and you are not worth my time. Now, get out of my way before I make you."

"Make me? You can't make me do anything, Ash."

I covered the distance between us and balled my hands into fists at my side. "You want to bet? If I were you, I would choose my next words carefully."

"Or what? You'll hit me? We both know the great Asher Buchannan doesn't lose his cool and doesn't like to lose control, so you're not going to do anything."

It took every ounce of self-control I had to stand there and not punch him.

"You know, I'm starting to think that negotiating with the FBI on your behalf isn't such a good idea after all."

"Fuck you, Asher. This isn't about the money or the reputation. You're just pissed because Caroline chose me over you, even with the knowledge that we would have to go on the run and go into hiding. She still chose me over a comfortable life with you and that really bothers you, doesn't it?"

I stood up straighter, a flicker of annoyance pulsing through me. "Why would that bother me? You both did me a favor, remember?"

Jeffrey's lips twisted into a sneer. "I know it bothers you, Asher, because I know you. We've known each other since college, and I know Caroline meant something to you. You were even planning on proposing to her."

I dug my nails into my palms and held myself still. "Don't you have anything better to do than spy on me? Or are you just a piece of shit on all fronts?"

Jeffrey threw his head back and let out a low, humorless laugh. "And there it is. The crack in the great Asher Buchannan's mask. You're not as perfect as you want people to believe."

"And you're shittier than you pretend to be."

Jeffrey stood up straighter and glared at me. "At least I'm not some emotionless robot."

"At at least I didn't stab my friend in the back for money and then come crying to him after to fix all my problems. Caroline might have chosen you, but she's already regretting it because she knows you would sell her out for the chance to make more money."

Jeffrey made a low growling sound and shoved me. "Shut the fuck up. You don't know what you're talking about."

"I know exactly what I'm talking about. You just can't stand the truth."

Jeffrey shoved me again, but this time I bared my teeth at him. "Caroline chose me because she wanted to."

I snorted. "Yeah, you keep telling yourself that."

He aimed for my stomach and lunged. At the last second, I moved to the side, and he raced past me, bristling with anger. He skidded to a halt a few inches away and spun back around to face me. Then he growled and threw the full force of his weight behind a tackle, knocking us both to the ground.

My heart was pounding in my ears as we rolled around on the pavement, grappling to get the upper hand. I punched him squarely in the face, and the sickening crunch reverberated inside of my head. Then Jeffrey threw his head back and head-butted me, sending me sprawling backwards onto my ass. Blood poured out of my nose and stained the pavement below.

I used the back of my hand and launched myself through the air and knocked Jeffrey to the ground. He made a low wheezing sound when the breath left his body. I climbed on top of him and pinned his feet to the ground, landing another solid punch to his center. Jeffrey twisted his head to the side and howled, a crazed look in his eyes.

Slowly, I drew my lips back and snarled at him. "Calm the fuck down. You're embarrassing yourself."

"You're the one who is embarrassing yourself."

I grabbed Jeffrey by the scruff of his neck and lifted his face up off the ground. "You're the one who's flat on your ass, so you might want to re-think your statement."

Jeffrey drew his lips back and spat in my face.

Slowly, I used the back of my hand to wipe it away and pulled him up to his feet. Then I pushed him away and blew out a breath. "Enough. This isn't going to solve anything."

Jeffrey staggered a few feet away and ran a hand over his face.

When he came at me a third time, I squared my shoulders and put him in a headlock. He squirmed and thrashed as we spun in circles. Abruptly, we came to a stop, panting and wheezing as a small crowd gathered around us, with Savannah in the center. She glanced between the two of us, her phone held up to her face. In the distance, sirens wailed, slicing through the morning air.

A murmur rose through the crowd.

With a frown, I released Jeffrey and took a few steps back. "I'm not going to fight you."

Jeffrey scowled and spat out a mouthful of blood. "Coward."

"You can tell yourself whatever you want to feel better, Jeffrey. It's over."

And I had no interest in continuing this fight with Jeffrey.

Not only did I have no interest in being fodder for the town gossip, but I also didn't want to keep going round and around in circles for no reason. Up until a few weeks ago, I had considered Jeffrey to be one of my oldest and dearest friends, but as I stood across from him, watching as he struggled to take his breath, I began to realize that he had never been my friend.

Jeffrey had only kept me close for his own benefit.

Every word dripping out of his mouth was filled with venom and jealousy, and I couldn't believe it had taken me this long to figure out. Although he didn't know it yet, his entire relationship with Caroline had an expiry date, and it only lived in the shadows of what we had because it was the kind of person she was.

I almost pitied Jeffrey for not realizing the truth.

But he had made his decision and made mine so much easier.

Beating him to a pulp wasn't going to make me feel better, and it wasn't going to turn back the clock.

By the time the police arrived, two men were standing in between us, trying to calm Jeffrey down. The crowd around us fell quiet, with the exception of Savannah who had witnessed the entire thing and provided a statement, and the officers talked to both of us at length before allowing us to leave.

Before heading for my car, I gave Savannah a quick look over my shoulders.

She had a strange look on her face that I couldn't identify.

Inside the bar, it took a few minutes for my eyes to adjust, and when they did, the first thing I noticed was the smell.

Followed by the sparse number of patrons spread out, nursing their drinks and wearing vacation expressions. My shoes squeaked against the hardwood floors as I made a beeline for the bar and pulled up a stool. A blond-haired bartender finished drying off a mug before he wandered over to me.

"What can I get you?"

"Whiskey," I replied, pausing to peel off my jacket and drape it over the back of the chair. "You got any nuts?"

He ducked behind the counter and pulled out a small bowl, stopping to fill it with an assortment of nuts. Then he shifted away and selected a bottle of whiskey off the shelf. Out of the corner of my eye, I watched him pour it before he slid it over to me. With a frown, I spun around in my stool and scanned the area around me, dimly lit and with quiet music wafting through the speakers.

It was depressing.

And it suited my mood perfectly.

As I sipped on my whiskey, I kept replaying my encounter with Jeffrey over and over in my head. A part of me wondered if I should've done things differently, but the other part of me knew that I had taken it easy on him. Given that we had known each other for years and had seen each other through a lot, Jeffrey deserved a lot worse.

He should've been grateful that I had no interest in drawing blood.

Besides, he's going to be stuck with Caroline. Isn't that punishment enough?

In a strange way, the two of them did deserve each other.

I spun back around to face the bartender, picked up my drink and tilted it in his direction. "Here's to bad decisions."

The blond-haired bartender gave me a polite smile.

By my fourth drink, I was hunched over my seat and peering at the nuts in my bowl. The bartender re-appeared in my field of vision, his brown eyes wide and focused. "Do you need anything else?"

"I don't think so."

"You sure?"

I glanced up at him, and my vision went blurry around the edges. "You know what I need? I need Caroline and Jeffrey to leave. I think I liked it better when I didn't know where they were and all they've done is cause problems for me."

The bartender cleared his throat and took my bowl away. He returned with another bowl full of nuts and tossed a rag over his shoulders. "Caroline your ex?"

I nodded. "I was going to propose to her, and I didn't know shit."

"You must've loved her."

I paused and signaled for another shot. "I thought I did but now that she's back, I think it was all in my head."

I had wanted to believe it was love.

On paper, Caroline and I had made all the sense in the world. As a self-made businesswoman, it was what had attracted me to her in the first place. Caroline was also the first woman I'd been with to make me feel like I could have it all.

And I'd fallen for it, hook, line and sinker.

Fucking moron.

"And Jeffrey is the man she left you for?"

"He was my best friend," I replied, with a shake of my head. "I know it's such a cliché, but I really didn't see it coming. The two of them tricked me. They took my money and now they're back to finish the job."

The bartender frowned and poured me another drink. "Shit. I'm sorry, man."

"So am I. I don't even know why I'm listening to them. I know they don't care. I know they're just trying to use me."

The bartender began to wipe the counter next to me. "You should tell them to fuck off since they're making you so miserable."

"I want to, but I want my money back, and I want them to pay."

"Damn straight, and they should pay too."

I lifted my drink up and squinted at him. "But it won't change anything. It's not going to change a damn thing."

No matter how much I wanted it to.

"You need to forget all about them," the bartender offered, after a brief pause. "Go out and find yourself a nice woman and let her make you feel good. Screw 'em, you know."

Immediately I thought of Savannah, and her smile.

And the concern on her face as I'd driven away from the wellness center without acknowledging her.

I had no idea what the hell I was doing with her.

All I knew was that being around felt easy, natural.

Like I'd been doing it my whole life, and the more time I spent around her, the more I wanted to get to know her. Although there was still a lot I didn't know, I could already tell that she was the kind of woman worth sticking around for.

Worth fighting for.

And I was the goddamn idiot with the baggage who couldn't even admit that he liked her.

"I can be that woman for you, honey."

I tilted my head to the side and regarded the blonde-haired woman in cut-off shorts, a tight top and blood red nails. She sat down on the stool opposite me and leaned forward, giving me a generous view of her cleavage.

"Is that so?"

She placed a manicured hand on my chest and nodded. "I can be whatever you want me to be, sugar."

I looked down at her manicured hand and back up at her face. "I'm not good company."

She shifted closer, and the sickly sweet smell of her wafted over me. "It doesn't matter. We can do whatever we want, and you can be whoever you want to be. I won't judge."

When she leaned back over the bar, she pulled her purse closer to her and took out a cigarette. She held one out for me and flicked the lighter on. Then she placed her own cigarette between her lips and lit it up, the red and orange flames giving her a strange glow.

Taking her home was exactly what I should do.

Because it was the distraction I needed after a day like today.

But I couldn't get Savannah out of my head, nor could I shake off the feeling that doing anything with this woman would be wrong.

She blew out a puff of smoke and offered me another smile. "I know it gets real lonely around this time of year because Valentine's is coming up. I promise I'll make it worth your while."

I sucked in a long breath and blew out a ring of smoke. "Thanks, but I should get going."

Slowly, I rose to my feet and rummaged through my pockets. After setting down out a few crisp bills, I stumbled in the direction of the door, my jacket draped over my arm. Outside, the sun was beginning to set below the horizon, bathing the world in hues of pink and purple. I let the cigarette fall to the floor and ground it out with the heel of my shoe.

Then I set off at a leisurely pace, with no real destination in mind, my mind still filled with thoughts of Savannah.

CHAPTER 18

- SAVANNAH -

"Gem, I've got to go. I've got a client." I set the phone down on my desk and straightened my back. "Hi, welcome to Divine Delight. How can I help you?"

The elderly women let the door click shut behind her and shuffled over to me, looking frail and small in her too large clothes, and her sunken eyes. I stepped out from behind the desk and greeted her with another smile when she came to a stop.

She stood up straighter, glanced around and looked back at me. "I don't know. My granddaughter told me that she came here, and she enjoyed it."

"I'm glad to hear your granddaughter has had a positive experience. Here, why don't you sit down?"

I led her to the set of couches we had set up, overlooking the water through the glass windows. Slowly, she sat down and placed her purse in her lap. "It is a very beautiful place. My granddaughter was right."

I sat down opposite her and folded my hands in my lap. "Thank you. A lot of our rooms overlook the water too."

"Oh, that's lovely. What is that smell?"

"Incense and rose water," I replied, with another smile. "We have them on sale if you'd like to look, Mrs...."

"Cooper," she offered, giving me a shy smile. "Elaine Cooper."

"It's nice to meet you, Mrs. Cooper. Let me just see if I can find the receptionist for you."

With that, I sat up straighter and glanced over my shoulders. Valerie sat at her desk, twirling her fingers around her hair and with her phone pressed to her ear. I frowned, stood up and tried to wave her over, but she wouldn't look over at me. Instead she spun around in her chair, so she was facing the window, and her voice rose.

I was beginning to wonder if I had made the right call hiring Valeria.

While she did have a lot of experience in the hospitality department, having worked in several hotels and B and Bs in neighboring towns, she didn't seem to understand what her duties entailed. As Asher's assistant, she was meant to be organizing his schedule, answering his calls and making sure to plan out his entire day in the smoothest way possible. Since reviewing her credentials, Asher had also offered her the position of receptionist, until we were able to find someone suitable.

Unfortunately, Valerie had taken her second position as more of a suggestion than an actual responsibility. Whenever Asher stepped out of the office, which was more often than not in the past few days, she went back to her desk and sat there, taking phone calls and scrolling through her laptop. Whenever I tried to get her attention, she pretended not to see me.

And I was trying not to let it bother me.

It had only been a few days since she was hired, and I didn't want to be the one to cause problems for her. Now and again, I considered bringing Asher into the loop and letting him know how she behaved when he wasn't around, but I didn't want to be that person. Starting over in a new office was hard enough without being under scrutiny, and I already knew how to pick up the slack when she wasn't doing her job.

You're letting her off the hook too easily. This is her job. It's not your responsibility to cover for her, Sav.

Except going to Asher with this still felt weird.

I wasn't sure where the two of us stood, or how I was supposed to behave around him and until I did, I didn't want to make things worse between us. With a sigh, I gave up on trying to get Valeria's attention and turned my attention back to the silver haired woman sitting across from me, looking a little lost and out of place.

Poor thing.

When I sat back down in front of her, she sat up straighter, looking visibly relieved. "No luck?"

"I can show you the incense sticks later," I offered, pausing to give her a smile. "Before we do that, let's see if we can figure out what kind of package you want."

Her eyebrows drew together. "Package?"

"For your spa treatment," I clarified, pausing to pull the stack of brochures towards me. I flipped one open and set it down on the coffee table in front of us. "We offer facials, the steam room, a licensed masseuse and a waxing option. We've also got a hair salon if you want to make an appointment there."

She glanced between the brochure and my face. "I don't know. My granddaughter didn't tell me what kind of package she got."

"We can call her if you want."

Mrs. Cooper nodded and rifled through her purse. "Oh, I don't have a charger."

Out of the corner of my eye, I saw the front door open, and Asher stepped in. He frowned when he didn't see me behind the desk, his blue eyes wide and intent. Then his expression softened when he saw me sitting across from a client, with a brochure flipped open. When he made his way towards us, I sat up straighter and held myself still.

My stomach erupted into butterflies when I caught a whiff of him.

He smelled like sandalwood and sage, a heady combination that went straight to my head. I sat up straighter and cleared my throat. "Mrs. Cooper is trying to decide on the package she wants. She says her granddaughter loved it here."

"There's a lot of options," Mrs. Cooper told him, with a shake of her head. "I'm sorry. I don't mean to waste your time."

Asher sat down next to her and pulled the brochure towards him. "Not all, Mrs. Cooper. We're here to help you relax and have a good time. Why don't we look through the options together?"

With a small smile, he flipped the brochure opened and moved closer to her. "You know you can customize your own package."

Mrs. Cooper's face lit up. "You can?"

Asher nodded. "Absolutely, and you're in luck. Today is half off day for senior citizens."

Mrs. Cooper beamed. "It's my lucky day."

"It definitely is," Asher agreed, with another smile and a quick look in my direction. "Ms. Parish can get you set up with whatever you need, including the discount. So, why don't I explain to you what happens during every service and then you can tell me what you'd prefer?"

Mrs. Cooper paused. "Will you make a recommendation if I can't choose?"

"Whatever you need, Mrs. Cooper."

Mrs. Cooper turned, so she was facing him completely. She hung on his every word as he described, in great detail, all of the services that were being offered and what to expect. By the end of his explanation, she was holding his hand, and her face split into a wide grin. Asher, on the other hand, was treating her with such kindness and patience it was almost as if I was seeing another person.

I had never seen him act this way before.

And I couldn't take my eyes off of him.

Seeing a softer, gentler Asher made him all the more irresistible and left me with a strange swell of emotion in the middle of my chest. Now and again, he glanced over at me to offer more information, but he didn't need to. He did, after all, know the wellness center like the back of his hand and including me in the conversation was out of politeness than any real necessity.

But I still appreciated it.

Fuck.

Why couldn't he have just been polite and dismissive?

I didn't want to see Asher this way because it made harder for me to keep my distance and justify not pursuing something with him. It was one thing for me to tell myself that Asher was closed off and incapable of opening up to people. It was another thing entirely for me to watch this entirely different side of him that made my insides feel like jelly.

Every time he looked at me, another part of me melted.

It was almost embarrassing how much attention I was paying to him when I should've gotten up to leave. By the time he was done helping Mrs. Cooper, Asher rose to his feet and held his arm out to her. She tucked her hand into the crook of his elbow, and he led her away, to the rooms in the back. On his way past his office, he paused to give Valerie a confused look. She had her chair pulled up and was typing away intently. As soon as she noticed him looking at her, she paused to give him a bright smile.

I frowned at her back.

Asher returned a short while later and paused at Valerie's desk. He exchanged a few words with her while I stepped back behind my desk. Once he was done, Asher made a beeline for me, a thoughtful expression on his face. Valerie glanced up at him and furrowed her brows together. Then she looked over at me and glared.

I had no idea what her issue was, but I was pretty sure that Asher hadn't liked what he saw.

Or what he didn't see.

And it wasn't my fault Valerie couldn't do her job properly unless Asher was around.

When he reached the front desk, Asher took one hand out of his pocket and placed a hand in front of him. "Thank you for dealing with that."

"Me? You were the one who swooped in and completely saved the day. I had no idea what I was doing."

Asher shrugged. "She just needed a little patience and guidance."

I cleared my throat. "You were really good with her."

Asher tilted his head to the side and studied me. "She reminds me of my grandmother. She even has the same first name."

My lips lifted into a half smile. "That's really nice. I bet your grandma's really proud of you."

Asher's expression turned serious. "I don't know if she was. She died before the company really took off, so she never got to see what I made of it."

"I'm sure she was proud of you anyway, regardless of whatever successes or failures you have. It's what grandmas are for."

Asher paused and nodded. "Yeah, you're right."

"What was she like?"

Silence stretched between us.

He was quiet for so long I began to wonder if I'd crossed another invisible line. Slowly, Asher shifted from one foot to the other, took both hands out of his pockets and placed them on the table. Then he turned so he was facing me directly, his expression open and vulnerable.

"She had a really big heart, and she always made everyone feel warm and welcome. When I was with her, it didn't feel like anything bad could happen, you know."

I released a deep breath. "It sounds like she was amazing."

"She was, and I always wanted to make her proud," Asher added, in a lower voice. "I know I screwed up a lot when I was younger, but she never gave up on me."

I leaned over the table, and our eyes met.

I couldn't look away.

Nor did I want to.

Up close, I could see every individual lash and the flecks of gray in his blue eyes. It felt like everything else stopped existing, like we were suspended in time and no one else mattered.

"I'm really glad you had a grandma like that."

Asher cleared his throat. "Me too. I'm really lucky I got to know her and be close to her."

When he looked away, the knots in my stomach unfurled, and I could breathe again. Then he shifted to take out his phone, and I caught another whiff of his intoxicating cologne. Each whiff was doing strange things to my insides and making me feel like we were the only two people there.

For now, it almost felt like we were.

And I wanted to believe it.

Because I liked seeing this side of Asher, the harder and sharper edges dulled, giving way to something softer and more vulnerable. While I hadn't known what to expect when Asher walked in and saw me sitting with a client, the last thing I expected was for him to sit down with the client and give her his undivided attention.

He wasn't as grumpy or cold hearted as he made himself out to be.

On the contrary, I had seen snippets of it here and there, but now I knew for sure that underneath the polished surface was a man with a heart of gold. As I stood there, studying him and waiting for my heart to stop pounding wildly against my chest, I began to wonder about who Asher really was.

And why had he allowed the world to harden him?

Was it Caroline who had driven him to this?

Or his father leaving them behind?

Or was it both?

The thought of what Caroline must've done to push him to this didn't sit well with me. I turned it over and over in my head until Asher glanced up from his phone and back at me. I stood up straighter and clasped my hands behind my back.

"Why didn't you call Valerie to help you?"

"I tried, but I couldn't reach her."

Asher raised an eyebrow. "Savannah, if you have a problem with Valerie, I need you to tell me."

"I don't have a problem with her."

Asher gave me a pointed look.

I blew out a breath. "Okay, fine. There are still a few kinks we need to work on with her performance, but I'm sure we'll get there."

Asher shook his head. "You can't make excuses for her if she's not doing her job properly."

"I'm not."

"You are. It's just the kind of person you are. You like to give chances."

"There's nothing wrong with that."

Asher tilted his head to the side and frowned. "No, but only if you're doing that with the right people. Otherwise, you're just allowing others to take advantage of you and bleed you dry."

I lifted my chin up. "No one is taking advantage of me."

Asher's eyes moved over my face, and the flutter in my stomach started again. A tingling sensation started at the tips of my toes, through the base of my spine and all the way to the top of my head. I held myself completely still, afraid that if I made any sudden movements, the spell would end.

Like an idiot I didn't want it to.

I wanted to stand there with Asher and pretend we were having a normal conversation.

I wished he wasn't my boss, and the man who wanted to change the town.

And I wished I didn't work for him, so I could reach across the desk, pull him to me and kiss him senseless. Instead, I laced my fingers together and ignored the heat blossoming in the center of my stomach, and slowly, Asher's eyes moved back up to my face, and I held my breath.

I could look into his eyes forever.

Asher's lips lifted into a half smile. "You know you also remind me of my grandmother."

"What?"

"She had a big heart too," Asher added, his smile never wavering. "No matter how many times people hurt her, she always forgave them."

I cleared my throat. "I don't think I'm that forgiving."

"I don't think that's true."

"I don't think you're as much of a hard ass as you want people to believe."

Asher's lips twitched. "Is that so?"

I nodded. "Yesterday when that guy, you friend or whatever, kept trying to goad you, I saw you try to avoid a fight. You didn't even fight back until you didn't have a choice."

Asher shrugged. "I didn't see the point."

"Exactly. For a self-proclaimed grump, you handled yourself well."

Asher's expression grew amused. "Thanks."

I unlaced my fingers and reached between us. Then I placed a hand on top of his, feeling the warmth seep through me. "I'm sorry you had to deal with that."

Asher searched my face. "I'm sorry you had to see it."

I shook my head. "Don't be."

Because I liked getting to see the different sides of Asher. Knowing he was able to rise to the occasion and protect his own had filled me with a strange stirring. It grew as I looked at him and realized how deep my feelings for him really ran. As much as I hated to admit it, and against my better judgment, Asher had found his way into my heart.

And I didn't know if I wanted to yell or celebrate.

Either way, I knew it couldn't be a good thing.

Not only did he still have a lot of things to deal with, especially with the arrival of his ex and former friend, but I also had my own scars to contend with, including whether or not I wanted to give Kayden a second chance. Although I knew I should know better, I also couldn't help but feel like I shouldn't jump the gun.

At least with Kayden I knew what I was getting into.

Asher, on the other hand, was unfamiliar terrain, making it hard for me to tell left from right or up from down. When Asher's phone rang, slicing through the thick tension in the air, he gave me an apologetic smile and pulled it out of his pocket. He went into his office, shut the door behind him, and I sagged.

Losing myself in Asher was not a good idea.

Not if I had no way of guaranteeing I'd survive.

ALICIA NICHOLS

CHAPTER 19

- ASHER -

"This is a good deal."

Jeffrey shoved the file back over the table and folded his arms over his chest. "I don't think so."

I frowned. "You came to me for help, and I got you what you wanted. The FBI is offering you a generous deal. Take it."

Jeffrey glanced over at Caroline who was picking at her nails. "We didn't risk our lives for this."

Will slammed his hands on the dining room table and scowled at them. "You didn't risk your lives at all. It's three years in prison followed by two years of mandatory community service, and it is a good deal. You're not going to get a better one."

I sat up straighter and leaned forward. "And the FBI has agreed to keep your records sealed to give you a fresh start when you're out."

"We don't want any prison time."

Will snorted. "You should've thought of that before you stole money and decided to use the wellness center as a front for money laundering."

Jeffrey stood up and fixed his gaze on me. "I don't know what you told the FBI, but I'm sure it's your fault we didn't get a better deal."

I snorted and leaned back against my chair. "I don't have that kind of influence over the FBI."

"Bullshit." Jeffrey bared his teeth at me, and his eyes tightened around the edges. "We want a better deal, and we're not budging on this."

"Then you're going to have to prove you're worth it first. Since I'm willing to bet you're not, this is what you get."

Jeffrey said nothing.

Will pushed himself off the table and exhaled. "I told you that they were wasting our time. Mr. Buchannan. They're not here because they want to help. They're trying to sell their cooperation to the highest bidder."

Caroline glanced up, and her expression hardened. "Of course we are. Do you have any idea what we would be risking if things go sideways?"

I looked over at Caroline. "This is a good deal, Caroline. You and I both know that is."

And it was time to bring this charade to an end once and for all.

Having spent the past few days in negotiations, the last thing I wanted was to be spending my Friday sitting across from them at a dining table in my house while they found reasons to pick apart the deal that could finish this. Since they had committed so many crimes, the FBI wasn't willing to drop all charges, even if they offered valuable information helping them target the mob. While I couldn't understand the FBI's reasoning, it wasn't my place to judge their methods.

Caroline and Jeffrey were, after all, still criminals.

Flipping on the mob to save their own skin didn't change that.

If anything, it made me question their motives even further.

Staying loyal to the mob would've at least gotten them some respect, but more and more, I was beginning to realize there was very little they wouldn't do to save themselves. Throwing me under the bus hadn't even registered on their radar, and although it made me sick to my stomach to think that our years together hadn't meant anything, I knew I'd make my peace with it in time.

As far as they were concerned, it wasn't personal.

"I'm the one who's handling these negotiations," Jeffrey interrupted, stiffly. He stepped into my line of vision and placed an arm around Caroline's shoulders. "Don't talk to her."

I pushed my chair back with a screech and stood up. "I'm not here to waste time with this. Either you want to take the deal, or you don't."

Jeffrey and Caroline exchanged a look.

"Let me perfectly clear, not taking the deal is up to you. I can't force you either way, but if you don't take the deal then all bets are off."

Caroline's head snapped up, and she stared at me. "What do you mean?"

"I've been patient, and I've let a lot of things go, but I've got my limits."

Jeffrey stiffened. "Are you threatening us? Is that why you asked to meet at the house? So no one would see what kind of man you are?"

"I'm the kind of man who doesn't like to be screwed over," I told him, pausing to glance between the two of them. "You two should consider yourselves lucky that I'm even willing to negotiate at all considering what you've done."

Settling out of court was the best option for all parties involved.

Even Jeffrey knew it, but he just wanted to drag this on because his pride was hurt. I had seen the blue and purple bruise underneath his eye and on his jaw when he walked in, and I hadn't felt the slightest bit of remorse. Will had taken one look at him, and his lips had curled into a smug smile. Caroline, on the other hand, had spent the entire time avoiding my gaze and acting like she didn't want to be there.

Which was fine with me.

I didn't care how they made their peace with it, only that they did.

Because dragging this on further didn't make any kind of sense.

Not when we all wanted the same thing.

Bringing an end to this was the only way to move forward, and I had never been one to hesitate when it came to pushing back and ruffling a few feathers. Given that they'd known me for years, I had half expected the two of them to be prepared, but I was beginning to realize that they had spent the past few years seeing right through me. All these years later, I was nothing more than a means to an end.

And once all of this came to an end, it was likely that they wouldn't give me a second thought.

The thought filled me with relief.

Jeffrey made a low noise in the back of his throat and moved away from the table. "Caroline told me that it wouldn't come to this. That we could make you see reason, but I guess she doesn't know you as well as she thought."

"No, she doesn't."

Caroline stood up and reached into her coat. She pulled out a file and set it down on the table with a thud. Without looking at me, she pushed it across the table, and Will reached his hand out. His face gave nothing away as he looked between the two of them before flipping the file open and skimming through the document. Once he was done, he swore and slammed the file back down onto the table.

With a frown, I picked the file up and lifted it up to my face. "Are you fucking kidding? What the hell is this?"

"You're being sued for emotional damage," Jeffrey told me, his lips twisting into a smirk. "We've got a good lawyer, and he's got a good case too."

Will took the file out of my hand and tossed it onto the table. "This will never hold up in court."

"Won't it? The FBI's evidence is circumstantial at best, so even if they do go to trial, there's no guarantee they'll be able to prove any of us did it."

Caroline smiled. "This isn't the first time we've taken the FBI for a ride."

I fastened a button on my jacket and stood up. "This is horseshit, and you know it."

Jeffrey shrugged. "Maybe, but considering how much damage has been to your reputation and that of the company's, I'm thinking you're going to want to pay whatever we want to make this go away."

"I am not going to advise him to settle," Will snapped, his gaze swinging angrily between the two. "You're bluffing, and you don't have a case."

Caroline took Jeffrey's hand in hers. "We'll see you in court then."

With that, they spun on their heels and hurried out of the house, hand in hand. As soon as they were gone, Will twisted to face me and folded his arms over his chest. "I know you've been trying to settle all of this quietly—"

"No more playing nice," I interrupted, with a shake of my head. "If they don't like the deal then we take it off the table and leave the FBI to deal with them."

"There's enough to question them, and I'm sure it'll be enough to link them to the crimes."

"It has to be."

Since they had chosen to take the hard way out, I had no choice but to do the same.

Either way, I was going to bury them.

A short while later, Will and I came out of the house and made a beeline for my car. In the car, he spent the entire time on the phone, trying to do damage control. When I pulled up outside the wellness center, he pushed the door open and wandered away. I stared at his back for a few moments before I locked the car and hurried up the path.

So much for keeping things civil and having a reason to celebrate.

I had spent all morning and half of the afternoon trying to come up with a plan. Knowing that I had not only failed, but I had also walked into another labyrinth of problems irritated me to no end. I had expected the feeling to stay with me throughout the day until I walked through the door and saw Savannah on a ladder, hanging up red and white streamers.

The reception area looked like it was decorated by cupid.

But I couldn't help the smile that lit up my face when I saw Savannah singing along to the music wafting through the speakers. She hummed to herself as she took a tac out of her mouth and pinned up another balloon. Slowly, she climbed down the stairs and rubbed her hands together. When she spun around, a smile lighting up her face, my heart grew to twice its size.

And fluttered uncertainly.

Savannah really was something else.

Her smile faded when she saw the look on my face. "I did ask if you were okay with me putting up decorations for Valentine's Day."

"I am."

Savannah tilted her head to the side, and a furrow appeared between her brows. "So, what's that look on your face?"

I stood up straighter and cleared my throat. "What look?"

She paused and shook her head. "Nothing."

"Need a hand?"

She gave me a grateful smile. "Yeah, I'd appreciate that."

In silence we worked together, while I kept sneaking glances at her, confused at the strange swell of emotion in my chest. Over the past few weeks, Savannah had grown from a thorn in my side to someone I couldn't imagine not being around. In spite of my best attempts to keep her at bay, she had wormed her way into my heart, and I had no idea how to get her out.

Or if I even wanted to.

"I love Valentine's Day," Savannah announced with a grin. "I know you're probably going to tell me it's some holiday invented by corporations to sell candy, flowers and chocolate, but I don't care."

"It is a holiday invented by corporations."

Savannah and I set the brightly wrapped boxes down, and she placed both hands on her hips. "Like I said, I don't care. I love the idea of having a whole day dedicated to love."

"Why?"

Savannah paused. "Why not? I think we all need reminding, you know. Because we get so busy with life and all the drama, and we forget to appreciate each other."

I grunted and didn't say anything.

Savannah threw her hands up in the air and sighed. "Yeah, yeah. I know. I sound like a hallmark movie. Kayden, my ex, used to say that I needed to get my head out of the clouds and come back down to Earth."

"Ah, yes. The asshole. Why would you even listen to him?"

Savannah shrugged, and her expression turned uncertain. "I didn't, but what do I know anyway? It's not like I've had the best luck with love."

"I'm sure your luck will change," I offered, after a lengthy silence during which we hung up some more balloons. "I wouldn't worry."

"Who's worried? I can't wait to realize I found the right person and figure out why it didn't work out with anyone else."

Holy shit.

Savannah was making me feel things, all sorts of feelings I'd buried deep down because I didn't want to confront the truth. For the longest time, I had settled in life and in relationships because I hadn't felt like anyone could ever look at me and see, much less love me. Being with Savannah made me realize, that for the first time in a long time, I wasn't the problem.

Savannah couldn't possibly love someone like you.

Except I couldn't deny that I wanted her to.

Having gone my whole life believing that I didn't deserve love, first when my father abandoned us and then by a long slew of girlfriends, all of them incapable of seeing the real me, I had all but given up on the idea. Hell, I'd even convinced myself that it just wasn't in the cards for me.

And I had my peace with it.

Or so I thought.

Savannah was changing everything for me and making me doubt myself.

I couldn't decide if the churning in the center of my stomach was relief or terror.

All I knew was that she made me want to be different.

She made me want to be better.

Having spent years developing a façade and perfecting my no-nonsense exterior to keep people at a distance, I was beginning to realize I had it all wrong. Being a closed off, career focused go-getter hadn't made me any happier. If anything, it made me miserable and other than allowing me to get ahead of the game and stay on top, career-wise, it had driven everyone I loved away.

I rarely saw my mother, and if it weren't for the fact that my sister constantly reached out to me, I probably wouldn't have a relationship with her either. As Savannah and I wandered around the reception area, hanging up decorations and making small talk, everything started hitting me all at once. Not only did I no longer want to be the practical, self-serving man I pretended to be, but I also had no interest in any of the strings attached with it.

Needing that persona to survive was one thing.

Allowing it to take over and become me was another.

When we were done, Savannah gave me a bright smile that had my heart doing somersaults inside of my chest. I gave her a small smile in return and escaped into my office, letting the door fall shut behind me. As soon as it did, I went behind my desk, sat down and took my phone out of my pocket. Then I scrolled through my contacts and stopped at my sister's number.

She picked up on the third ring, sounding breathless and confused. "What's wrong?"

"Is that any way to talk to your older brother?"

Liz chuckled. "No, but I can't remember the last time you called me, so I thought something must be up."

"I deserve that."

"Is everything okay?"

"Liz, do you think I'm a good person?"

Liz said something in the background before her voice came back on, clearer than before. "What are you talking about? What happened?"

"I've been thinking about some things since I got here...."

"Is this about that woman I heard in the background the other day?"

I paused and ran a hand over my face. "Yes, but I didn't come here to start something. I'm here to run a business."

Liz snorted. "Big brother, you might be a smart businessman, but when it comes to real life, you're kind of dumb."

"Excuse me?"

"No offense or anything, but it's pretty clear that you like her. You haven't called me in years, Ash. This is a pretty big deal."

"I'm not that bad."

"You're not," Liz admitted, with a sigh. "Look, I know we've never talked about it, but I know that dad leaving was hard. And I know you were close to him."

I sat up straighter and frowned. "What's that going to do with anything?"

"Since he left us, it's like you're afraid to stop moving, like you don't want your feelings to catch up with you or something…I don't know."

"When did you become a shrink?"

"I'm your sister, and I notice things. Just because I don't talk about them doesn't mean I don't notice," Liz replied, after a brief pause. "I know you did what you had to do in order to survive, but you don't have to be that person anymore."

"What if I don't know how to be anything else?"

"Get to know yourself again," Liz suggested, a smile in her voice. "You're already on the right path, Ash."

"When did you get so wise?"

"I've always been wise. You've just never noticed because you were too busy trying to be a hotshot businessman."

I choked back a laugh. "Fair enough. I probably deserve that."

And I didn't want to go back to being a self-centered robot, even if it meant standing still and not running away from my problems anymore.

Liz was right.

It was time for things to change.

"You and mom should come visit. I've got plenty of room in the house."

"I've heard Lockwood Creek is beautiful."

"So, you have been keeping tabs on me."

Liz scoffed. "Of course I have. I'm your sister. It's part of the job description."

I rolled my eyes. "I don't remember that part."

"Do you remember the part where you buy mom and I all kinds of expensive gifts to make up for being cold and distant?"

I burst into laughter. "You're definitely making shit up."

"It could be true."

I twisted in my seat, saw Savannah through the glass and smiled to myself. She was leaning over the counter, talking to a client, and her entire face was animated. When she smiled, another wave of emotion rose over me.

I was not going to screw this up.

And I was not going to break Savannah's heart.

CHAPTER 20

- SAVANNAH -

"I didn't hear you come in last night."

I put a hand over my mouth and yawned. "Yeah, I went for a walk along the beach when I got off of work."

Gemma spun around to face me and lifted the mug up to her lips. "Is that what we're calling it these days?"

"I really did go for a walk."

"Alone?"

"Uh-huh."

Gemma took a sip of her drink and set the mug down on the counter behind her. "Why don't I believe you?"

I shrugged. "Because you have trust issues."

"We're not psychoanalyzing each other first thing in the morning. It's too early for this shit."

I snorted. "You're the one who started it."

"You do realize that the whole town is talking about you and Asher, right?"

I blinked. "What?"

"Yeah, apparently Kayden saw the two of you getting all cozy and stuff, and he's been running his mouth."

"Fuck."

"My offer to kick his and ass and key his car still stands," Gemma pointed out, pausing to link her fingers together. Her lips lifted into a devious smirk. "I can come up with a few more ideas if you want."

I shook my head and pulled the refrigerator door open. "No, I've got this. I need to go to work."

"On a Saturday?"

"Yeah, I've got a few things to take care of."

Gemma gave me a knowing look. "Have fun with Asher. Don't do anything I wouldn't do."

After taking my lunch bag out of the fridge, I made a beeline for the door. I paused with my hand on the knob and craned my head over my shoulders. "You do realize that there is a lot you have done."

Gemma winked and took another sip of her coffee. "That's the point."

"You need to go out more."

"So do you."

I rolled my eyes. "When are you moving out again?"

"Love you too, Sav."

With another shake of my head, I hurried outside, and into the brusque early morning air. I slung my bag over my shoulders and walked past rows and rows of two-story buildings. Little by little, the manicured lawns and driveways gave way to shops and boutiques, with their owners getting ready to start their day. On my way past, I waved at them and hiked my purse higher up my shoulders.

In the distance, the wellness center glistened underneath the morning sun.

I couldn't imagine having the wellness center torn down.

WEDDING NIGHT STRANGER (MR. BUCHANNAN)

Over the past few weeks, it had become something of a second home to me, even with all the disagreements with Asher. Not only had the two of us reached an unspoken agreement, calling a truce as we did, but I also enjoyed getting to see the other side of him.

There was a lot more to Asher than met the eye.

With a sigh, I took my key out of my pockets. They jingled as I shoved the key into the lock and pushed the door open, then flicked on the light switch. Once the bright lights came on, my mouth fell open.

The entire place was decked with streamers, balloons and teddy bears, all in red and white. Of the decorations that were hung up, only a few of them were the ones Asher had helped me with. I dropped my bag onto the floor, took a step forward and glanced around, realizing that there were dried rose petals strewn onto some of the shelves, in between the books and products on display.

It looked far better than anything I could've come up with.

I kicked the door shut with back of my leg and ventured further into the office. As I did, I flipped on the rest of the lights and smiled at the rest of the decorations, leading up to Asher's private office. When I pressed my face to the glass, I saw a vague outline in the dark, draped over his couch.

With a frown, I twisted the knob and the door creaked open.

Asher's shoes were on the floor, along with a pile of his clothes leading up to the couch. He had an arm draped over the back of the couch, the other resting behind his head. A blanket was draped over him, leaving his legs to stick out. I smiled, crouched in front of him and lifted the blanket up to his chin. Then I tucked it into his side and bent down to pick up the clothes. Once I set them down on one of the chairs, I spun back around, and I realized Asher was watching me.

His blue eyes were wide and unfocused, and his hair was unkempt, but it was the sexiest thing I'd ever seen. There was something about seeing Asher, his eyes still heavy with sleep, and his carefully construed mask nowhere in sight, that got to me.

Seeing him this vulnerable made my heart give an odd little twinge.

Asher had stayed late at the office to finish the decorations, knowing how much it meant to me.

I was overcome with the desire to kiss him.

Instead, I clasped my hands behind my back and cleared my throat. "The decorations look amazing."

Asher threw off the cover, revealing the rest of his body, clad in boxers and a white sleeveless top. My throat turned dry as I drank him in, eagerly taking in every muscle and every crevice on display. He shifted from one foot to the other and stretched his arms up over his head, revealing the smooth taut muscles of his stomach.

Shit.

Get a grip, Sav. Just because he helped you decorate doesn't mean anything.

Except it did because I knew Asher was a cynic.

He didn't believe in Valentine's Day, much less going all out with decorations. Yet, I had spent most of the day yesterday telling him everything that I knew about the day, and its history, and he had listened intently, never once correcting me or changing the subject.

It was a little unnerving.

When Asher was done stretching, he lowered his hands to his side and ran a hand over his face. "It's Saturday. What are you doing here?"

"I wanted to get some more decorating in, but you beat me to it."

Asher's lips lifted into a half smile. "I'm glad you like them."

"Thank you. No one's ever done anything like that for me."

Asher tilted his head to the side, and his expression turned serious. "It's a good thing you're the one who found me. I don't think I can handle more gossip."

I frowned. "I'm sorry."

Asher ran a hand through his hair and blew out a breath. "It is what it is. I'll handle it."

He took a step forward, tripped on the carpet and went sailing forward. I lifted my arms up on either side of me and caught him before he collided with me. My arms flailed at my sides and reached for the nearest thing, knocking a vase onto the floor with a crash. Then the two of us were sprawled on the carpet, water and glass flying in every direction. I shifted, and Asher was on top of me, a stunned look on his face.

I burst into laughter and groaned. "When I came in here to help you, this isn't what I pictured."

"You didn't expect a display of coordination and grace?"

I laughed harder. "I can definitely see it now."

Asher propped himself up on his elbows and looked down at me, a strange glint in his eyes. "I can think of worse ways to spend the morning."

"Yeah?"

Asher bent down to kiss me, and I melted. "Definitely."

When we shifted, I tilted my head to the side and sighed.

Kissing him like this felt right.

Like there were no boundaries between us.

Slowly, Asher leaned back and rose to his feet. He held his hand out to me and glanced around the office. "We've made a mess, haven't we?"

I giggled and laced my fingers through his. "We have."

"Let's get cleaned up first then we can take care of the glass," Asher suggested, before tugging me in the direction of the bathroom. He stopped in the doorway, flicked the light on, then Asher tugged me into the bathroom and kicked the door shut with the back of his leg. As soon as it clicked shut, he pressed me up against the wall, and his mouth claimed mine. I made a low noise in the back of my throat as I linked my fingers over his neck.

He was addicting.

And I couldn't get enough.

With a low growl, Asher pulled me to him and maneuvered us towards the shower. He kept one hand on the back of my neck, and the other pulled the curtain aside. Then the sound of water filled the room, and Asher drew back to look at me. He took every inch of my skin, from the top of my head to the soles of my feet, leaving goosebumps wherever he looked.

Slowly, he smiled and lifted my shirt up over my head.

My skin felt like it was on fire.

But I didn't care if I burned from the inside out so long as we burned together.

Asher threw the shirt over his head and reached for my jeans. In one quick move, he flicked the button, and I watched, my heart hammering against my ears as he knelt down and pulled my pants down to my ankles. My eyes didn't leave his face as I stepped out of them and shivered.

Was this what it felt to be worshipped?

To have every inch of me fawned over?

Because I didn't want it to end.

Asher's fingers glided over my thighs and up to my waist. I wound my fingers through his hair and threw my head back. "You can't imagine how good this feels."

His mouth moved over my bare skin, leaving a trail of heat in his wake until he reached my center. Slowly, he rose back up to his feet and pulled me, so we were pressed against each other. I kept one hand through his hair and tugged on his shirt, until it joined the heap on the floor. His eyes were dark and wide with hunger as he tugged on the waistband of his boxers.

As soon as he pulled it down, my mouth widened at the sight of him.

He was big.

And he was all mine.

My heart was hammering wildly against my chest as my mouth found his. Wave after wave of desire built up and rose within me. Then I lowered myself onto the tile floors and kissed the tip of his member. He made a low growling noise that had the blood pool in my stomach.

A part of me knew we shouldn't be doing this, especially in his office bathroom, but the other part of me didn't care. After everything the two of us had been through, we deserved to be happy.

Especially if it meant being happy with each other.

I tilted my head back to smile at Asher before taking him into my mouth. He gripped the back of my neck, the powerful muscles of his thighs clenching. With a moan, I licked and sucked, tasting every inch of him until he was hard. The fire in my veins burned stronger, washing away every last doubt and every last insecurity.

Till there was no doubt in mind that Asher and I weren't wrong.

We never were.

It wasn't long before steam filled the room. Asher threw his head back and moaned, the sound reverberating inside of my head. I tilted my head back to look up at him, our eyes met, and all of my feelings dove to the surface. Abruptly, he pulled me to my feet and kissed me soundly, till my head was spinning, and my lungs burned.

When the need for air became too great, Asher hoisted me up and set me down in the shower stall. His eyes moved over every inch of me. "You're so fucking beautiful, Savannah. Fuck, you have no idea how hard it is to try and stay away from you."

I grabbed a fistful of his hair and pressed my mouth to his. "We shouldn't have to."

Asher made a low guttural sound and stepped into the shower. He maneuvered, so I was standing underneath the shower head, hot water sliding down my back and over my face. I pushed my hair out of my eyes, sucked in a harsh breath and nipped on his lower lip. His mouth parted, and my tongue darted in, allowing us to begin a sensual battle for dominance.

Without warning, Asher pushed me so my back was pressed against the cold, hard wall. Then he lifted my arms up over my head. He wrenched his lips way and pressed hot, open-mouthed kisses down the side of my neck and over the slope of my chest.

"You have no idea how hard it's been to keep my hands to myself."

I bucked and muttered something incomprehensible underneath my breath.

With each kiss and each lick, he was making all of my defenses come undone, and I couldn't seem to care.

Not when it felt this good to give in.

Asher released my hands, so they fell to my sides. After giving me another searing kiss, he lowered himself onto the floor and looked up at me. His eyes didn't leave my face as he used two fingers to push aside my wet folds. With a smirk, Asher buried his mouth into my center, and my entire body erupted.

Wave after wave of pleasure washed over me as I writhed and spasmed against him. Asher's fingers moved up to my waist, and he dug his nails into the sensitive flesh there. He flicked his tongue back and forth, pushing me closer and closer to the edge of oblivion. My entire body felt like it was on fire as the force of my orgasm ripped through me, leaving my breathless, panting and clinging to Asher like my life depended on it. Once my vision cleared, and I could breathe again, I looked down at him, and my heart sputtered.

Asher's head was still between my lungs, and the look he gave me sent another jolt of desire racing through me. His eyes darkened before he growled. Suddenly, his mouth was moving again, ravaging me until I couldn't think of anything else. My hands moved to the back of his neck, and I grabbed a fistful of his hair and bucked.

Again and again, I ground against him, needing to feel more of his mouth.

Of his hands.

Of him.

Everywhere, all at once.

He kept one hand on my waist, and the other moved down to my legs. In one quick move, he lifted my legs over his shoulders, giving him better access. I pressed my back against the wall and listened to the sound of his heavy breathing. Droplets of water slid down his face and over his back. When another orgasm washed over me, he pressed a hand against my stomach. I thrashed against him, riding out my high and feeling like I was going to explode into a million pieces.

As soon as I could drag in a mouthful of air, I pulled Asher up to his feet and kissed him, tasting myself on his mouth. His mouth moved from my lips to my neck and up to my ears, tugging on one lobe then the other.

"I could taste you all night, Savannah."

"You should." I breathed before my hand darted between us. He eased into me, and I stilled, every inch of humming with electricity. "You feel so good, Asher."

Asher thrust into me and groaned. "We should stay like this."

"Yes."

Asher's head dropped into the crook of my neck as he eased out and slammed back into me. "Jesus, you have no idea how crazy you make me. Look at how hard you make me."

I wriggled my hips and whimpered. "Oh, Asher. Mmm."

Over and over, Asher eased out and slammed back into me, drawing out my release until I was clawing at his back.

I needed more of him.

More friction.

More of his hands all over my body making me feel things I only ever felt with him.

I raked my hands over his back before letting them fall to his waist. Then I hoisted myself up and wrapped my legs around his torso. My entire body burned where he touched, and I couldn't get enough of it.

The primal, desperate look on his face almost sent me over the edge.

He made a low noise somewhere in his chest, and I purred. Asher leaned back to look at me, and the look in his eyes sent the butterflies in my stomach into a frenzy. He pressed his mouth into mine and thrust, so he filled me all the way to the hilt.

When he lowered his head to take one nipple between his mouth, I threw my head back. "Fuck, Asher. I don't ever want this to stop."

"It doesn't have to." Asher switched to the other nipple, flicking and sucking as he did. "It's just you and me, baby."

I let my head fall against his chest and inhaled, the smell of sandalwood and sage washing over me. "Yes."

"I've got you," Asher maintained, in a thick voice. "Fuck, Savannah."

I sunk my teeth into his flesh, and my eyes rolled to the back of my head.

It had never felt like this with anyone, and now I knew why.

Asher was the only one meant to make me feel this way.

This was how it was meant to be between us.

When I drew back to look at Asher, and held my gaze, I exploded again, taking him with me as I did. His entire body jerked and writhed, and I clung to him for dear life until he set me back down on my feet and pulled me in for a hug.

Then he reached for the bar of soap, the tender expression on his face making my heart melt. "Let me do this."

I nodded. "Okay."

CHAPTER 21

- ASHER -

I kept feeling her gaze on me through the glass, but I didn't mind. Every now and again, I snuck glances at her, images of our time together in my office playing out in my mind's eye. Over and over, I saw Savannah splayed out on the floor underneath me, color in her cheeks and a familiar glimmer in her eyes. Then I saw the two of us in my private bathroom, a thick cloud of steam between us and nothing else. Whenever I blinked, I imagined Savannah tilting her head back and giving me that devastating smile of hers.

The one that went right through me and left me feeling unnerved.

Like I had been turned inside out, and Savannah was the answer to a prayer I hadn't even known I had.

Fuck.

What the hell was she doing to me?

With a slight shake of my head, I wrenched my gaze away from her and turned my attention back to the laptop and the same paragraph I'd been reading for the past hour. Over the past few days, I had done everything I could to push the feelings back and let things go back to normal. Unfortunately, the harder I tried to resist Savannah, the more I found myself drawn to her. In the mornings I came in and looked for her first and lingered at her desk while I drank my coffee.

In the afternoons, I found excuses to call her into my office, so we could chat while eating our lunch. And on my way out in the evening, I kept finding reasons to give her a ride home, and when I pulled up, she didn't get out right away. Instead, the two of us had spent the past few days finding more and more reasons to spend time around one another, and I couldn't bring myself to walk away.

Damn it.

While I knew the optics of our situation wasn't great, considering I was in her direct chain of command, I also knew that remedying it by going to HR wasn't an issue. The real problem was the circumstances under which the two of us met. I had met Savannah while she was still in her wedding dress and trying to get over her ex for Christ's sake. And although she had no idea, my emotional baggage wasn't any better than hers between being stabbed in the back and facing serious federal charges.

I didn't want to drag her into the middle of all that with no clear end in sight.

Granted, both Caroline and Jeffrey had broken and given the FBI a few powerful names, enough that the FBI was drafting up an immunity deal for them, but in typical cowardly fashion, the two of them were playing it safe. Considering the kind of trouble they were going to be in once the mob found out they were rats, it made sense that they were playing things close to the vest.

Even if did frustrate me to no end.

The FBI might have been willing to let them roam free, giving them the illusion of normalcy, but I wouldn't have been as charitable. I didn't trust either of them. As far as I was concerned, Caroline and Jeffrey needed to be brought in regardless of the information they provided. Since they were still criminals, I couldn't understand why there wasn't some kind of punishment. Will had spent the past few days discussing the details with me and explaining why, exactly, they likely weren't going to be serving any kind of time.

Slippery bastards.

It made me wonder what else they had been hiding from me.

And for how long.

WEDDING NIGHT STRANGER (MR. BUCHANNAN)

Had they been playing me the entire time and playing the long game?

Or was the decision to rob and frame me a spur of the moment kind of thing?

Either way, it didn't matter because the end result was the same and cutting them loose now would not only be stupid, but I might as well take the knife and stab myself in the back just to get it over with. Although I hadn't seen hide nor hair of them since my altercation with Jeffrey, I knew they were keeping tabs on me and hiding in the shadows.

Sooner or later, they were going to come back out, and I had no idea what was going to happen then. A part of me wanted this entire nightmare to be over, so I could get back to focusing on the business and doing damage control. The other part of me wondered if I was going to be satisfied without drawing blood. Granted, their testimony would exonerate me, and the company would remain unblemished, but the damage had already been done.

Nothing was going to go back to the way it was.

Even if they do go away, the rumors won't. There will always be people who whisper and point and form their own conclusions about you and the company. Caroline and Jeffrey made sure of that.

With a frown, I finished the rest of the email I was working on and held my fingers over the keyboard. Then I typed up a response and sent it out. Once I was sure it went through, I stood up, stretched my arms up over my head and threw a quick glance over my shoulders. Savannah sat at her usual spot at the front desk, nodding along to the music, a smile hovering on the edge of her lips.

Goddamn it.

Her smile made go weak in the knees and having her around was making it harder and harder to focus on what I needed to get done. Without the trial being put to rest, the permits for the server farm were on hold, and I was stuck trying to make the most of the wellness center. While it had grown on me since my arrival a few weeks ago, and we had a steady stream of clients on a daily basis, I didn't want to lose sight of why I was really here.

You didn't even want to run the wellness center, remember?

A short while later, when I walked out of my office, Savannah was already at the front door, peering through the glass. I stopped to admire her, my stomach giving an odd little twinge as I did. When I inched closer, her hands flew to her mouth, and her eyes widened. I covered the distance between us, and she spun around to face me.

"I just saw Gemma fall."

I placed a hand on the small of her back and led her outside. "Come on. We can take her to the hospital ourselves. We're closer."

Quickly, we hurried out the door and in the direction of the protestors who had stopped chanting and were gathered in a semi-circle. Savannah pushed her way through, and I followed close behind. Once we reached Gemma, the two of us crouched and carried her between us. She was hobbling, wearing a dazed expression, and blood pouring down the side of her face. In silence, we loaded her into the backseat of my car, and I peeled away from the asphalt.

Minutes later, I pulled up outside the hospital on the outskirts of town and skidded to a halt. Wordlessly, Savannah pushed the door open and stumbled out, waving her arms over her head. The glass doors to the emergency room whooshed open, and a team of professionals hurried out with a stretcher, making a beeline for us. In spite of her protests, Gemma was loaded onto the stretcher, and the two of us followed in her wake.

Although Savannah wasn't saying much, I could see how worried she was about her friend. She kept glancing over at her and back at the medical staff, as if she expected something different. Gemma, on the other hand, while disoriented, hadn't stopped complaining about the fuss everyone was making.

It filled me with no small amount of relief.

Once I stepped in through the doors, the smell of disinfectant hit me first, followed closely by the sound of shoes squeaking against the linoleum floors. Bright florescent lights flickered overhead, and I saw medical staff rushing past us in either direction. Slowly, Savannah walked up to the main desk and a silver haired woman in pink scrubs glanced up at Savannah.

While they talked, I drifted away and came to a stop in front of the vending machine.

Savannah materialized at my side a moment later. She ran a hand over her face and blew out a breath. "She still needs to be examined before they can tell me anything, but they're saying it's not serious."

"Good. I'm glad." I took out a crisp bill and fed it to the machine. Then I pressed two buttons and waited. "I'm sure she'll be fine. We got her here right away."

"It's a good thing you have a car."

"It's a good thing you saw what happened."

She held my gaze and frowned. "I don't even know why they were so close to the wellness center."

I shrugged and reached for the energy bars, pausing to hand her one. "Here. You're going to need this."

Savannah sunk into the nearest chair and stretched her legs out in front of her. "I hate hospitals."

"Me too."

Savannah peeled back the wrapper and took a small bite. "Usually only family is allowed, but Gemma's family lives in another state, so they said they'll make an exception for us."

I pocketed my energy bar and sat up straighter, the metal chair digging into my back. "You can have my slot. I don't mind."

Savannah took another bite of her wrapper and fixed her gaze on me. "Are you sure? I'm sure she'll be happy to see a familiar face."

"I'm sure she'll be happy to see your face. I'm just the designated driver."

Savannah snorted, a half-smile on her face. "You're a lot more than that."

I nodded. "I'm also a pretty face. I know."

She rolled her eyes. "Modest too."

"Of course."

She gave me one last look before she looked away, watching another couple walk across the room to the front desk. I crossed one ankle over the other, sank lower into my seat and brushed my hand against Savannah's. I was surprised when she laced her fingers through mine.

Her hand felt warm and solid.

Like she was tethering me to her.

Except I was the one who was adrift at sea, and without Savannah, it felt like I would keep drifting until the water swallowed me whole. Out of the corner of my eye, I saw Savannah finish her energy bar and toss the wrapper into the nearest bin. It spun in a circle before it landed in the middle.

"You're full of surprises."

"I used to play basketball in school," Savannah replied, without looking at me. "I didn't even know I could still do that. It was actually how Gemma and I met."

"Yeah?"

Savannah tilted her head in my direction, and her expression turned thoughtful. "Yeah, she was a cheerleader."

"I can't imagine Gemma as a cheerleader."

I had only ever seen her as a cutthroat insurance broker. She didn't seem like the sports type.

"I was surprised when she went to business school," Savannah continued, her eyes moving back to the main desk and staying there. "And when she told me she was going into insurance, I thought she was kidding."

"Why? It's a smart choice to go into insurance. It's a stable and lucrative job."

Savannah pulled a face. "Yeah, but it feels kind of soulless to me, no offense. I mean, you're basically charging people for worst case scenarios then paying up when things don't pan out."

"It's better to have that kind of security though, and it's not just for worst case scenarios. It's also to make sure you can get things taken care of and quickly too."

Savannah snorted. "I have never seen insurance companies take care of things quickly."

"Fair point. Investigations take time."

"If anything, they drag things on as long as possible so they don't have to pay out." Savannah stood up and shoved her hands into her pockets. "I'm going to go see if they can let me in to see her. I'll be right back."

I watched her walk away, the knots in my stomach tightening.

I hated not being able to ease her pain.

Or do anything other than sit there and wait for better news.

A heartbeat later, she was being led through a set of double doors. She glanced over her shoulders at me, and I gave her a small smile. Once she was gone, I stood up, wandered outside and patted my pockets until I found what I was looking for.

I placed the cigarette between my lips and inhaled. Although Gemma and I were on opposite sides of this, I was relieved to hear she was going to be okay, especially because of how much she meant to Savannah. Given how worried she was, I was glad I was able to help in some way. Knowing that

Savannah would've been here alone if it weren't for me was unthinkable.

I was suddenly glad that I hadn't left the office for lunch.

As much as I hated hospitals, there was nowhere else I would rather be.

Once I ground out the cigarette and threw it into the bin, I wheeled around to see Savannah through the doors, searching for me. Our eyes met, and her lips lifted into a smile. Quickly, I covered the distance between us and stopped a few feet away.

"She's cranky and wants to go home, but she's going to be okay. She only needed a few stitches, and she'll be out of here by tomorrow morning."

I released a deep breath. "Good. I'm glad."

Savannah nodded. "Me too."

"Why don't we go to the cafeteria? I'm sure if you stick around long enough, they'll let you go back in."

She lifted her gaze up and search my face. "Don't you need to get back to the office?"

I shook my head. "They can manage without us. Come on, I've got a craving for bad cafeteria food."

Savannah's lips lifted into the ghost of a smile. "Sure."

During the elevator ride upstairs, I reached for her hand, and she let me hold it. The doors pinged open, and I led her out, and we followed the signs until we reached the cafeteria, situated outdoors, with a glass dome overlooking the late afternoon sun, and a sky full of clouds. With one hand, I tugged on the door, and she stepped through, pausing to give me a warm smile over her shoulders.

It was the kind of smile I would've given anything to keep on her face.

Savannah chose a table near the edge, underneath a patch of light, and overlooking the city. As soon as she sat down, she pulled her chair forward and brought her head to a rest in her hands. I walked backwards to the line, and my eyes didn't leave her face until I returned with a few turkey and cheese sandwiches and mugs of coffee. Her expression lit up as she removed the lid and inhaled.

"Thank you for doing this."

I nodded and took a sip of my coffee. "Don't mention it."

Savannah took a sip and winced. "So, you know your way around a hospital, huh?"

"When my mom got sick, I spent a lot of time in the hospital."

Savannah's expression turned solemn. "I'm sorry. That must've been so hard."

"It was, but my sister and I had a good support system, and in the end, mom beat it, so it worked out. She's been in remission since."

"Shit. That's awful. I'm sorry you had to go through that. Honestly, I would've been traumatized. I doubt I would've been able to set foot in a hospital after that."

"It was hard, but we got through it. What about your family?"

Savannah cleared her throat. "Both my parents died a long time ago, and my sister and I don't talk anymore."

I reached across the table for her hand and squeezed. "I'm sorry."

Savannah shrugged, and her gaze moved to a spot over my shoulders. "So am I. I did try to have a relationship with her, but I guess it just wasn't meant to be."

I frowned and held her hand. "You don't have any more family?"

"They're out there. After my parents passed, they were around for a bit but then they kind of disappeared."

"That's shit, but it's their loss."

Savannah sighed. "It's what I try to tell myself. I guess it's better to have the right people by your side though. Like I'd rather be alone than have people in my life who don't have my back or who are only there out of duty or whatever."

"I get it."

Savannah's gaze moved back to my face. "Your ex?"

I stroked the inside of Savannah's wrist and something in me unfurled. "Caroline wasn't with me out of duty, but she was using me. The thing is….I thought she was it for me, you know. And Jeffrey would always be my best friend."

"Do you want to talk about what happened?"

"I don't know if there's much to say, honestly. Finding out that they stole money from me and that they wanted to use the business as a front for money laundering…yeah, I'm still trying to wrap my head around that."

I had no idea why I was telling her all of this now, only that it felt good to confide in Savannah and let the chips fall where they may. And it felt much better than I thought it would to unburden myself.

Savannah let out a low whistle, and her expression tightened. "Fuck. I'm sorry, Asher. I hope they're brought to justice."

"They're probably going to cut some kind of deal with the FBI in exchange for information."

"Is that why you were trying to warn me about keeping my nose out of it?"

I exhaled. "I know they look harmless, but they aren't. You should try and avoid them."

Savannah pulled a face before her expression turned serious. "Isn't there anything you can do?"

"Not at the moment."

Savannah paused. "Is there anything I can do?"

"This helps." I used my free hand to gesture between us. "Being able to talk about it without being judged."

Savannah winced. "I'm sorry about all the problems I've been causing. I should've have jumped to conclusions and made snap decisions without knowing the truth. It wasn't fair to you."

"It's okay."

"It's not. I want to make it up to you."

"You really don't need to. You had no idea or obligation to cater to my life."

She tilted her head to the side and studied me. "Is that why you want to shut down the wellness center? Because it was going to be used as a front?"

"The wellness center was meant to help us integrate and make some money while we got the permits, built the farm, etc. It was never meant to be a long-term project."

Savannah's expression fell. "Oh."

"But I meant what I said about there being nothing to worry about. I'm looking at a few other options while we wait for the permits to go through. I can't go into a lot of details, but I am taking this seriously."

Savannah's expression softened. "I'm glad."

I smiled at her. "Me too.

CHAPTER 22

- SAVANNAH -

"What's this?"

"I picked you up some lunch."

I pulled the bag closer to me and sniffed. "Are those dumplings?"

Asher leaned over the desk and smiled. "And kung pao chicken. I remember you telling me how much you liked it."

"Asher, the Chinese place is on the other side of town."

He tilted his head to the side and offered me a half smile. "Are we just stating facts now? I know where it is."

"And they don't deliver to the wellness center. I'm actually pretty sure the only reason they agree to deliver to my place is because they know me, and I've been a regular for years."

"Your point being?"

I reached for the bag of food and set it down on my desk. "You didn't have to go through all of this trouble."

But the gesture had my stomach doing somersaults, and it had me debating the merits of leaning over the desk and stealing a kiss.

Every single part of me wanted to.

Asher shrugged. "I wanted to. I knew you were going to have a hectic morning. How is Gemma by the way? I hope she's settled in okay."

"Yeah, one of the neighbors, Mrs. West, agreed to keep an eye on her while I'm at work. Gemma is on medication because of her concussion and needs to be taking it easy. "

"That's generous of Mrs. West, agreeing to watch her, I mean."

"The perks of living in a small town."

"True."

I cleared my throat. "Thanks for letting me come in late today. I wanted to be there when Gemma was discharged, and I wanted to be sure she got set up at home."

Asher nodded. "I'm happy to help. I'm sorry I couldn't be there."

"Be where?"

"At the hospital," Asher clarified, his eyes never leaving my face. "I wanted to come and help, but I've been in meetings all morning."

"I wasn't expecting you to come."

Although it would've been nice if he had, I knew that Asher ran a business and given everything he'd shared during our cafeteria date, I knew his hands were full. Between trying to bring Caroline and Jeffrey to justice and proving his innocence, it was a wonder he was able to function at all. Asher not only handed it well, but he also showed up to work every morning, ready to take on the world, and doing it fearlessly and without restraint.

For the life of me, I couldn't understand how.

If I were being investigated by the FBI, I would be a nervous wreck.

Leaving my house wouldn't have been an option, much less going to work, plastering on a smile and acting like it was business as usual. Yet, the more I thought about everything Asher had to endure since arriving, including the townsfolk busting his ass every step of the way, the more respect and admiration I had for him.

Asher really was something else.

And it made me care about him even more. Yet, despite knowing that Asher came with a lot more baggage than I realized, I wasn't afraid. If anything, it made me want to feel closer to him and help him navigate the unfamiliar terrain. While I didn't know much about Asher, since he kept everything close to the vest, the more I knew about him, the more I cared about him.

There was no doubt in my mind that Asher was innocent.

And I was sure he couldn't wait for his name, and that of his company's to be cleared. Although I had no idea what it was going to be like to navigate what we had, with the FBI on the fringes, it didn't bother me as much as I thought I did. Half of me expected the fear and nervousness to settle in, driving a wedge between us.

The other half of me was being incredibly calm and patient about the whole thing.

A little too calm for my liking, but it was better than freaking out.

Asher had that kind of effect on me, of making me feel like I could trust him even if the entire world was crumbling down around us. Even though I couldn't explain it, I knew that he wasn't guilty of the crimes he committed, I had seen proof of the kind of man he was firsthand.

And Asher Buchannan was a good, albeit grumpy grouch who needed to loosen the reigns a little.

When it came to Asher, I was well and truly in trouble because I knew that whatever it was between us, was no longer a fling or a mistake I could write off. Hell, I'd even considered asking him if he wanted to go to HR just so the two of us wouldn't have to sneak around at work. Pretending like he didn't matter to me as much as he did was exhausting, and I wasn't sure I wanted to do it anymore.

Not with the way I was feeling about him.

More and more, I was beginning to realize that Asher was the kind of person who understood me on every level. Since meeting him, he had gotten under my skin, challenged and surprised me every step of the way. While I had been reluctant to admit it, I finally knew why I hadn't been able to shake him off so easily.

I was well and truly head over heels for Asher Buchannan.

And I wasn't sure I wanted to fight it anymore.

Great timing, as usual, Sav. Come on, you know he's here on business, and after what his ex-did to him, it's likely that he's going to want to get involved with anyone, anytime soon. Wouldn't really blame if that was that case, would you?

Except I wasn't ready to write off Asher.

Not yet at least.

Every stolen moment, every kiss, every smile made me want to get to know him more. Ever since our interlude in the shower a few days ago, I hadn't been able to get him off of my mind, and I had stopped trying. I didn't want to pretend like I didn't have feelings for him or that seeing him didn't do strange things to my insides.

On the contrary, I didn't care who knew anymore.

Shit.

Why couldn't Asher and I have met under different circumstances?

And how in the hell were we supposed to make it work when we were both so damaged?

Asher waved a hand in front of my face, and his expression turned serious. "Are you okay?"

I blinked and took a step back. "Yeah, I was just thinking of when I'll have a chance to enjoy the food."

Asher took a step back and cleared his throat. "Why don't you take the day off? I heard there's a Valentine's Day fair."

"It's not just for one day. It's for a few days, so I can go later."

"You should still go," Asher maintained, pausing to give me a strange look. "I think you'll enjoy it, and you look like you could use for some time away."

"I can't. I have work to finish."

Asher waved my comment away. "Your friend was just in the hospital. This will all still be here when you come in tomorrow."

"I don't know…."

Asher leaned in and gave me a heated look. "Take the rest of the day off, Parish. That's an order. Don't make me take it back."

I blushed. "Well, if you insist…"

"I do." Asher studied me for a few more moments before he drew away. "You deserve to have some fun."

"What about you? You don't want to go?"

Asher paused. "It's not really my thing, and I do have some things to take care of."

I thought the two of us were making strides in the right direction, but something about Asher's answer filled me with disappointment.

Had I read too much into his gesture, and his generosity?

"Is everything okay?"

"No, but it will be."

I shifted from one foot to the other. "I'm here if you need anything."

Asher's expression softened. "I know. I appreciate that, but there's nothing to worry about."

I gave him one of my winning smiles. "Fine, then. I'll bring you back a caramel apple."

"Win me a stuffed bear," Asher joked, before taking a few more steps away, in the direction of his office. "The biggest one you can find."

"I've got pretty good aim."

Asher's laughter trailed after him and stopped when he shut the door to his office behind him. I stared at the spot he occupied, a ridiculous grin on my face. Slowly, I gave a slight shake of my head and sighed. Then I straightened my back, picked up my purse and takeout and made a beeline for the front door.

In the doorway, I paused to glance over my shoulders and found Asher watching me. He gave me a slow, lazy smile that sent shivers racing up and down my spine. Before I could talk myself out of it, I stepped outside and let the door click shut behind me. Overhead, the afternoon sun was warm on my face, and I set off at a brusque pace, the takeout bag swinging back and forth at my side.

A few blocks away, I heard the music and spotted a large red and white tower, made of cardboard and spray painted. As I got closer, I couldn't shake the feeling that I should've taken Asher with me, if only to give the two of us a chance to spend more time together.

Because the more I got to know Asher, the better I liked him.

When I rounded the corner, I saw the flower arch at the entrance, and the red and white streamers and smiled. Out of the corner of my eye, I saw a flash of movement and Gemma emerged, red-faced and triumphant. She skidded to a halt when she saw me and glanced away sheepishly.

"You're supposed to be resting at home," I laughed.

"Thought you could get rid of me that easily? I love going to the fair. I wouldn't miss it for anything."

"You could've gone later."

Gemma folded her arms over her chest. "It's only a few stitches anyway. Now, come on. Are we going in or what?"

"What did you do to Mrs. West?"

"She's over by the carnival games trying to win a teddy bear for her granddaughter." Gemma looped her arm through mine and pulled me along. "Come on. Let's go to the flowers station. I plan on winning this year."

"You have an unfair advantage since you own a flower shop."

Music rose and fell around us as we wove in and out of people.

Everyone around us was buzzing with excitement and dressed in variations of red and white. A few costumed bears were walking around, offering hugs to the children and pointing them in the direction of the crafts corner where children were scatted on tables surrounding a tree. Now and again someone got up to hang up a heart shaped paper from one of the branches and skipped back to their seat.

On the other side of the fair, nestled in between the cotton candy and fizzy drinks, I spotted the kissing booth, with a long line already forming, and a large thermometer in the background. Each kiss was worth five dollars, and by the end of the fair, all of the money was going to be donated to the local shelter in town.

Gemma clapped her hands together when she saw the flower decorating station and released my arm. "This is my year. I can feel it."

"I'm going to go check out the other games."

"Tell Mrs. West I'm fine," Gemma called out, over her shoulders, before rolling up her sleeves. "And bring me back a caramel apple."

"One for you and one for Asher," I repeated, with a smile. "You got it. Want me to win you a stuffed animal too?"

Gemma flipped me off before returning her attention to her bouquet.

I walked around, eating my food and enjoying the warmth of the sun on my face. When I threw out the takeaway containers, I smelled the popcorn in the air and smiled. While I wasn't sure if Asher would've enjoyed an event like this, with its confetti of colors and flurry of activities, I did know that I wanted him to be there.

More than I cared to admit.

I could picture us on the Ferris wheel together, holding hands and smiling. And when I blinked, I saw Asher in line to win a stuffed animal, sneaking glances at me the entire time.

The thought left a warm feeling in center of my stomach.

I really did have it bad for Asher.

With a sigh, I spun around and saw Kayden a few feet away, his hands shoved into his pockets. He did a double take when he saw me, and the easy expression on his face fell. He looked over my shoulders then back at me before folding his arms over his chest.

"I'm surprised you're not here with him."

"What are you talking about?"

"Don't play dumb with me, Savannah. I know you've been seeing the new guy in town. Ashmond or whatever."

"Asher," I corrected, with a frown. "And that's none of your business anyway."

Kayden took a step towards me and scowled. "You told me you were going to think about giving us a second chance. We were going to go away together, remember?"

"Okay, first of all, I never agreed. Second of all, you're kidding me, right?"

Kayden's eyebrows drew together. "Why would I be kidding?"

"You're really going to make me spell it out for you?"

Kayden stared at me and said nothing.

"You cheated on me multiple times, Kayden," I continued, aware of the glances being thrown our way. "And if that wasn't bad enough, you cheated on me with your ex's sister and got her pregnant, and you chose to tell me on our wedding day of all days. Why would I want to give you a second chance?"

"Because I told you the truth."

"You don't get points for coming clean after something like this. You only told me because you didn't want to get caught."

"That's not fucking fair—"

"Fair? You want to talk about fair? I've spent the past few weeks having to endure all of the looks people having been giving me. I had to call off my own wedding—"

"Now hold on a second—"

I held a hand up and gave him a withering look. "I wasn't done talking. I've let you say your piece, Kayden. Hell, I don't even know why I'm talking to you right now after what you did to me. You should be thankful that all I did was call off the wedding."

"So, you're dating someone else to get back at me? Is that it?"

"Oh, for fuck's sake, Kayden, not everything is about you. Believe it or not, I don't owe you any explanations or any reasons for why I choose to do what I do. What I do, and who I do it with is none of your business."

Kayden scoffed. "He's just some rich city boy who's going to going to leave you behind when he gets bored."

I pointed a finger at Kayden and bristled.

Fucking Kayden had a lot of nerve.

How dare he accuse Asher of the very thing he was guilty of himself?

I shouldn't have been as surprised as I was, considering the kind of man Kayden was, but I was feeling protective of Asher, who had been nothing but good and kind.

"At least he's honest about what he wants. I'd rather be left behind by him than manipulated by you."

Kayden threw his hands up in the air. "You've got to be kidding me. I'm offering you a second chance. I thought that's what you wanted."

I gave him an incredulous look. "Why in the hell would I want another chance with you? You are nothing but a sad and miserable human being who is always chasing after someone just to try and fill the hole in your heart. I feel sorry for you Kayden."

Kayden scowled and fumbled for words.

A half circle had already formed around us, and I was sure that by nightfall, we were going to be the talk of the town.

Again.

"You are never going to be happy," I added, my voice rising towards the end. "I don't think you even know how to be. You just keep chasing all these things you think are going to make you happy because you think it's what you're supposed to do."

Kayden made a low noise in the back of his throat. "Oh, you think you've got it all figured out, do you? The great fucking Savannah Parish has done it again. You don't know shit."

"Neither do you, but at least I have the balls to admit it."

Kayden's eyes tightened around the edges. "Don't come crying to me when it's over because I am not going to help you pick up the pieces."

"I wouldn't come to you if you were the last person in town. Oh and by the way, I cancelled the honeymoon reservation. Since I waited so close to the date, they're not going to be giving you a refund. Happy Valentine's Day, asshole."

Kayden opened and closed his mouth several times. With one last dirty look, he stomped off, pushing his way through the crowd. A smattering of applause rose through the crowd, led by Gemma. She pushed her way through, draped an arm over my shoulders and pressed a kiss on top of my forehead.

"Babe, I'm so proud of you. How do you feel?"

I paused. "I don't know. Do you think I overdid it?"

Gemma snorted and steered me towards the concession stand. "Are you kidding? If anything, you were way too nice. I would've definitely been harder on him."

At the front of the line, Gemma ordered soda, a few snacks, and we carried them back to a bench. Once we sat down, with the treats between us, I gazed ahead at the Ferris wheel and released a deep breath. While I hadn't meant to tell Kayden off for the way he treated me, it was a relief to know I wasn't still under his spell.

Now that the wool was no longer over my eyes, I was seeing him for the person he really was. Suddenly, I was beginning to realize that I had pinned all my hopes and dreams on the image of Kayden I had in my head, and not the actual Kayden who was capable of inflicting so much hurt and pain, without a care in the world.

Getting another woman pregnant might've been the best thing Kayden had ever done to me.

Otherwise, I wasn't sure if I would've gotten the courage to walk away for good.

In between bites of her corn dog, Gemma kept sneaking glances at me. "I know that look. Don't overthink it, Sav. You did the right thing."

"Honestly, I'm kind of glad I got it off my chest. The past few weeks, I've been tiptoeing around him not wanting to hurt his feelings, and I don't even know why."

Gemma used a napkin to dap her mouth. "Because you're a good person who cared about him even though he's a piece of a shit."

"Maybe."

"It's definitely true. He never deserved you, babe. And I'm glad you told him off. Now that you're finally moving on, he's just jealous."

I twisted to face her and frowned. "Do you think he really expected me to just sit around and wait for him?"

Gemma pulled a face. "With men like Kayden? It's hard to tell. I think he just liked knowing he could keep you hanging, but ever since Asher came into the picture, things have changed."

"It's not all Asher, you know."

Gemma smiled and took another bite of her corn dog. "I know, but you have to admit that a part of it is."

"I'll admit to nothing."

"It's okay to like someone you didn't think you were going to like," Gemma offered, in a quieter voice. "I know you and Asher didn't get off to the most conventional of starts, but it shouldn't matter."

"What do you mean?"

"I mean I know the two of you spent hours in the cafeteria yesterday, just talking."

My eyebrows drew together. "How did you even know that?"

"I was bored, and the nurse told me that the two of you made a cute couple, so I asked her to tell me more."

I rolled my eyes. "You couldn't find something better to do?"

Gemma picked up her drink and sipped on it. "No, you guys are much more entertaining and according to the nurse, the two of you looked madly in love."

I sighed. "I think she's exaggerating."

"I don't. I don't know Asher well, but I know you, and you're different around him. I'm not saying you should marry him or anything, but I do there's something there, and it's worth looking into."

"When did you turn into such a romantic?"

Gemma set her drink down and shot me a dirty look. "I've always been wise in the ways of love."

"Except when it comes to your own love life."

"Fuck you."

CHAPTER 23

- ASHER -

I glanced over at Savannah and exhaled. "I can't believe you got me to agree to this."

"We all agreed it was for the best," Savannah replied, without looking at me. "It's going to be fine."

"I finally get the chance to beat you," Gemma added, from next to her.

I raised an eyebrow. "I thought the point of this meeting was to mediate."

Savannah glanced up from the folder and cleared her throat. "The point is to try and make sure both sides get what they want, or as close to it as possible."

"I don't know why you brought in a mediating team," Gemma replied, with a shake of her head. "I can take Asher on all by myself."

"I seem to remember that you couldn't handle it the last time you and I went toe to toe."

Gemma scowled and flipped me off.

Savannah sighed. "This is why we need a team to mediate. They're going to make sure the protests decrease, but you're going to have to give something up, Asher."

I leaned back in my chair. "We already agreed they'd protest somewhere else."

"That was more for your benefit than ours."

"That was for the benefit of the wellness center," I pointed out, pausing to give Gemma a pointed look. "There are still people who work there, remember?"

Savannah glanced between the two of us. "The mediating team is going to be here soon. Do you two have to do this now?"

"There's no time like the present," Gemma replied, before turning around in her chair to face the windows. "This is a hell of a view by the way."

"It is."

Underneath the table, I reached for Savannah's hand, and she smiled. Having spent the past few days in one meeting after the next with the FBI, it was a relief to be sitting in the conference room across from Savannah, as if nothing had changed between us. While having Gemma there wasn't ideal, especially considering her desire to bury my business under mountains of paperwork, it was better than not having Savannah at all.

Although I didn't want to admit it, I had missed her.

More than I cared to admit.

And I had spent too much thinking about her over the past few days. In spite of the FBI being much closer to bringing the case to a close and clearing my name, there were still a few loose ends where Caroline and Jeffrey were concerned. The list of names they had provided, while useful, still needed to be verified before the final deal could be brought to the table.

Much to the dismay of Caroline and Jeffrey.

During the meetings with the FBI, I caught a few glimpses of them, and the two of them looked worse for wear. Although the two of them did their best to put up a façade, pretending like they still had everything in control, I could still see the cracks they tried so hard to hide.

But their inevitable defeat wasn't as satisfying as I thought it would be.

Instead of reveling in the fact that they were getting a taste of their own medicine, by being put in the microscope, it left me with a strange feeling in the center of my chest. Caroline and Jeffrey had been a part of my life for the past few years, and out of all the scenarios I imagined for the three of us, the two of them on the run wasn't one of them.

Neither was them being put behind bars.

Savannah has made you soft. The two of them deserve much worse after what they did to you, and they should be thankful that all you want is justice not revenge.

"They mediation team is running a little late," Savannah announced, after a lengthy silence. She squeezed my hand underneath the table before turning her attention back to the folder. "Do you guys want to discuss some of the points here before they come?"

Gemma spun back around and rose to her feet. "I'm going to get a quick massage."

"I thought you were trying to have this place shut down."

"No, I don't want this place to be a placeholder for a server farm that's going to ruin the water. There's a big difference." Gemma fixed me with a pointed look before tossing her hair over her shoulders. "I can still enjoy the amenities though."

"Massage room is the last door on the top floor."

"I'll see myself out," Gemma declared, a little too loudly. Once the door clicked shut behind her, I pulled Savannah's chair closer to me, and she gave a startled gasp. Then I cupped the back of her neck and pressed a kiss to her lips. She made an unintelligible sound in the back of her throat before she melted against me.

Savannah tasted like spearmint gum.

It was a taste I could lose myself in.

And I wanted to.

Her hands moved to the back of my neck, and she threaded her fingers through my hair, sending little pinpricks of desire racing up and down my spine. When I inched closer to close the gap between us, she made a low purring sound that had the blood roaring in my ears. Reluctantly, she wrenched her lips away and brought her head to a rest against my chest.

I smiled and pulled her to me. "What are you doing?"

"Trying to savor the moment," Savannah replied, in a muffled voice. "It's a good thing this glass is not see through."

I drew back to look at her, and my smile vanished. "You realize I would never put you in a position that would compromise your job, right?"

Savannah looked up at me and nodded. "I know."

"I know that you and I have a lot to figure out, but that's not going to affect your job here," I added, pausing to lace my fingers through hers. "Without you, none of this would've been possible anyway."

"I'm sure you and Gemma would've gotten here... eventually."

I snorted. "If we didn't kill each other first."

"You do bring out the competitive side in each other," Savannah acknowledged, with a smile. "It's kind of cute."

"You're cute," I replied, before lifting her hand up to my lips for a kiss. "Savannah, I—"

"You two can do this some other time," Gemma interrupted, loudly. "This is not the time or the place for this."

Savannah dropped her hand and looked over my shoulders. "That was a fast massage."

Gemma shrugged and went back to her earlier seat. "I changed my mind. I want to be sharp and alert during the meeting, so I just went to the bathroom instead."

Reluctantly, Savannah pried her fingers away from mine and sat up straighter.

A few moments later, the doors to the conference room were pushed open, and a group of four men and women came in, all similarly dressed in their khakis and button-down shirts. Wordlessly, they took their seats at the rectangular shaped table, then the redheaded woman at the head of the table pulled her chair closer and flipped the folder open.

"Welcome. I'm glad you could all make it today."

Silence settled over them.

The blonde glanced around, and her eyes lingered on me. "Mr. Buchannan, I understand that you wish to come to an agreement with the protestors."

"That's right."

The blonde twisted to face Gemma, who was seated closer to her. "And provided the two parties can work out an agreement, will you convince the other protestors to stop?"

Gemma nodded. "Of course. We just want what's best for the community."

The blonde nodded and smiled. "I understand. My name is Tiffany Walsh. I'm going to be conducting the mediating session today. My colleagues Brandon, Ryle and Alyssa are here to take notes and help make sure the negotiation is as smooth as possible."

"Will we really need that many people?"

Tiffany looked over at Savannah, and her expression turned serious. "Negotiations are serious, and it's important to prepare accordingly."

Savannah looked down at the file and I didn't say anything.

Seated at the head of the table, I moved my chair closer, my knee brushing against Savannah's. A flutter of impatience started in the center of my stomach and didn't stop until Savannah looked over at me, and it erupted into a swarm of butterflies, taking up residence in my stomach.

Damn it.

This wasn't meant to be happening.

Savannah was here to help mediate not be a distraction.

Yet, as far as distractions went, she was by far the best. Each time she drew her bottom lip between her teeth, or a furrow appeared between her brows, it made me want to kiss her even more. I half listened to Tiffany as she read out the terms of agreement, but the other half me only saw Savannah.

I had no interest in anything else.

Savannah and Gemma were the main reason I was in this meeting instead of letting someone else handled it. Little by little, the protestors were losing steam and before their flame could be extinguished, they were grasping at straws. While I understood and sympathized, I also wasn't going to put my company in the crosshairs in such a delicate position.

It was why I convinced the board to have a sit down to consider the terms.

The thought of having to fill them in after was already giving me a headache.

Tiffany cleared her throat. "Mr. Buchannan, there's a stretch of land overlooking the water, a few miles outside of Lockwood, and it currently does not belong to anyone. Ms. Hart has suggested that you purchase the land and file permits for the water rights there. That way, there will be little interference between your server farm and Lockwood's local charm and marine life."

I glanced over at Gemma who held my gaze. "That's assuming I can. Public land is much harder to secure permits for."

Gemma cut her gaze over to me and sat up straighter. "I can help you so will the mayor. And I know a good local lawyer."

"It sounds like a reasonable deal, Mr. Buchannan. This way, you can still keep your server farm, and the community still has access to the water without the sever farms."

I paused, and my eyes swept over the room. "If I were to begin trying to acquire the rights to that piece of land, how do I know Ms. Hart and the other protestors won't set up camp there?"

"It'll be in the contract," Tiffany responded, pausing to flip through the paperwork. "Your lawyer has also added a clause that penalizes any of the parties that violates the terms of the contract."

Will was good.

Better than good.

Even in another state he was still looking out for me, and I knew that if there was anything shady about the deal, he was going to find out. He was also going to make sure the deal was as good as I thought it was, and not a complete sham to get me to move my farm somewhere else.

"I will talk to the other protestors and make sure they understand what's at stake if they don't follow the terms of the contract," Gemma offered. "But we have another request too."

I raised an eyebrow. "Go ahead."

"We want you to keep the wellness center. I'm aware it was meant as a means to an end, but a lot of the towns people have grown fond of the wellness center, including myself, and it would be a shame to get rid of it now."

"I'll have to talk to the board," I told her, with a frown. "Go over the financials again and see if it's possible."

Gemma nodded, mostly to herself. "I think you'll be able to figure something out."

"Yes, it just might be."

Tiffany linked her fingers together over the table. "So both parties are in agreement regarding the movement of the server farms, and acquiring the water rights somewhere else?"

"Pending the board's approval," I reminded her, with another quick look around the room. "It'll be a majority vote, but I see no reason why it shouldn't go through. This way, we both get what we want."

Tiffany snapped the folder shut and stood up. "After the board's decision, we can reconvene and adjust the rest of the plan accordingly, if needed."

Savannah rose to her feet and led them out of the room with a smile.

Once the door clicked shut behind her, I stood up and fastened the first button on my jacket. "I have a meeting with the board of directors for later. I'll let you know how it goes."

"Good."

Silence stretched between us.

Gemma didn't make a move towards the door. She just stood there, studying me intently.

"Was there something you wanted?"

Gemma nodded. "Now that you mentioned it, there is. Do I need to give you another speech about Savannah?"

I raised an eyebrow. "Why would you need to do that?"

Gemma picked up Savannah's folder and held it to her chest. "She's finally getting over her douche bag of an ex. I would hate for you to turn out like him. I know things are changing between the two of you, so just don't fuck it up, Buchannan, or the server farm's future will be the least of your problems."

"You're not nearly as scary as you think you are."

Gemma scoffed. "And you're not as much of a tough ass as you want people to believe."

"Fair point."

On her way out, she paused at the door and glanced over her shoulders at me. "I'll see you around, Buchannan."

WEDDING NIGHT STRANGER (MR. BUCHANNAN)

"See you later, Hart."

Through the glass, I saw her walk up to Savannah who had the office phone cradled between her neck and shoulders. She glanced past Gemma and looked directly at me. The butterflies in my stomach erupted into a frenzy as I yanked on the knob and stepped out into the hallway.

I held her gaze until I couldn't anymore.

Then I sat down behind my desk, pulled the chair forward and let my fingers hover over the keyboard. Considering how important it was to resolve this peacefully, I was going to do everything within my power to make sure the board agreed to the protestors' terms. Not only was it in our best interest to find a peaceful solution, enabling us to move forward with our plans, but it also wasn't a smart move to make enemies of Lockwood Creek.

Especially if we were going to be neighbors.

The terms of the agreement were in my inbox, and I skimmed through them again, assuring myself that it was for the best. While nothing had worked out the way I wanted it since my arrival here, I was beginning to wonder if it was working out the way I needed it to.

Otherwise, what was the point of all of this?

With an exhale, my mouse hovered over the meeting icon, and I sat up straighter. After unfastening the first button on my suit jacket, I clicked on the icon. It wasn't long before several of the boxes in front of me had the board members' faces, all of them wearing identical concerned expressions.

"How did the meeting with the mediators go?"

"As well as can be expected."

Mr. Yang linked his fingers together over the table and peered into the camera. "Do they still want us to move the server farm somewhere else?"

"Yes, and as per the terms of the new agreement, we'd have to acquire the water rights further down, outside the town line to be precise, and we would have to find a way to ensure the wellness center stays open."

A murmur of disapproval rose through board.

Several members looked away and muttered something underneath their breath. A few started flipping through the folders in front of them, with each of them having their own copies of the agreements present. Finally, the head of the board Mr. Park Yang snapped the folder shut and cleared his throat.

"This is not the news we hoped for, Mr. Buchannan."

"I've had the lawyers go over the agreements, and I've had them scope out the area in question, and it's a good plan. Moving the server farms there, while more costly, is the best option to avoid any more issues with the locals."

Mr. Yang frowned. "What kind of issues would we face if we decide to move forward with our original plans?"

"Tearing down the wellness center is going to enrage a lot of people, including the mayor, and without his support, it's going to be hard to get the permits pushed through, meaning the server farm would be put on hold indefinitely."

Not taking the deal meant the town council, spearheaded by the mayor and his lawyer, would attempt to tie us up in litigation.

Although they didn't have the money or the resources we did, they had one of the best lawyers I had ever seen, and while I had never met him in person, I had seen his handiwork. Working side by side with the locals was the best option we had, and providing the town with more job opportunities was the kind of thing they wouldn't be able to deny.

Regardless of how they felt about having a server farm next door.

Another murmur of disapproval rose.

"We'll need to see a projection and budget sheet," Mr. Yang announced, after a lengthy pause. He unlinked his fingers, took his glasses off and began to polish them. "Provided the numbers make sense, we'll need to consider who will oversee the project."

"This project needs someone who is familiar with the locals and knows how to handle his own."

"You have someone in mind?"

"I'm going to oversee the project myself. Since I'm here, and it was my idea, I want to see this through," I announced, studying the board members' portraits. "It's the right thing to do."

Successful or not, I had poured too much time, energy and effort into this project to put someone else at the helm now. Staying behind ensured the transition was as smooth as possible and allowed me to deal with any other problems that arose.

It had nothing at all to do with me wanting to be close to Savannah.

At least not entirely.

Yeah, keep telling yourself that, Buchannan. You're crazy about her, you idiot. When are you going to admit it to yourself and her?

ALICIA NICHOLS

CHAPTER 24

- SAVANNAH -

"Why didn't you tell me to come to the signing? I would've been there."

Gemma held the yogurt cup up to her face and raised an eyebrow. "You have a very clear conflict of interest. Besides, I knew it was a good deal, and I knew that Asher was going to push for it."

"You couldn't have known."

Gemma licked the spoon and pushed herself off the counter. "Fine. I didn't know for sure, but I had a good feeling. It's why they took a few days to deliberate."

I ran a hand over my face and sighed. "So, I guess that's it. No more protests."

"Don't sound so disappointed."

"I'm not. I just…"

I had no idea what was going to happen next.

Now that the future of the server farms was secure, with the mayor and the town lawyer promising to help Asher secure permits for the water outside the town line, Asher's job was now done. He had come to Lockwood Creek to get the project up and running and now that it was off the ground, there was no longer a reason to stay. The wellness center, while not part of the original plan, was still going to remain open, and all Asher had to do was find someone else to run it.

Already people were buzzing about who he was going to choose.

I, on the other hand, couldn't care less.

Not when it meant losing Asher when I was finally getting to know him.

Little by little, he had shown me different sides of himself, leaving me wanting to know more, and I couldn't believe this was how it was going to end. A part of me was happy that the entire issue was resolved, with few problems arising, but I had to admit that I was going to miss having something that tethered us together.

Kept us close.

Without his constant presence at the wellness center, what happened next?

His focus was going to have to be on the server farm, and everything that entailed, and it made me miss him already.

I didn't know what Asher and I were to each other outside of the wellness center, and the little bubble we'd created for ourselves.

Hell, I didn't even know if there was a future once he returned to the city.

Without the forced proximity, would he even still want me?

Fuck.

How had I let myself get so caught up that I forgot about our expiry date?

Because you're a hopeless romantic. That's why. You wanted to believe that there was still time for the two of you to figure things out.

But time was out, and we were still stuck in the same place.

Gemma waved a hand in front of my face and frowned. "You should talk to Asher."

I blinked and took a step back. "I don't know, Gem. I don't know if there's anything to talk about. Once he finds a replacement to run the wellness center and the rest of the project, he'll leave. And that'll be that."

Gemma finished off the rest of her yogurt and tossed it into a bin. "I don't think you should jump to conclusions, Sav. You should talk to him before you go assuming things. At least find out where you really stand."

I knew Gemma was right, but I didn't want to admit it.

Hearing him say the words that would bring everything crashing down around me was terrifying, and it would be too much for me to bear. Asher had gone from being an attractive stranger in the bar, to a grumpy boss, to someone I had grown comfortable around and looked forward to seeing, all in the span of a few weeks.

And it wasn't fair that he was going to be ripped away from me before we even had a real chance.

I cleared my throat. "We had a good run, Gem, but we both knew what it was."

"Don't be an idiot and don't overthink this," Gemma warned, with a shake of her head. "I bet he's going to call you to talk any second now."

"Since when you are a fan of his?"

"Asher has a lot of issues, but he's a good guy." Gemma shrugged and snatched her sweater off the back of the chair. "Anyway, I've got to go. I've got an order I'm supposed to work on."

"It's Saturday."

"It's for a wedding." Gemma brushed past me and pulled the door open. "Hey, Asher. Right on time."

I spun around, saw him standing in the doorway in his dark jeans and button-down shirt, and my stomach gave an odd little flip. He and Gemma exchanged a quick nod before he looked over at me, and his lips lifted into smile.

"Can I come in?"

My throat turned dry as I nodded. He stepped in and paused to close the door behind them, and the swarm of butterflies in my stomach erupted. Wave after wave of nervous energy rose through me, but I tried to ignore it. Then he covered the distance between us, pausing a few feet away. "Gemma told you the good news?"

"Congratulations."

Asher's smile faded, and his expression turned serious. "The board isn't too happy, but they'll adapt."

I swallowed. "I hope so. When are they sending your replacement?"

Asher took a step forward, his eyes never leaving my face. "Next week."

"Oh."

"She's going to be running the wellness center herself."

A lump rose in the back of my throat. "I see."

I had known it was coming, but it didn't stop disappointment from taking root in the center of my stomach.

"But I insisted that I stay to oversee the rest of the project myself," Asher continued, his lips lifting into half a smile. "I'm the best person for the job since people here are used to me."

"You what?"

Asher chuckled and took my hands in his. "Maureen will be running the wellness center. I'm staying to oversee the server farm project."

"I don't know. Do you really think you can handle it?"

Asher's lips twitched, and his hands moved to my waist. "I know I can."

"Good. Wouldn't want you investing in something big if you weren't ready for it."

"I still want you to be the office manager," Asher told me, in a quieter voice. "But I also want you to be my liaison during meetings with the town council, the mayor, any other disgruntled protestors."

"I'm sure there are other people who are more qualified—"

Asher shook his head and bridged the rest of distance between us. "I only want you, Savannah. No one else."

He wrapped his arms around me, and my breath hitched in my throat. "What do you say?"

"I...I have no idea what to say," I admitted, in a thick voice. An unfamiliar swell of emotion rose and unfurled in my chest. "This is not what I was expecting."

Asher searched my face. "Me neither. I didn't come here looking for anything."

"I know."

Asher kept one hand on my waist, and the other moved to the back of my neck, sending a jolt of desire racing through me. "But now that I've found you, I don't want to leave."

My heart was hammering wildly against my chest, and I had to remind myself how to breathe. Being around him made it hard to think and harder to hold onto common sense, but I didn't mind much.

Not if it meant he was staying.

"I don't want you to stay because of me."

Asher's brows furrowed together. "Why not?"

"Because if it doesn't work out, you'll resent me for keeping you," I whispered.

Asher shook his head. "I won't. The entire time that I've been here, I've been chasing after something without even knowing what it was, and after I met you, everything just clicked."

I held my breath as a single tear slid down my cheek.

Asher used the pad of his thumb to brush it away. "I know we've both got some baggage, and we've been through some shit, but that's exactly why we're right for each other, Savannah. You're the one that I want. I want you to be the one to call me out on things, and I want you to be the one to open my eyes when I'm being stubborn."

My lips lifted into a half smile. "Even when you think it makes me a pain in the ass?"

Asher chuckled before pressing a kiss squarely to my lips. "Especially then."

Half of me was afraid that I'd wake up alone in bed, with the realization that it was all a dream. The other half of me could hardly believe that Asher was standing in front of me, telling me everything I needed to hear. Rather than packing up and leaving me behind, Asher wanted to stay right here.

With me.

Fucking hell.

"Well, in that case, there's no else I'd rather annoy."

"Even a cynical grump like me?"

"Especially a cynical grump like you," I added, softly. "With a heart of gold. You can't fool me, Asher Buchannan. I can see right through you."

Asher kissed me again, harder this time.

For a while, we stood there, clinging to each other until the need for air became too great. Wave after wave of emotion rose within me, and my heart felt like it was going to explode.

Slowly, Asher wrenched his lips away and pressed hot, open-mouthed kisses down the side of my neck and my jaw. His hands moved from the back of my neck to my waist, and he squeezed.

I wanted to stay like that forever.

Asher bent down and hoisted me into his arms. He carried me across the carpeted hallway, to the room at the end and stopped in the doorway. With a smile, he lowered his head for another kiss, making my head spin as I grabbed a fistful of his shirt. Even with my body pressed against his, it still wasn't enough.

I needed more.

I needed him.

His mouth, his touch, and the feel of his naked body pressed against mine.

He made a low noise in the back of his throat as he stepped in through the doorway and kicked the door shut with the back of his leg. The blood was roaring in my ears as Asher set me down on my feet and drew back. His eyes were wide and full of raw hunger as he took me in, drinking every inch of me till it felt like I was about to explode.

Into a million pieces all at once.

He drew me to him again, but this time he pulled my shirt up over my head. Goosebumps broke out across my flesh, and my eyes stayed on his face, not wanting to miss a single moment. Asher tossed the shirt aside and reached for my jeans, momentarily fumbling with the zipper before he pulled it down, leaving me in my bra and panties. I made a low sound of impatience, and helped him out of his own clothes, offering me an unencumbered view of his tanned, glistening body.

He was the most beautiful thing I had ever seen.

And I had never felt more exposed nor more desired in my entire life.

Asher touched me gently, like I an illusion that would disappear if he moved too fast. "You're so beautiful, Sav. I can't fucking believe how lucky I am."

"I think I'm the lucky one here."

His hands moved up and down my bare arms, but he kept a few inches of space between us. "We're both lucky we found each other. There's nowhere else I'd rather be than right here."

A wave of impatience rose through me as I reached for him. "Oh, Asher. You have no idea how much it means to hear you say that."

He held my wrist in his hand and used his other hand to unhook the clasp on my bra. Once my breasts spilled forward, he released my hand and lowered himself onto the carpet.

When he looked up at me, everything else ceased to exist.

Nothing else outside my room mattered.

Using his teeth, he pulled my panties down over my thighs and down to my ankles. Breathlessly, I stepped out of them, and my fingers went to his hair. With a moan, I wound my fingers through his hair and marveled at the feel of his hot mouth on my flushed skin.

Everywhere he touched, he claimed.

I was his.

Only his.

Asher continued to press hot, open-mouthed kisses along the inside of my thighs until he reached my center. I held my breath as his fingers moved to my waist, and he dug his fingers into the sensitive flesh there. Then his tongue darted out in between my wet folds, and my mind careened to a halt.

Holy shit.

"Oh, Asher. Oh, God. I...I've never felt this way about anyone."

WEDDING NIGHT STRANGER (MR. BUCHANNAN)

How did each time with Asher feel better than the last?

How did being with him feel so right?

"Good because I love being the only man who can make you feel this good."

Like he devoured me whole while I braced myself against him.

My grip on the back of his neck tightened as I bucked against him. His tongue moved back and forth, making the pool of desire in my stomach grow molten. Wave after wave of desire built up within me until my vision turned white. I was moaning and chanting his name when the force of my orgasm ripped through me, leaving me breathless and panting.

Rivulets of sweat down slid down my back and the sides of my face.

When my feet touched the carpet again, Asher released his grip on my waist and rose up. He kissed me, soundly, and I tasted myself on his lips, a heady combination that made my knees go weak. Asher maneuvered us backwards, so my knees hit the back of my bed.

As soon as they did, he drew back and climbed onto the bed. I sat up on my legs and met him halfway, eager and desperate for his mouth on mine. He smiled into the kiss, tasting like mint mouthwash and coffee. My head spun, and I felt lightheaded I pushed him onto his back and grinned.

Then I threw one leg up on either side of him.

He lifted his head up and pushed my hair out of my eyes. "I like this side of you."

"I like that you bring out this side of me," I said, in a thick voice. I placed one hand on either side of the headboard and stilled. Asher lifted his hips up off the mattress, and in one quick move, he was inside of me, filling me to the hilt.

Every part of him fit against me.

Like two pieces of a puzzle.

"That's it, baby. I could stay like this forever."

I ground myself against him, wanting to take all of him inside of me, so there were no more barriers between us. "We should."

Asher dug his nails into my waist and lifted his hips up off the mattress. Tears pricked the back of my eyes, and my lungs burned with effort. The swell of emotion in my chest only grew stronger.

Slowly, I placed my palms down on the mattress and looked into his eyes. Asher didn't break our gaze as we moved together, taking and giving in equal pleasure. Each stroke, every movement, each look drove away any last doubt I had until I was sure that we were all that mattered.

The two of us were meant to be like this.

Asher's eyes darkened with desire as he pushed my hair back and kissed me, pouring every ounce of emotion he could into the kiss. I moaned and nipped on his bottom lip. His answering groan made the hairs on the back of my neck rise, and the butterflies in my stomach explode. Our tongues began a sensual battle for dominance that made my head spin.

Suddenly, I was falling again, hurtling over the edge with nothing but Asher to anchor me. I lowered my head, held his gaze, and saw the depth of emotion shinning there. Asher pressed his lips to mine, pouring all his emotion into the kiss. My entire body writhed and spasmed as I rode out my high, chanting his name the entire time. When my lungs stopped burning, and my vision cleared, I gave one final buck and collapsed against him. I held him to me and stroked his back as Asher's hips rose up. I didn't look away as he gave a few more thrusts before his body jerked and writhed.

He called out my name as his own release came.

Then he held me to him, and I laid my head to a rest on his flushed chest, over the pounding of his heart. The sound of our heavy breathing filled the room as did the smell of him, a combination of sandalwood and lemon scented soap that had my stomach doing somersaults. With a smile, I rolled off of him, and

WEDDING NIGHT STRANGER (MR. BUCHANNAN)

he draped an arm over my shoulders. When he tucked me into his side, I let my head fall into the crook of his neck and threw a leg up over him.

It felt right to be here with him like this.

Like I'd been doing it my whole life.

His fingers moved to the back of my head, to massage my scalp. "It's a good thing I came over."

I giggled and pressed a kiss to his neck. "Yeah, it's a good thing you did."

Asher drew back to look at me, and his thumb traced my jaw. "I wouldn't have it any other way. I want to be here, with you."

I reached behind my neck and adjusted the pillow, so my neck was propped up. Asher twisted, so he was on his side, facing me directly. He pulled the cover up over us and leaned over to me to tuck it into the sides.

"So now that you're stuck in this town…"

Asher chuckled. "I wouldn't call it stuck."

"Okay, so now that you're stuck in this town, what's next?"

Asher pressed a kiss to my forehead before settling back down, sending another wave of warmth coursing through me.

I was crazy about this man.

"I don't know yet. There's this woman I'm crazy about. I think I have a good shot."

"You do. I'm happy you're staying," I whispered, my eyes never leaving his face. "You have no idea how happy I am."

Asher's lips curved into a smile. "I've got a pretty good idea."

I studied every inch of his face, from his smooth angular jaw, and the light stubble there, to the way his long lashes curled. When my eyes moved back up to his face, and I saw the warmth there, my smile vanished. With a frown, I pushed myself up and stared at him.

We couldn't be happy together.

Not yet.

"What about the FBI?"

Asher rubbed his nose against mine. "You don't have to worry about that. The deal I've been negotiating has changed."

"What do you mean?"

Asher leaned back, and his expression turned serious. "Caroline and Jeffrey are going to be charged, but it's going to be for less prison time since they cooperated."

"Is that a good thing or a bad thing?"

"I'm just glad it's over and that my name, and the company's, will be cleared." Asher's hands moved to the back of my neck, and he played with the hair there. "I don't know how it's all going to play out, but my lawyer is feeling confident."

"You must have a really good lawyer."

Asher kissed the tip of my nose and huffed a laugh. "I do. God knows I haven't made the past few weeks easy for him."

"You should give him a bonus or something."

Asher's expression turned amused. "Any other ideas you want to tell me about?"

I ran my fingers through his hair. "I've got a few."

"Before you tell me about them, there's something really important I want to ask you."

"Okay."

"Will you be my Valentine?"

I burst into laughter. "Valentine's Day was a week ago."

"So?"

"I don't think it counts anymore."

Asher climbed on top of me and pressed kisses down the side of my neck. "Does that mean you don't want to?"

I wriggled against him. "Of course I want to."

Asher pinned my arms over my head and gave me a wicked smirk. "Good because I've got a few good ideas about how we can celebrate."

"Do they involve this bed and takeout?"

Asher nodded and lowered his head, so his lips were inches from mine. "It's like you read my mind."

I closed the gap between us and locked my fingers over his waist. "I'm glad we're on the same page."

"Fucking finally."

ALICIA NICHOLS

CHAPTER 25

- ASHER -

"Stop trying to peek."

"I am not trying to peek."

I squeezed her hand and chuckled. "Yes, you are. You've been dying to know what's happening since I picked you up."

"Because you're in cahoots with Gemma."

I laughed again and brought her hand up to my lips. "I am not in cahoots with Gemma. She just helped me plan something."

And for that I was grateful.

Gemma and I might not have seen eye to eye since my arrival, but when it came to Savannah, we were in complete agreement. Since I'd already missed Valentine's Day, I had spent the past few days trying to come up with a way to make it up to Savannah and show her how much she meant to me.

A short while ago, when I arrived to pick Savannah up, she was buzzing with excitement. In her knee-length blue dress, with her hair falling in loose waves around her shoulders, she was the most beautiful woman I had ever seen.

I'd barely been able to take my eyes off of her.

A few blocks away from the beach, I had taken out a blindfold. Savannah hadn't been happy, but she had humored me and put it on. A few minutes later, when I had led her out of the car, she almost stumbled and fell face first. Since then, she had been trying to sneak glances, and I had been doing my best not to laugh at her.

I loved how curious she was.

It was one of the many reasons I was crazy about her.

With a smile, I kept my hand on the small of her back and stopped at the edge of the sand. Then I helped Savannah out of her flats. She used both hands to hold onto me and sniffed, a smile hovering on the edge of her lips.

"Are we at the beach?"

"Yes."

"Are we going for a midnight swim?"

I continued to tug her forward, in the direction of the table set up a few feet away from the water, with a single tablecloth in the center, and a uniformed waiter already waiting for us. When he spotted me, I gave him a nod and a smile. The waiter, who wore a black and white uniform, pulled out both chairs out and poured a generous amount of wine into both glasses. Once we inched closer, I saw the single candle in the center, and the smell of cinnamon and salt wafted through the air.

My stomach grumbled in response.

Savannah laughed. "Somebody is hungry."

A heartbeat later, her stomach made a low noise that had her draping an arm over her middle. "Oops. I spoke too soon."

I patted her hand. "It's okay. My plan involves food."

"The actual edible kind?"

I helped Savannah lowered herself onto the chair and untied the blindfold. "You should get your head out of the gutter."

Savannah blinked and glanced around, her mouth forming a surprised O. She tilted her head to the side, saw the waves crashing onto the shore a few feet away, and her face lit up. Then she looked back at me as I sat down across from her and reached for her hand. Wordlessly, the waiter came and set down a plate of garlic bread in the center.

"You did all of this?"

"No, I hijacked the table for us."

Savannah squeezed my hand, and her smile grew wider. "We'd better hurry up and eat then before we're chased away by pitchforks."

"Pitchforks? I think it would be more like rotten tomatoes."

Savannah used her free hand to reach for the glass of wine. "That's a waste of perfectly good tomatoes."

I eyed her over the rim of my own glass and smiled. "I agree. I can think of a much better use for food."

A blush stole across Savannah's neck and stained her cheeks. "What happened to getting my head out of the gutter?"

"I can't help it if you're the sexiest woman in the world."

Her blush deepened. "Thank you. You're not so bad yourself."

I chuckled and took a long sip of my wine, which burned a path down my throat before settling in the pit of my stomach. "I know we're late to the party, but I wanted to do something to celebrate Valentine's, and Gemma helped."

Savannah withdrew her hand and leaned back against her chair. "Italian food and a moonlight dinner? Yeah, you're going to make it really hard for yourself."

"Why is that?"

"I can't imagine anything topping this." Savannah made a sweeping hand gesture before she reached for her drink. "You're setting the bar way too high for yourself."

"I like a good challenge." I craned my neck over my shoulders and gestured to the waiter. He nodded and returned with two bowls of tomato soup. With a flourish, he set them down in front of us before disappearing again. Savannah picked up her spoon and inhaled.

I studied her face, bathed in the pale glow of the moon, and my stomach gave an odd little lurch. When she glanced up at me, and I heard the waves crashing against the shore, it was drowned out by the sound of my heart pounding in my ears. Savannah's other hand snaked across the table, and she laced her hand through mine, sending a jolt of electricity racing through me.

With a smile, I picked up my own spoon. "Italian food is a good choice."

"It was my parents' favorite. Whenever we had a fancy dinner at home, it was what my mom made."

"Your mom had good taste."

Savannah nodded, a thoughtful expression on her face. "She did. So did my dad."

"I would've loved them, I'm sure."

"They would've loved you," Savannah replied, softly. She gave my hand another squeeze before returning to the soup. "This is delicious by the way."

"It is." I paused. "There's something I have to tell you."

Savannah glanced up, and her brows furrowed together. "Why do you look so serious? Are you about to tell me that you're a spy or something?"

"I could pull off the bond look."

Savannah huffed a laugh. "I could not pull off being a bond girl."

"I disagree. I think you'd make a great bond girl."

Savannah finished her soup and dabbed her lips with the napkin. "Is that what you wanted to tell me?"

I shook my head. "I wanted to tell you that the board has agreed to find an alternative energy method for the wellness center."

Slowly, Savannah set her napkin down and looked across at me. "I didn't even know that was possible. Won't the servers be too far?"

"We're looking into alternative sources of energy, like solar power."

Savannah's mouth broke out into a smile. "I think that's great. Won't it be hard to manage something like that with the size of the wellness center?"

"That'll be up to the research and development team to figure out."

Savannah blew out a breath. "That's amazing. I thought you were just being nice when you told me I could stay on as office manager and liaison."

"You didn't think I would let this fall apart, did you? It's been on my mind since the first mediation meeting. It just took some time."

Because the board hadn't been easy to convince.

Proving to them that moving the server farm was in our best interest was one thing. Asking them to approve another budget for the wellness center, which wasn't even in the original plan, was another. Initially, half the board had been resistant to keeping on the wellness center for much longer than a few years, much less investing to have it become a permanent fixture.

The other half had known that keeping a wellness center, in the middle of a seaside town, was a stroke of a genius, one that set it apart from the competition. While I hadn't seen the appeal in the beginning, more and more I was beginning to see how beneficial it was to keep the wellness center on it and invest in it to become more than a side project.

Given how successful it was already, it had the potential to do better.

And I knew the townspeople agreed by the overwhelming positive reception I had received since the announcement of our deal. Not only were the protestors gone, off to find another cause to rally behind, but the town's reluctance to accept me had long since given way to something warmer and a lot more welcoming.

It had been too long since I felt accepted as I am.

And I owed most of that to the extraordinary woman sitting across from me.

"I take it the board wasn't too happy with another change in the plan," Savannah commented, her expression turning concerned. "Is there anything I can do to help?"

"I've got this," I said, with a smile. "They'll take some time to come around completely, but they know a good opportunity when they see it. Otherwise, they wouldn't have agreed."

Savannah reached for her wine and finished it all. She looked over my shoulder and signaled to the waiter. He materialized, poured some more wine and took our soup bowls away. Then another waiter returned with a different tray, carrying two plates of pasta, with steaming hot marinara sauce and meatballs in the center.

"Wouldn't it have better to work on this later?"

I picked up my fork and knife before glancing over at her. "What do you mean?"

"Wouldn't it have been better to wait until the FBI closed the case? There's a lot of heat on you right now, and I don't think you should risk angering the board any further. Couldn't they, like, fire you or something?"

I set my cutlery down and reached into my pocket. "You haven't seen it, have you?"

"Seen what?"

With a grin, I held the phone up to my face, the bright screen making me squint. After finding the video, I handed the phone over to Savannah. Her expression changed from confused to thrilled in the span of a few seconds, one hand flying to her mouth in surprise. Once the video ended, she watched it again, tears filling her eyes and spilling over.

Savannah sniffed and handed me the phone back. "Asher, why didn't you tell me? This is huge news."

"I thought you had seen the statement like everyone else. It's not every day the FBI issues a formal apology."

Savannah reached for the glass of water and took a long sip. "Exactly. What about Caroline and Jeffrey?"

"Five years in prison, and they have to pay a fine," I told her, in between sips of my drink. "And they have to reach a settlement with my company for damages."

Savannah made a low noise in the back of her throat. "I can't believe you didn't tell me any of this sooner."

"I'm pretty sure the whole town has heard by now."

Savannah pushed her chair back, and it fell backwards with a thud. Then she came to a stand in front of me and held her hand out. Once she pulled me to my feet, she drew me in for a hug, and I lingered. I wrapped my arms around her waist, buried my face in her hair and exhaled.

She smelled like freesias and jasmine.

I wanted to bottle the scent up somewhere.

And I wanted to stay like this with her forever.

After weeks of uncertainty and not knowing if my life's work was going to go down the drain, it was with no small amount of relief that I was exhaling. Not only was I satisfied with the punishment doled out to Caroline and Jeffrey, but I also knew that an apology from the FBI was going to go a long way in restoring my name, and the company's. Although we still had some work to do to dispel the shroud of mistrust for good, I looked forward to rebuilding.

Every step of the way.

"We should eat before the food gets cold," Savannah murmured, without pulling away. "I'm just so happy for you."

I drew back to look at her and kissed her. "We could celebrate in other ways."

Savannah giggled and squirmed out of my arms. "We can do that later. Right now, I want to enjoy this nice meal prepared for us."

I brought her hand up to my lips for a kiss. "I like the sound of that. I love you, Savannah Parish, and I can't wait for us to get naked later."

Savannah laughed and pushed herself up onto the tips of her toes to kiss me. "I love you too, Asher Buchannan."

With an exhale, the two of us sat back down, and Savannah reached for her cutlery. She kept glancing over at me until I lifted up my wine glass and held it up to hers. Savannah touched her glass to mine, a strange glimmer in her eyes before she went back to her food. Once we were done, and the plates were cleared, I pulled her to her feet and placed both arms around her waist.

In the distance, the soft strings of a violin played, slicing through the warm night air. Savannah brought her head to a rest against my chest, and we swayed to the music, the smell of her perfume lingering in the air. With a smile, I spun her out and waited for a few seconds before spinning her back into my arms. She returned, flushed and laughing, and her face lit up with warmth and humor.

Then I dipped her backwards and kissed her until we were both out of breath.

When I set her back on her feet, she was breathless and unsteady on her feet. "I could get used to this."

I kissed her again and took her hand in mine. "Good. Let's get out of here. I've got dessert waiting for us at home."

Together, we took off at a brusque pace, kicking up sand as we did. She didn't stop laughing until we reached the car, and I pressed her against it. I placed my arms on either side of her and kissed her until the warm feeling in my stomach erupted, and her eyes shone brighter than the stars overhead.

I could not get enough of her.

Nor did I want to.

With a growl, I pulled away from her and went around to the driver's side. In the car, she reached for my hand and held it the entire way, the stroke of her finger sending pinpricks of desire racing up and down my spine. I gripped the steering wheel with my free hand, and it took every ounce of self-control I had not to bring the car to a halt on the side of the road and pull her to the back seat.

Every cell in my body screamed for her.

When I skidded to a halt in front of my house, I killed the engine, and we both hurried out of the car. My heart was pounding in my chest as I pushed the door open and reached for her. She kicked the door shut with the back of her leg as I reached for her and crushed her to me. Savannah made a low noise in the back of her throat that had my head spinning.

She hoisted herself up to lock her legs around my waist, and all the blood rushed to my groin. I growled into her mouth and carried her through the dark and into the bedroom. There, I set her down on the bed and took a step back. Once I flicked the lamp on, flooding the room in florescent lightning, she stood up and shimmied out of her clothes.

"Are all these flowers for me?"

I nodded, and my hands went to the buttons of my shirt, flicking one after the other in quick succession. "Only the best for you, Ms. Parish."

Savannah stepped out of her dress and kicked off her heels. "You shouldn't have, Mr. Buchannan."

"I absolutely should have."

Savannah covered the distance and batted her lashes at me. Her hands went to the zipper of my trousers, then she helped me push down the trousers, so I was standing in my boxers. Her lips crashed on mine, hungry and yearning as we moved backwards and fell onto the bed. I dropped one hand between us and stroked her. When she moaned, I slid one finger and another into her wet folds.

She arched her back and smiled into the kiss. "You're very good at that."

I kissed a spot underneath her ear and lowered my head to her chest. "You haven't seen anything yet."

Savannah threw her head back and laced her fingers through my hair. She bucked and ground against me until her breathing quickened. Her grip on the back of my hand tightened as her body writhed and spasmed, her orgasm washing over her. Once her vision cleared, she gave me a look that sent another wave of desire over me. Without warning, she turned around, so her back was facing me and propped herself up on all fours.

I couldn't hear anything past the pounding in my ears as I positioned myself at her back. Then I pressed a kiss to the back of her neck and growled. "I can't get enough of you, Sav."

Savannah ground against me and whimpered. "Who says you have to?"

Slowly, I eased out and slammed back into her until the sound of our breathing filled the room. Each sound, each taste, each touch drove me more and more insane until the rhythm changed. Suddenly, we were moving with wild and animal-like abandon, starving for each other. Savannah came again, crying out my name as she did.

My own release followed soon after, and I held myself against her for a while.

Little by little, when my vision returned, I collapsed against the mattress and pulled her to me. Savannah snuggled into my side and pressed a kiss to my cheek. I dropped a kiss on top of her forehead and let my eyes flutter closed.

For the first time in a long time, I wasn't thinking about what came next.

Or where we went from here.

All that mattered was that we were together.

And I wouldn't change a single thing about how we got there.

THE END

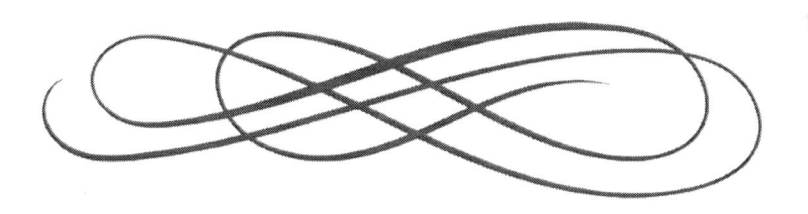

WHAT'S NEXT?

Out of interest, who would you like me to write about next?

Fill out this survey: https://bit.ly/3j8tJ8V

It doesn't contain invasive questions at all, I promise. Let me know what other stories you'd like to see.

In the meantime, be sure to check other series that I have going on.

SHIVER OF DESIRE

MR. WEST, BOOK 1 – 5

If you've enjoyed Savannah & Asher's story, know that there's an ever-growing collection of Small Town Billionaires! Begin with "Mr. West's" steamy and sweet romance in "Shiver of Desire"!

READ "SHIVER OF DESIRE" HERE NOW:

https://mybook.to/ShiverOfDesire

He'd taken me for granted, and I'd let him, thinking I could change a man like Cooper West

We used to date years ago.

Now he's back in town for his father's funeral.

Despite the heartache, he's still the only one who can make my heart race and my mind go blank.

He looks good.

Like he hasn't spent the past two years tossing and turning, wishing he'd gotten on a plane to come back for me.

I always did have a habit of getting too attached.

I just didn't think Cooper would be the one to leave me hanging.

Why does he still have such an effect on me?

ALICIA'S AUTHOR NOTES

Did you enjoy this steamy read from my bestselling Millionaire Doctors' Club series?
Great news, you can check out a FREE sneak peek to the next story in the series on the next page!

Much love xoxo

Alicia Nichols

REALITY LOVE (PREVIEW) (MR. FORESTER - INSTALOVE SPARK)

I'm torn between the man who used to love me and the man who now does.

Tonight I'll choose one man on a reality dating show I just joined and for the next seven weeks, we'll be engaged.

But not everyone's a stranger.

Wayne holds my past, and Luke holds my heart.

The producers are hell-bent on making it difficult for our love.

All in the name of ratings.

I don't want to be some shiny new thing that he can drop once he's had his fill.

Will I find the perfect forever love I seek, or will I get my heart broken again?

CHAPTER 1

- SOPHIE -

Private conference lounge, California office of the Love At First Sight Studios

The camera zooms in on a pretty blonde seated on a plush brown armchair, one leg crossed over the other at the knee. The blonde smiles shyly and tucks her hair behind her ear, resting her hands on her lap.

"I'm Sophie Montrae, I'm twenty-seven years old, and I'm so thrilled to be selected for this season of Love At First Sight." *She throws her hands up with jazz fingers, and suddenly lets out a nervous, bubbly laugh.* "This is so exciting! Ahahaha!"

Cut to shot of Sophie slowly sipping coffee from a wide, white mug. She looks up and smiles serenely for the camera.

"On this show, I'm going to get the opportunity to pick my own happily ever after. Tonight, at the cocktail party, I'm going to choose the one man I feel the biggest connection with, and for the next seven weeks, I'm going to be engaged to this man. At the end of our time together, we'll get to decide whether we want to get married and spend our whole lives together, or whether we need to break up and call off our happy ever after... forever."

Sophie bites her lip. The camera slowly zooms in on her face, letting the viewers see the glint of sunlight and apprehension in her blue eyes.

"I'm hoping I make the right choice, because this decision has the potential to affect the rest of my life. No pressure, right?"

WEDDING NIGHT STRANGER (MR. BUCHANNAN)

I cradle my glass of champagne close to my chest and survey the grand ballroom from under my lashes.

Coyness won't do me any favors in finding my perfect man tonight, but the men here seem to be eating it up. Since the night began, I've had no shortage of guys coming up to me to strike up an innuendo-filled chat. The past thirty minutes have flown by with different men trying to sweep me away every few minutes, making me feel like I'm walking through a whirlwind. It's why I'm here—hiding in a corner of the ballroom behind a giant potted plant that's as tall as I am.

I've got a room full of men, all wanting to meet me, and it's up to me to decide which of these men is going to get a chance to potentially be my life partner.

And I've only got an hour left to make my choice.

With the ball completely in my court, I'm not so sure I want to continue with this show. I knew what I was getting into, of course, going into this, but being here right now, everything is just so… overwhelming.

How does one decide the person they want to marry with just one conversation? The producers have banned me—and everyone else at this party—from revealing personal details about my career and family. Here, I'm a blank slate, with no ideas of prejudice or prestige laid upon me for everyone's judgment. Here, I'm just a name, and anything someone wants to figure out from me can only be figured out from my looks, clothes, body language and personality.

The catch? If I'm a blank slate, so is everyone else.

And I've never been very good at playing detective.

What am I doing here? I wonder. Am I really so desperate for love that I would sign up to be here, on a reality dating show that forces near-perfect strangers to marry in seven weeks, on the off chance that I might actually find the one?

"Yeah, you are, Soph," I admonish myself under my breath. "You're exactly that desperate. And if you've got an hour left to make this pay off, you need to get out there and do something to make it work."

What's my alternative? Go home to my musty little flat and my two dogs knowing that yet again, I'm destined to be alone for all my life? I don't think so.

Taking a deep breath for confidence, I smooth down the drape of my bright red gown. I fix the neckline till my halter straps lay flat against my clavicle, and re-adjust my grip on my champagne glass.

"You've got this, Soph," I mutter. "Get out there and kick some ass, and go get some ass. You've got this in the bag."

It's weird to be talking to yourself all the time, I know. But I'm the kind of woman that needs pep talks, and I'm also better than anyone else at giving myself pep talks. Do I have another choice?

Tell that to the six men who have left me in the past because of "my little quirks."

I've got to do this. I've got to. I owe it to myself to prove that I'm not unlovable. That it's not me, but them. That no matter what my trainwreck of a romantic past has been oh so eager to tell me, I'm still a goddamn catch.

I'm doing this for me.

I take a big gulp of champagne, letting the bubbles fizz encouragingly on my tongue. And with a final glance around the ballroom, I step out from behind my potted plant and re-enter the fray.

Not even five steps towards the ballroom floor, I'm accosted by my first hopeful wannabe.

"I'm Jamie," he says, freaking *sliding* into place in front of me—how does one slide on a thick brocade carpet like it's a wet bathroom floor?—and greeting me with a charming smile, "and you look absolutely ravishing tonight. Are those stars in your eyes, or are they just that beautiful? Because you could easily pass for a celestial being."

"No," I say flatly and turn around.

Pep talks are well and good, but there is only so much bullshit I'm willing to put up with.

Another guy comes up to me soon and looks me up and down, clutching an overly full glass that smells strongly of rum. No. Just no. "You're sexy as hell," he drawls, cheeks already flushed red from drinking. "I could show you a good time if you came home with me tonight. What do you say? Let's blow this popsicle stand."

My left eye twitches.

"No," I respond, "and I happen to find people who use phrases like 'let's blow this popsicle stand' extremely tedious, so that's another no. No squared."

He grins in slow surprise, like he's impressed with me. "Ooooh, she *feisty*. I like it." He leers. "How 'bout this? I've got a popsicle you can blow, and I guarantee you're gonna love it."

I'm shocked into silence with the extent of my disgust. I can't believe they allowed this man to be on TV.

I look around for the nearest camera man desperately, and he grimaces behind his camera and nods back. I escape before Drunk Popsicle Guy can blast me with another whiff of his rum-dosed breath, and I watch from the corner of my eye as the camera man signals one of the studio's security personnel to escort him out of the ballroom.

Oh, the tragedies of an open bar. Free flowing drinks and loose lips—such a toxic combination.

I can guarantee that the producers are going to cut my delightful little interaction with that man from their final edits. Sleazebags like him don't belong on one's 'quest to find love', after all.

Rolling my eyes, I take another large sip of my champagne and continue to make my circuit around the room.

This is what happens when you have a love-hate relationship with reality TV that extends to my kind of extreme. You end up finding yourself as a contestant on a dating show to find love, while derisively questioning every second of the hateful experience.

I still believe in fairytale love. A part of me will always be the little girl who hid under the blankets with a torch every night, rereading my precious hardcover collection of princess stories. The teenager who curled up beside her mother on the couch every December for our traditional Hallmark movie marathons. The adult who looks with longing at the couples holding hands during their morning walks at the park outside my flat.

And this ballroom is magical, like something straight out of a Jane Austen adaptation. I'm wearing a beautiful dress the producers outfitted me in, a gorgeous yet risqué piece I'd never have dared to choose for myself, and my hair is done up in such a pretty, elegant twist. With earrings dangling from my lobes and the glimmering silver chain at my neck, dressed to the nines, I feel like a modern-day princess.

But when you're searching for your fairytale love among seven other women, while your every footstep is being tracked and every expression is being watched like a hawk twenty-four seven by a camera crew and eventually, by five million viewers all over America... well, some of that magic starts to be lost.

There are a bunch of striking men in this room, but none really my type. They seem eager to please, eager to charm. They prowl like predators; there's nothing honest or genuine about them. And with seven other ladies on the prowl for them, they have no qualms dropping me like a hot potato to chase someone else the second they can tell I'm not interested.

I like my men a little less... shiny.

When my champagne flute is drained, I go over to the bar to get a refill. I feel exhausted, and a little like I've failed—maybe I didn't come here fully *expecting* to find my happily ever after, but I did come here to give it a proper go, and can I really say I've tried if I can't even find a guy to have this experience with? I want to try. I want to fall in love. I want to build a connection with someone, anyone, in this room.

I just don't know how.

Already, I can see some of the other ladies on the show with me starting to couple up. Kelsiey Davies—spelled with an i-e-y, she was extremely insistent to remind me—is out on the dance floor with Jamie The Slider, their dark heads bent close. The streaks of cobalt blue in Kelsiey's hair stand out among the small crowd of dancers. I feel a little jealous.

"Can you top up my champagne, please?" I ask the bartender, tipping my empty glass towards him.

Don't look at the happy couple, Sophie. Don't go there. Just don't go there.

The bartender fills my flute to the brim with a knowing little smile. I shrug back sheepishly and hope the cameras aren't catching any of this.

And then my eyes flit to the side, just absently, and I don't have room in my suddenly fuzzy brain to wonder if the producers are going to use my footage to paint me as a borderline alcoholic, because my heart fucking stops.

Leaning against the opposite corner of the bar counter is the sexiest man I have laid eyes on in my life.

He's wearing a light gray suit. Sure, almost every man here is wearing a suit, but this guy is really wearing his suit. Or rather, his suit is wearing him. Broad shoulders taper down into a trim waist, power visible in every muscle, and his biceps seem large enough that I could fashion his suit sleeves into a pair of pants for myself and they'd fit right over my thighs. Y'know, if I wanted to wear his suit as pants. Which I don't. I think.

Maybe the champagne is starting to get to my head.

But more importantly, even as a side profile, his face looks familiar. His hair is a honeyed light brown, cropped short at the sides with the longer top swept back into a neat, high coif. His face is clean shaven but for the merest hint of golden-blond stubble at the edges of his jaw, and even lost in thought, his gaze looks piercing.

He brings his glass of whiskey absently up to his lips, and even as he continues staring into space, it tilts his head a little more towards me.

Suddenly, I remember where I've seen him from.

Without thinking, I pick up my full glass of champagne and head towards him. I slip in beside him and lean an elbow against the counter—partly to act casual, and partly to support myself because wow, my knees are suddenly so very weak.

Luke Forester looks even more handsome now than he did a year ago.

Holy shit, this must be fate.

END OF PREVIEW

Read Mr. Forester's Complete Novel Now Here:
https://mybook.to/RealityLove

ACKNOWLEDGEMENTS

ALICIA NICHOLS

Writing a book is the result of many minds and interactions coming together. Inspiration, experience, and insight is gathered from everywhere, and this shows in how this all finally comes together.

I want to begin by thanking you, the readers, who become a part of these stories by reading, reviewing, recommending, and buying the books. It is thanks to you that people like me get a chance to keep tapping into our imagination and sharing new stories. Thank you for your ongoing support.

Thank you also to the team at Light Age Media. Without Erynn, Jordi, and several others, this would not have been possible. You have breathed life into these stories and made it so that they could engage with a wider audience.

I also wish to thank Ty, Marty, Ja, and Josh who have guided my way to publishing and have opened up my world of what was possible from my laptop and with determination. I now feel much more empowered to keep sharing these stories as a way of life.

A special thank you to my Advanced Reader Group who have offered valuable insights early on to improve the story. If you're willing to write your honest reviews and read the books, prior to them being released, here's how you can become a part of it.

Join my ARC team here: https://bit.ly/3NPTOba

A note of gratitude also goes to my early teachers at writing school. I had always wanted to write novels and here's me putting my words where my mouth was. A huge thanks also to the incredible doctors, nurses, and medical staff that I've come to know through my family, from direct experience, and in your continued dedication to your craft. You are truly special.

And thank you to my friends and family who want to see me continue to do what I love. I appreciate your support on this journey and for this craft.

OTHER BOOKS BY ALICIA

COVETED

DR. STONE, BOOK 1

Begin a steamy new series with Dr. Stone. "Coveted" will set you on a course to a satisfying romantic HEA.

And it's FREE. It's an e-book I give to you just for signing up to my newsletter. You won't find it anywhere else.

Also, be sure to check out more dreamy doctors in my "Millionaire Doctors Club Series".

READ "COVETED" HERE NOW:

https://dl.bookfunnel.com/46pg16ndzd

I can no longer deny how my doctor makes me feel.

And he might just feel the same way.

His smooth, tanned face peering intently at me makes me go weak in the knees.

Dr. Stone moves from around his desk and comes to stand in front of me.

My heart skips a beat at his proximity.

I shudder and melt into his embrace, realizing that it had been too long since I'd been held.

The only problem is, he's also my doctor.

DR. WALKER

COMPLETE SERIES, BOOKS 1 – 5

Begin a steamy new series with Dr. Walker. "Daddy Neighbor" will set you on a course to a satisfying romantic HEA. Be sure to check out more dreamy doctors in my "Millionaire Doctors Club Series".

START READING "DR. WALKER" HERE NOW:
https://getbook.at/DrWalkerBoxset

Who is my new neighbor?

All I know is he is a caring father who drives fast cars and…

…he's breathtakingly gorgeous.

Chills run over my skin from hearing his voice and I don't see signs of a wife.

One night he accidentally catches me staring into his bedroom from mine.

I don't want to seem like a stalker, so I decide to introduce myself the next day.

Something is mysterious and exciting about him. A mystery I can't wait to unravel.

And I'm not sure how I feel about that.

DR. PIERCE

COMPLETE SERIES, BOOKS 1 – 5

Maybe a new start is all your heart yearns for. Even if your life is in shambles and you're forced to return home, back to square one. Will you take a chance at love, even if it requires everything you have left to preserve it? Swoon your way to a satisfying HEA. Start reading Dr. Pierce's series today!

START READING "DR. PIERCE" HERE NOW:

https://mybook.to/DrPierceBoxset

Doesn't he realize that he's the most important thing to me?

But I'm not sure he feels the same way and my love dream is slipping away.

This is my crazy night out before I return home to face my life.

I'm broke and soon might also lose my fashion shop.

Not looking forward to returning to the small town I once left to live my dream.

I eagerly dive into this Mystery Man's arms and his deep blue stare.

Consumed in his kiss, I feel aflame for him.

His are the eyes I saw in my dream.

But before we get too far, he dashes out to save a life, and I don't even have his number.

He's only in town for tonight.

I won't see him ever again, will I?

DR. CARTER

COMPLETE SERIES, BOOKS 1 – 5

If you don't believe in that everlasting love nonsense of romance novels, think again. Dreamy Dr. Carter will leave you satisfied and wanting more. Start reading his series today!

READING "DR. CARTER" HERE NOW:

https://getbook.at/DrCarterBoxset

I wasn't expecting to meet my future husband at the doctor's office.

Well, he doesn't know it yet.

But I can't introduce myself if I'm hiding behind a couch after breaking in.

All for a good cause, I think. I'm helping my friend hide a secret from her fiancé.

How can I meet this gorgeous Viking god in a more fitting scene?

Until by chance we meet.

DR. MACLEAN

COMPLETE SERIES, BOOKS 1 – 5

You've been introduced to Makayla, Dr. Cole Stone's BFF. Now you get a chance to read her own journey to find love. With a Dreamy Scottish Doctor of all things! Read Dr. MacLean. Begin with "Lady of Scots" and dance your way to a satisfying HEA. Start reading his series today!

READ "DR. MACLEAN" HERE NOW:

https://mybook.to/DrMacleanBoxset

At first, the six-year age difference between Ryan and I had been a cause for concern.

Now I love every minute of it.

Ladies' man. Billionaire. He's some kind of Scottish Lord.

My doctor friends want him as a donor for their research.

So, I'm the one who has to lure him in at this important fundraiser event.

Across the room, Ryan makes his way toward me.

His lean and muscled body is outlined by the dark suit he's wearing.

Each step towards me feels determined and filled with purpose.

He stops directly in front of me, his lips curve into a smile.

And the entire world melts into the background.

I've got to get a grip. I'm not here to make goo goo eyes at a Scottish lord, right?

DR. BLACKMORE

COMPLETE SERIES, BOOKS 1 – 5

Swoon over this new dreamy doctor and ride the wave of Hollywood love in this new steamy rom-com. Squirm and laugh your way to a satisfying HEA. Start reading Dr. Blackmore's series today!

READ "DR. BLACKMORE" HERE NOW:

https://mybook.to/DrBlackmoreBoxset

If word gets out that we're no longer together, millions of fans would be disappointed.

But the man that really sends shivers racing up and down my spine is forbidden to me.

Fans believe I'm still dating my obnoxious co-star.

That's only to save my acting career and the show.

The problem is that I can't avoid the man I fantasize about: Dr. Blackmore.

He oozes sex appeal without even trying.

I rehearse scenes with him to make my character in this TV medical drama more believable.

Do I really want to derail my career for his love when he has nothing on the line? Or does he?

DR. WRIGHT

COMPLETE SERIES, VOLUME 1

If you've enjoyed Jenny & John's story, there's more!

This collection features all my dreamy doctors. Dreamy Dr. Wright will leave you satisfied and wanting more.

Start reading his series today! His Complete Series, Volume 1, with books 1-5 is available.

READ IT NOW HERE

https://getbook.at/DrWrightBoxset

DR. PARK

COMPLETE SERIES

Begin a steamy new series with Dr. Park. He'll set you on a course to a satisfying romantic HEA.

START READING "DR. PARK" HERE NOW:
https://getbook.at/DrParkBoxset

He's moved on, is happily married, and has a family.

I came here partly for him. Was I a fool in denial?

I'm still getting over Cole, the doctor I've had it bad for the last 10 years.

I hate knowing that I'm still hung up on him.

But I have to restart my life. No longer do I want the jet-set lifestyle.

Meeting the right guy and starting a family together feels like such a long shot right now.

I deserve someone who is willing to fight for me and has my back.

I'm nowhere closer to my dream and can't wait to have a stable life.

No sooner said, I meet Dr. Max Park by chance at a convention.

He's seeking investors for his clinics.

But I can't avoid noticing a strong, charming, confident man, perhaps a bit rough around the edges.

What a delicious Lumberjack Hottie.

I don't want to get ahead of myself.

What is it with me and all these doctors? Is my heart aching that bad?

DR. GRANT
COMPLETE SERIES

Love reveals second chances. Even if it seems to have eluded you for years, love is right around the corner. This is Jenny and John's story. Read Dr. Grant and leave your door open for love to a satisfying HEA. Start reading his series today!

START READING "DR. GRANT" HERE NOW:
https://mybook.to/DrGrantBoxset

After two years, I'm ready to put my husband's death behind me.

He and I never really loved each other.
Most days he rarely gave me a second thought.

So, when my friend suggests that we go out next week, I hesitate.

There'll be a silver fox doctor I know from way back in school.

He's handsome and successful.

I once had a thing for him, but never acted on that feeling.

I've been a hermit for two years, and I'm ready to make a change in my life.

Is there still room for me in the outside world? Do I even know how to flirt again?

DR. HAYES
COMPLETE SERIES

Secret relationships in the fashion world. What could go wrong? When love is real, fake blows out the window. But not all is what it seems in this steamy romcom. With Dr. Hayes' new series, find out how love shines through to a satisfying romantic HEA.

START READING "DR. HAYES" HERE NOW:

https://mybook.to/DrHayesBoxset

Liar. Cheater. Dirtbag.

I rehash all the ways Baston duped me with his devil smiles and lies of omission.

He played me so easily for such a fool.

As a fashion photographer, I'm no stranger to looking at perfection.

Yet this guy has something about him that sets him apart entirely.

I can't avoid keeping my eyes off him.

How can I get to know him without this chick who is my archnemesis standing in the way?

DR. CAMPBELL
COMPLETE SERIES

Saddle up for the cowboy! A second chance gets steamy in this small town full of secrets. Maybe that's why these two need a fake marriage. But can she resist the heat from the fireman turned cowboy? And can she trust him? Find out with Dr. Campbell's new series and trot away to a satisfying romantic HEA.

START READING "DR. CAMPBELL" HERE NOW:

https://mybook.to/DrCampbellBoxset

Should I fake-marry the cowboy so I don't lose my ranch… and my new life?
I've never cared much for cowboys or their hats.
Until now.
Enter dreamy cowboy to the rescue when my car breaks down.
He's tall, tanned, and flashes one of his abundant sexy smiles.
After my divorce, my grandmother's inheritance helped me start over in a small Montana town.
Out of habit, my right hand slips to the ring.
I promised myself I'd pull the ring off before I got there.
Soon I find out this small town harbors a few secrets.
Secrets that will get me into a fake marriage with this cowboy.
Can I even trust him? How did I get myself into this mess?

DARWIN BROTHERS

COMPLETE SERIES, BOOKS 1 – 5

If you've enjoyed Ivy & Blake's story, know that the Darwin family has a backstory! Read their steamy and sweet romance in "Darwin Brothers"!

READ "DARWIN BROTHERS" HERE NOW:

https://mybook.to/DarwinBrothersBoxset

How can I confess my exciting affair with my best friend's older brother?

I might be better off fleeing from the Darwin brothers all together.

The last thing I need is a whirlwind romance that makes me second-guess my sanity.

I've made plenty of mistakes in the past.

We almost lost our family ranch because of them.

And I almost lost my sister.

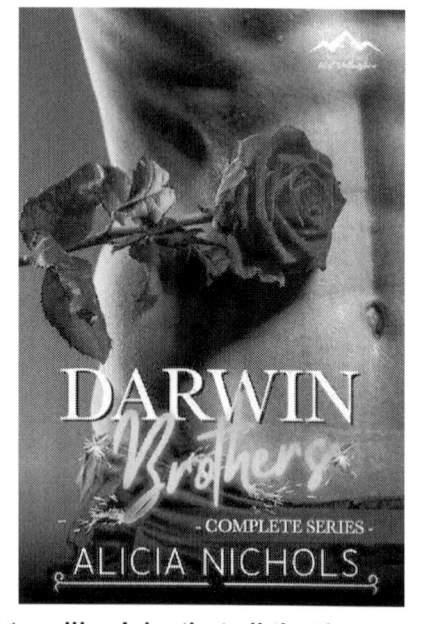

It was partly thanks to firefighters like Jake that all that is behind us.

He has a special aura and is so effortlessly sexy.

He's been nothing but gentle and caring.

Should I give this firefighter a chance? And will his love redeem my heart?

DADDY'S OFF LIMITS

MR. DALTON, COMPLETE SERIES

Love finds you in the small town of West Yellowstone. Sensual bachelors and single daddies fill the steam of whirlwind romances. ♥ **The Bachelors of West Yellowstone is an ever-growing collection.** ♥ **Begin "Daddy's Off Limits" to ride your small-town love with a guaranteed and satisfying HEA!**

READ "DADDY'S OFF LIMITS" HERE NOW:

https://mybook.to/DaddysOffLimits

I knew from the look on his face that he was praying I wasn't carrying his baby, and it broke my heart.
Was I crazy for wishing the opposite?
It doesn't matter if he's my dad's best friend or that he's single.
Blake Dalton is off-limits.
Nothing can happen between us.
Much less now that I'm his daughter's nanny.
I remember years ago going to bed battling fantasies about him.
Carved by the god of beauty himself, he's always the most handsome man in the room.
Back then it didn't matter if he barely paid me any attention.
I'm an adult woman now and have more control.
But the moment my eyes catch those smoky gray lights of his, I'm again sparked with desire.
I'm so screwed with this new job.
How am I supposed to stay in the same house with him all day if just being around him makes my brain a mess?

CONNECT WITH THE AUTHOR

Read Alicia's book catalog

https://viewauthor.at/AliciaNichols

https://amazon.com/author/alicianichols

Connect with Alicia and sign up to her email list here:

https://dl.bookfunnel.com/46pg16ndzd

Follow Alicia Nichols' Facebook Fan Page:

https://www.facebook.com/alicianicholsauthor

REVIEW THE BOOK

P.S. Readers:

It means the world to me that you bought my book. Your feedback is very important to me.

I'd like to ask you a small favor. Would you be so kind to leave an **HONEST** review on the site where you purchased it?

Thank you so much!

Review My Book Here:

https://mybook.to/WeddingNightStranger

Much Love!

Alicia

Printed in Great Britain
by Amazon